A Norman de Ratour Mystery

LOVE POTION MURDERS in the
MUSEUM OF MAN

ALFRED ALCORN

ZOLAND BOOKS
An Imprint of Steerforth Press
Hanover, New Hampshire

First published in serial by Salon.com in 2001.

For information about permission to reproduce
selections from this book, write to:
Steerforth Press L.L.C., 45 Lyme Road, Suite 208,
Hanover, New Hampshire 03755

Library of Congress Cataloging-in-Publication Data

Alcorn, Alfred.
 The love potion murders in the Museum of Man : a Norman de Ratour mystery /
Alfred Alcorn. — 1st ed.
   p. cm.
 ISBN 978-1-58195-231-5
 1. Aphrodisiacs — Fiction. I. Title.

PS3551.L29L68 2009
813'.54 — dc22
                              2008044688

FIRST EDITION

the
LOVE POTION
MURDERS in the
MUSEUM OF MAN

1

It is with reluctance and foreboding that I trouble these pages with an account of a tragic, unseemly, and suspicious incident here at the Museum of Man. I say "reluctance" as I do not wish to serve as amanuensis to a nightmare. Nor do I wish to prompt iniquity with words. I would rather, on this lovely evening, sit back and gaze out of my high windows at the Hays Mountains, where I can see the first flares of autumn touching with scarlet and gold those rolling, mist-tendriled hills. But write I must. Because yet again I have a presentiment of evil uncoiling itself within the womb of this ancient institution.

Let me start with this morning. Just as Doreen was heading down to the cafeteria for our coffees, Lieutenant Tracy of the Seaboard Police Department appeared in the doorway of my fifth-floor domain. Dapper as ever in charcoal suit, buttondown off-white oxford shirt, and plaid tie, the officer reminded me that he took his coffee black. The amenities of small talk attended to, the door closed, we got down to business.

"I'm here to see you, Norman, about the Ossmann-Woodley case." His tone indicated that he spoke off the record.

"Ossmann-Woodley," I repeated with a sigh, not entirely surprised. "I was under the impression, Lieutenant, that the case was too riddled with imponderables to begin an investigation. It's most unusual, I know, and not a little embarrassing for the museum, given Professor Ossmann's affiliation."

Thanks to the tabloids and those television programs devoted to the tawdry and the sensational (for which my dear wife, Elsbeth, has a decided weakness), much of the world knows that, just a week ago, Professor Humberto Ossmann and Dr. Clematis Woodley, a postdoctoral student, were found dead quite literally in each other's arms; indeed, in an unequivocally amorous embrace.

Foul play, other than double adultery — they were both married — has not been ruled out. In short, we have two corpses and enough circumstantial evidence to indicate *corpus delicti*. For instance, a security guard found them, not in some comfortable bed or even on the couch available in a nearby office, but on the floor of one the laboratories. There, judging from the disorder — an overturned chair, some smashed pipettes, and a terrified white rat running loose — their lovemaking had been spontaneous and energetic, if not violent. Rape does not appear to have been involved inasmuch as Professor Ossmann was a smallish man, a good two inches shorter and twenty-five pounds lighter than the formidable Dr. Woodley, who played rugby for Rutgers, albeit on the women's team. Moreover, neither participant had disrobed in a manner suggesting premeditated lovemaking. Professor Ossmann's trousers and boxer shorts were down around his ankles, and Dr. Woodley's panties had been clawed off, but by herself, judging from the fragments of matching material found under her fingernails.

Finally, both victims, if that is what they are, entertained a deep and abiding antipathy for the other. Professor Ossmann had blocked Dr. Woodley's appointment to a tenure-track position a year or so back. Dr. Woodley for her part had taken to calling Professor Ossmann "Pip" to his face, "Pip-squeak" being the nickname colleagues used behind his back.

I know the case in considerable detail, not only from the lurid and often inaccurate coverage in the *Seaboard Bugle*, but also from briefings I arranged between the SPD and important university officials in an attempt to keep the rumor mills from working overtime.

The postmortems, done by the venerable Dr. P.M. Cutler, have provided only preliminary findings. The Medical Examiner reported gross inflammation of the genitals of both parties, who otherwise presented no signs of trauma or assault. Professor Ossmann succumbed to a coronary thrombosis while Dr. Woodley died of massive systemic failure when her blood pressure, for which she was taking medication, dropped below what is necessary for life. Curiously enough, according to Dr. Cutler, despite prolonged sexual activity, no evidence of ejaculate was found. Whether Dr. Woodley had experienced a physiological orgasm could not be determined with any certainty. Assays on blood chemistry, other bodily fluids, stomach contents, and organs are presently being conducted and should tell us a lot more as to what happened on that Friday night in early September when the lab was deserted except for those two.

Sergeant Lemure, Lieutenant Tracy's blunt-spoken deputy, put the matter in words of a characteristic crudity, which I will refrain from repeating here.

The lieutenant regarded me closely. "Officially, Norman, it is a low-priority case because we cannot determine whether it's a murder, an accident, or some kind of bizarre suicide pact. But something about this case reeks."

His remarks struck a chord, if nagging doubts can be said to resonate. Despite myself, I have acquired of late a knack for suspicion. It's related, no doubt, to my work with the Seaboard police on what have come to be called the Cannibal Murders, which gained Wainscott University, the museum, myself, and others such notoriety a few years back. Indeed, the account of those grisly events that I kept in my journal at the time was subsequently entered as evidence in the case against the Snyders brothers. Published initially over my objections, it was well received in those circles devoted to the "true detective" genre.

Moreover, I have found that working as a private sleuth — or a public sleuth, for that matter — sharpens one's apprehension of those slight discordances that indicate the presence not so much of clues but of what might be termed "negative clues" — the dog that doesn't bark. It makes one aware of anomalies within anomalies, life being full of the anomalous, after all. And this case, if a case it be, is loud with silent hounds.

While I was thus cogitating, Doreen came in with the coffee. The dear girl had been offered a higher salary to go back to her old boss, Malachy Morin. But she told me she wouldn't even consider it, calling the man "a serial groper." She has a new beau and has finally ceased inflating out of her mouth those gaudy-hued, condom-like bubbles of gum.

After Doreen had withdrawn and closed the door, I noted the obvious. "We have no real evidence of foul play. At least not until the lab tests come in."

The lieutenant lifted an eyebrow at the implied collaboration in the "we," as though both realizing and acknowledging that we were once again, however unofficially, a team.

"No real evidence, it's true," he said. "It's as though someone got there before the bodies were discovered and tidied things up."

"Really?" I was somewhat taken aback. I had not been told of this before.

"Yes, and there are a few other details you might be able to help us clear up."

"Well, I'm at your service, Lieutenant," I said, trying to dissemble a shiver of excitement as my pulse quickened. The lieutenant's request for assistance made real what had heretofore been little more than a premonition. Indeed, I have developed a keen predilection for the blood sport of murder investigation. For that's what it is, at bottom, a blood sport. And deeper, in the darker reaches of my heart, I could also feel that strange craving for the reality of evil, if only for something to confront and vanquish.

Lieutenant Tracy smiled. He has one of those smiles the scarcity of which makes it the more appealing. "I knew I could count on you, Norman. And also on your discretion. My visit here, strictly speaking, is unofficial."

I nodded. "What is it that I can tell you that you think will be of help?"

"Could you tell me, what exactly was Professor Ossmann's connection with the Genetics Lab?"

His question made me frown. The Genetics Lab has over the past couple of years changed beyond all recognition. The Onoyoko Institute, suffering in the general stagnation of the Japanese economy and the blaze of bad publicity in the wake of the Cannibal Murders, has long since gone, replaced by the Ponce Research Institute. Though nominally nonprofit, the Ponce has proved an absolute boon to the museum. It has given us the wherewithal to resist persistent attempts on the part of the university to take us over on terms other than those ensuring the integrity and longevity of this institution as an actual public museum.

I chose my words carefully in responding to the lieutenant's question because, truth be known, I was not entirely certain what constituted the late professor's connection with the lab. I cleared my throat. "Professor Ossmann, as you know, was a consultant at the Ponce, as the institute is generally called. He worked on therapies having to do with the cardiovascular system, which was his primary research interest."

As I paused, the lieutenant leaned forward. "You seem skeptical of your own description."

"I am," I said. "This can go no farther than this room, but I've suspected for some time, Lieutenant, that Professor Ossmann was as much an *agent provocateur* for the university administration as an active consultant."

"In what way?"

"He played an active role in the higher councils of the university. He served on the New Millennium Fund Steering Committee. He was on the somewhat controversial Benefits Subcommittee of the Faculty Reform Committee. He also served for a while as chair of the Steering Committee on Governance. In fact, it was during his tenure in that last position that he and I had one or two significant disagreements."

The lieutenant said nothing, but his listening appeared to intensify.

"The same old story," I said. "Wainscott wants to take us over. We, the museum, were the subject of a long report by Ossmann's committee. My own Board of Governors rejected the report outright."

"How did he end up over here?"

"We have a goodly number of consultants from the university who have contracts with the institute. It remains something of a sore issue between the university and the museum."

"Why is that?"

"Money," I said and smiled. "Lieutenant, I don't want to bore you with the endless petty politics that go on in institutions of higher learning, but it's clear to me now that the university is trying to get its hands on the museum for nothing less than the income it can derive from the research done in the Genetics Lab under the auspices of the Ponce Institute."

His brows knit in thought as I went on. "And they might have succeeded had we not had in our employ a canny young attorney named Felix Skinnerman who has been handling our affairs with Wainscott for nearly two years now. He has learned, for instance, that the university's charter was amended during the heady days of the nineteen sixties to the effect that no faculty member can benefit directly from research, patents, royalties, and the like taking place under university auspices or on university grounds."

The lieutenant shrugged. "Why doesn't Wainscott simply amend its charter?"

I related in some detail how they could not change the clause without the unanimous consent of the Board of Regents — which, by charter, has to include three faculty members, one of whom reliably objects.

"How does all this connect with Ossmann?"

"It doesn't really," I continued, "except to provide the context for Ossmann's activities in the lab."

"Activities?"

"He was something of a troublemaker. He liked to object, to talk a lot about issues. He liked to speak to the press."

"But enough so that someone would want him out of the way?"

"Perhaps. I mean, if he was about to blow the whistle on some shady dealings or some off-the-books research. Of course I may be mistaken. I'm sorry, Lieutenant, but I feel like I'm offering you little more than wretched stalks."

The lieutenant smiled and rose to go. We shook hands. "That's all any of us are doing right now, Norman, clutching at straws. But if you hear anything . . ."

"Of course," I said. "We will stay in touch."

I finished my coffee alone. The lieutenant's visit reminded me anew that the unfortunate deaths of these two people, both estimable in his and her own way, have cast another shadow over the Museum of Man. While both were on the faculty of Wainscott University, they were, as biochemists, under contract to the institute directly and to the Genetics Lab indirectly. The shadow is real, darkened by the press, which has hounded me daily, all but accusing the museum of perpetrating a cover-up.

Indeed, the university's Oversight Committee, a claque of inquisitorial busybodies, has requested "in the strongest terms" that I attend a meeting to discuss "its concern with the unseemly recent events in the Genetics Lab." I have responded to Constance Brattle, who still presides over the committee, reminding her that I have myself (for my own good reasons) remained an *ex officio* member. I said I would acquiesce to her request but only if it was clearly understood that where the museum was concerned, the committee's involvement must remain purely advisory. I also stipulated that the press was to be excluded and all statements kept privileged. I reminded her that, as Director of the Museum of Man, I was as concerned as she in maintaining the high repute of both the university and the museum.

Strange how, when you start to worry about one thing, it leads you to worry about something else. For instance, no one has heard for some time from Cornelius Chard. Corny, the Packer Professor of Primitive Ethnology in the Wainscott Anthropology Department, inveigled the museum into underwriting some portion of his expedition to the Yomamas. It's a venture I tried to talk him out of. There's been considerable unrest in the area, apparently because of logging operations.

The Yomamas are a small tribe who inhabit an all-but-inaccessible plateau astride the Rio Sangre, one of the more remote tributaries of the Amazon. The tribe, according to Corny, are the last "untouched" group of hunter-gatherers left on earth. He also contends that they are the last people in the world actively practicing cannibalism. He has gone virtually alone to witness, as he puts it, the actual thing. He says he wants to refute once and for all what he calls, in questionable taste, "the cannibalism deniers."

Where he raised the majority of his funding, I don't know. It's one of those mysteries. He claims it's a perfectly legitimate source that will in no way taint the objectivity of his research. His very protest makes me wonder. I do know he associates with some strange people.

Through Elsbeth, who goes way back with Jocelyn, Corny's wife, I have gotten to know the man better, perhaps, than I might have wanted to. He's an advocate of anthropophagy and author of *The Cannibal Within,* among other works. I never go to dinner at their home without wondering what, exactly, it is we're eating.

I believe Corny organized his Rio Sangre expedition because, though he won't admit it, he's envious of all the publicity Raul Brauer has been getting for his book *A Taste of the Real.* Brauer, some people may remember, was involved in the cannibalism of a young volunteer on the Polynesian island of Loa Hoa back in the late sixties. His account was something of *succès de scandale* and is, I've been told, being made into a movie.

Still, it's a relief to get these things down on paper if not off my mind. Now I must brace myself for another meal out with Elsbeth and her friend, the food critic Korky Kummerbund.

For the life of me I cannot see what Elsbeth sees in "the restaurant scene," as she calls it. What is this cult of the gustatory that seems to have afflicted half the good people of Seaboard? What has happened to the days when one simply went to a restaurant of good reputation, ordered a recognizable dish and a decent wine, enjoyed it, paid for it, and left?

I have nothing against Korky; he is an engaging young man,

and he is devoted to Elsbeth. But the food! I scarcely recognize any of it anymore. And the menus. They read like parodies of pornography. Then we have to sample one another's portions and, worse, talk about them. I have small relish in "savoring the complexity" or "thinking with my taste buds," as Elsbeth and Korky urge. For me, the life of the digestive tract and the life of the mind do not mix. Of late I have hankered simply for a plate of old-fashioned beef stew served with mashed potatoes and peas.

But I really don't want to complain, certainly not about Elsbeth. My world, after all those years of barren bachelorhood, has been utterly enriched by her presence, by her vitality, by her love. Our happiness is very nearly a public scandal. We have become the toast of Seaboard's better tables. Last year we won the waltz contest at the Curatorial Ball. Ah yes, and those little *billets doux* we leave for each other! No, I do not complain. A meal out from time to time in some new bistro is small sacrifice on my part for the woman I love.

This evening we're to go with Korky to the Green Sherpa, a restaurant that specializes, they tell me, in a fusion of Himalayan and Irish cuisines. I can't imagine what they'll be serving, no doubt some kind of braised yak with boiled cabbage gotten up to look like something exotic.

2

It is another beautiful day, despite the rain and the wind, which began this morning and has been blustering about most of the afternoon and rattling the windows here on the fifth floor of the museum. Though now Director, I have kept my old corner office, with its view of the hills to the west and that stern and rockbound coast to the north of Shag Bay. Ah, yes, the beauty of the world, even in — especially in — an autumn rain.

I am surrounded by beauty within as well. Which is to say I have redecorated my office, jettisoning the mournful array of plaques and citations I accumulated over more than three decades as Recording Secretary, a position, I'm afraid, I have allowed to lapse somewhat. To replace them, I have truffled through the storage bins and closets deep within the bowels of this magnificent old pile and come up with some rare treasures.

Just over the door, I suppose to remind myself of my executive responsibilities, I have mounted an elegantly shaped nineteenth-century executioner's sword from the Ngala of the Congo. It has a wide short blade, crooked in the middle into a sickle shape just wide enough for a human neck. In a glass case I have a marvelous Chinese robe of silk satin embroidered with a swirl of peacocks, butterflies, and flowers, all in brilliant hues. And on the mantel over the fireplace (which I have kept in working order), there's a figurine of Eros with a dog, a piece that by rights should be on display in the permanent exhibits.

In my more Machiavellian moments, I have considered resurrecting a pair of shrunken heads, a missionary and his wife, if I'm not mistaken, that I came across in the Papuan storage area. I have thought of putting them in a glass-fronted case near my desk with a curtain I could draw aside when meeting with people I want to disconcert. But for the nonce I have made do with a montage of fantastic funereal masks from Melanesia.

Speaking of which, I cannot, in the wake of Lieutenant Tracy's visit yesterday, get out of my mind the unseemly deaths of Humberto Ossmann and Clematis Woodley. I have a feeling my good friend knows something about that bizarre tragedy that he's not telling me. Elsbeth and I were away at the time of the deaths, staying with a friend of hers in Boston and visiting museums. As a result, I didn't get back until well after the crime scene, if that's what it was, had been restored to some semblance of normality.

I also missed, according to Doreen, a veritable plague of grief counselors who descended on the museum telling people not to hold back their feelings. Doreen, who has the sturdy good looks of a backcountry girl, said one of the group, a student from the Divinity School, came by several times and left his card. When she finally told the young man that she had never met either of the victims and hadn't really given them much thought, his disappointment was such that she had to spend time consoling him. And, apparently, one thing led to another.

The good lieutenant called again this morning and wondered aloud if it would not be a good idea for me to try to contact Worried. He is the anonymous tipster who works in the Genetics Lab and proved instrumental in solving the Cannibal Murders. I told the lieutenant I would put out an e-mail to all in-house addresses, asking "Worried" to please contact me when he gets a chance. Worried may be able to tell me something relevant about what that collection of wily eggheads are concocting over in the lab.

But Woodley and Ossmann. I am perfectly willing to consider the possibility that they were murdered or, in one way or another, murdered each other. But how? Murder requires an instrument. But what? Some *elisir d'amore*? Are they brewing up some magic love potion over there in the lab? It seems too cartoonishly Larsonesque to imagine them sipping some philter from a dripping retort and then transmogrifying into sexual monsters. But stranger things have happened.

As I am Director of the museum, of which the Genetics Lab remains an integral part, one might suppose that I could simply walk in there and demand to know what's going on. Ah, the illusion of power. People tell you either what they want you to know or what they think you want to hear. The truth? Another of those illusions by which we live. I don't know. But if murder has been done, the truth must out if justice is to prevail.

Which reminds me, I received a call today from Malachy "Stormin'" Morin, "the lead blocker of the consolidation team," as he calls himself. He asked to schedule a meeting between me and "the big-money guys" in Wainscott's development office. Mr. Morin and other worthies in the Wainscott bureaucracy persist in the fiction that "the consolidation process" is actually happening.

Mr. Morin, who ought to be languishing in jail for the grotesque way he caused the death of young Elsa Pringle, fancies himself my boss. He has somehow managed to insinuate his blustering persona and considerable bulk — he's six feet, six inches and four-hundred-odd pounds — into the Wainscott hierarchy as Vice President for Affiliated Institutions. I have to keep reminding him that the MOM is affiliated with the university strictly on its own terms and that he has absolutely no authority concerning our affairs. But for the sake of good relations, I did agree in principle to meet with "the big-money guys," telling him I would get back to him.

On a more positive note, I have received word from Corny Chard. It came by way of a telegram, the diction of which made me think of the old days. (You might call it telegramese, a dying literary convention.)

NORMAN
HAVE REACHED HEADWATERS OF RIO SANGRE
STOP LOGGING AND UNREST EVIDENT STOP HAVE
SET UP BASE CAMP STOP WILL PROCEED WITH
MINIMAL CREW TO YOMAMA AREA STOP BEST TO
EVERYONE STOP
CORNY

On an even brighter note, I have been invited to attend the inaugural Cranston Fessing Memorial Lecture that my good friend Father S.J. O'Gould, S.J., is to give in November. It has a curious title: "Why Is There No Tuna-Safe Dolphin to Eat?" There's to be a dinner afterward, a black-tie affair, to which Elsbeth and I have been invited.

Speaking of dinner, our evening at the Green Sherpa was not a success. The proprietor, a strange fellow named Bain, fawned all over us, especially when he noticed Korky Kummerbund tucking in his napkin. Korky took it all in good grace, politely refusing to let Mr. Bain, who managed to appear both obsequious and threatening, pick up the tab. Korky did allow one special dish "on the house" to be sent over. Still, it was disconcerting to have Bain, a big blond fellow in a tunic-like outfit who spoke British English with a foreign accent, hovering over us through half the meal.

I had some sort of pummeled goat while Elsbeth, always game, had what looked like the remains of a rodent. She hasn't felt well ever since. Indeed, I'm beginning to worry about her. So it was with some relish that I read Korky's review of the place in today's *Bugle*. He concluded a quite thorough savaging of the food with, and I quote: "Despite its elevated ambitions, the Green Sherpa serves up little more than a pastiche of yak-whey chic and tortured potatoes in a mushy chinoiserie cuisine that induces the gastric equivalent of altitude sickness."

But Elsbeth. I'm afraid my love is starting to show her age. Although still full-bodied with abundant dark hair (thanks to chemicals, of course), fresh coloring, and brilliant agate eyes, the ravages of time have not left her untouched. There's a stoop to her now, a fine wrinkling about the eyes, the slightest tremor in her hands. I should talk. I'm getting a bit long in the tooth myself and a bit stringy, as tall ones are wont to do. But I've kept a good deal of my perpetually thinning hair and am at least not a candidate for a shaved head. So many men look like convicts these days. And I will not go into the unspeakable puncturing that young people do to their various bodily parts.

Oh, well, just like the old days, I'm off on my own to the Club tonight. Elsbeth assures me that, though not up to going out, she is perfectly capable of taking care of herself. Still, I do worry about the dear girl.

3

Dear Mr. Ratour,

I got your message loud and clear. Maybe I should have told you this sooner, but nobody around here, not on the maintenance crews, anyway, thought that the Ossmann-Woodley thing was suspicious. I mean the researcher types get up to all kinds of things you wouldn't believe. Back in August one of the security guys was going over a tape from a camera no one knows about and he found footage of one of the research assistants, a really good-looking babe, doing two guys at once. Anyway, he modified it and put it out on the Internet as one of those things you can e-mail to people. Home movies stuff if you know what I mean. You can click on the icon down below and watch it yourself though I don't think it's evidence of anything. Anyway, everyone around here just thought the two professors [sic] that died got carried away and you know shit happens. But now that the newspapers are saying it's under investigation and all that stuff, I maybe ought to tell you that about a week before it happened, I heard Professor Ossmann arguing with another researcher. Ossmann kept saying things like the core discovery is mine and you know it. The other guy who sounded like he was from Minnesota kept answering something about how he figured out the experimentation and without that they wouldn't be where they were. Dr. Penrood, he's the English guy who complains about tea bags all the time, tried to act like the referee. I don't understand him that well because he sounds like he's talking through his nose but he kept saying something about it being a team effort. But I don't know what they were talking about. I'll let you know if I find out anything else.

Worried

I confess it was at the expense of some qualms that I clicked on the icon and watched the nearly ten minutes of indistinct but quite graphic video footage that unrolled on my screen. I scrupled that the possibility of its being evidence in the Ossmann-Woodley case outweighed any invasion of the already violated privacy of the individuals involved.

I found it oddly moving, inasmuch as amateur erotica can be far more stimulating than the professional "soft" stuff that Elsbeth, who has a weakness for the meretricious, occasionally finds on the so-called adult channels. The woman involved in this incident, a well-fleshed blonde, knelt away from the camera on all fours fellating a man whose face was obscured in shadow. The second gentleman, back to camera, copulated vigorously with the woman *au chien,* so to speak. I thought it would be interesting, for forensic purposes, to hear what they were saying, if anything. Perhaps the tape could be enhanced enough for us to learn who the three individuals are. I am not being prurient in this matter. For a sleuth the most seemingly incidental knowledge can be crucial. Nor am I interested in the morals of these individuals. Regarding affairs of consensual activity among adults I subscribe to the dictum of my friend Israel Landes: Keep it private and don't scare the horses.

I did venture another e-mail to Worried, asking if there was any possibility of an enhanced version of "the tape," perhaps with sound. I have to risk that he may think me interested for pornographic reasons.

I also called Dr. Rupert Penrood's office and arranged to meet with him Thursday morning after he gets back from London. Penrood is the Director of the institute, and I have yet to have a really good chat with him about the incident. It might be helpful to find out exactly what Professor Ossmann and the gentleman with the Minnesota accent were arguing about.

On my own initiative I moved last week, with the backing of the Seaboard Police Department, to secure those offices and files Professor Ossmann and Dr. Woodley maintained in the lab. Because it is not yet officially a murder case, the SPD balked at the cost of hiring a forensic biochemist to examine the lab notes, work in progress, computer files, and anything else of relevance to the case left behind by both researchers.

I have come up with an elegant solution. It turns out that Nicole Stone-Lee, the daughter of my good friends Norbert Stone and Esther Lee, is not only a doctoral candidate in biochemistry but also knowledgeable about the areas in which both Ossmann and Woodley were involved. After an interview that went very well, I hired her as a special consultant to the museum. She is to report any findings both to me and to the Seaboard police. I'm sure that if the Wainscott Counsel gets wind of this arrangement, all hell will break loose. But frankly, I don't care. Were I to wait on their acquiescence, any important data would be long gone.

Quite as an aside, I must say I was taken with Ms. Stone-Lee. What a gorgeous race of hybrids we are breeding! With her combination of animation and repose, with that delicate molding of the face, and with a reddish tinge to her features, she makes me feel my own genes are just a bit dated. She is also a distinct pleasure to work with.

Which is more than I can say about the University Oversight Committee. While I have acceded to the committee's entreaty to meet with me on the Ossmann-Woodley matter, I remain concerned about that body prying into the affairs of the museum. I have gone on record, I have put it in writing, that the museum desires to maintain "cordial and mutually beneficial relations" with the university. Indeed, as a token of our goodwill, I have continued to sit on the committee in an advisory capacity, at the same time informing the university that the committee's warrant where the museum is concerned likewise remains advisory.

The fact is that the Oversight Committee, hypersensitive to every ingenious whim of group disgruntlement, has become little more than a tool of the Select Committee on Consolidation, whose sole purpose, as I see it, is to take over the MOM lock, stock, and endowment through any means whatsoever. Indeed, they might have achieved their goal had there not been a series of serendipitous events, chief among them our financial independence.

For this I have to thank attorney Felix Skinnerman, who was referred to me by Robert Remick, the chair of the Museum's Board of Governors. In the wake of the Cannibal Murders, we were in desperate straits. The Onoyoko Institute, which had indirectly been subsidizing a lot of our operations, withered to a mere name with the virtual collapse of Onoyoko Pharmaceuticals. It is no exaggeration to say that we were on the brink of total capitulation to the university. And our submergence into Wainscott would have left us without a shred of real identity.

In this crisis the Board gave me complete discretion and some sound advice. Remick, who spends most of his time now in the Virgin Islands, not only put me on to young Skinnerman but advised me as well to take careful stock of the museum's assets and possibilities before consigning them to the university.

I have to confess I had my reservations about hiring Felix. In the course of a routine background check, I found that he had been fired from his father's company. Izzy, who knows the Skinnermans, told me the story. After finishing law school, Felix reluctantly joined the family's gift business, a firm, apparently, to whom people of means "outsource" their present buying for holidays and special occasions. It appears that Felix, bored with employing his considerable talents handling consumer complaints, inserted a bogus ad into the firm's online catalog for a "tastefully embossed gift certificate for the services of Dr. Jack Kevorkian, the perfect present for that elderly loved one who has lingered too long."

It caused quite a row in the family, according to Izzy, but also generated a good number of serious inquiries. It was only the first of several pranks. The following Christmas he listed in the catalog a "Cheeses of Nazareth," which he called a "Selection of dairy products from the Holy Land tastefully packaged on its own cheeseboard in the shape of a cross."

Felix, who has the charm of being slightly oblivious to his immediate surroundings and the marred, rugged good looks resulting from childhood acne, told me at our first meeting to sign nothing until we had done an assessment. How the scales fell from my eyes! True, we had debt, but people were coming in droves to see the Diorama of Paleolithic Life so that, as Felix put it, gate receipts were up. More than that, he convinced me we were sitting on a gold mine. We had "name recognition," office space to rent in the Pavilion, and state-of-the-art systems already installed in the Genetics Lab.

It was on that basis that we began negotiating with the Ponce Research Institute. The terms include a share of the royalties for any new treatments developed in the lab by the Polymath Group, its main research arm. The institute moved in and within days was hiring, on a consulting basis, researchers from the Medical School and Wainscott's highly respected Department of Biochemistry, many of whom had previously worked for the Onoyoko Institute.

Not only does the Ponce pay us a princely sum for renting the premises — it is a four-story structure, after all — but we have already received substantial royalties on NuSkalp, a biosynthetic hair transplant available in what the literature calls "designer tints." The institute has recently begun human testing of ReLease, a morning-after medication for hangovers that has, admittedly, caused some controversy.

The university threw an absolute fit in the course of all this, and the aftershocks of its continuing attempts to coerce us into a misalliance by resorting to legal measures can still be felt. Wainscott even tried to keep its faculty from signing up, but to no avail. So all in all the MOM is doing quite well, but we must remain ever-vigilant.

On quite another topic, the whole Raul Brauer escapade continues at full tilt. Readers of the account of what happened a couple of years ago will recall that Professor Brauer and several other Wainscott worthies admitted to cannibalizing a youth on the Polynesian island of Loa Hoa back in the late sixties as part of a "re-creation" exercise in anthropology.

Just as the ruckus created by the publication of Brauer's book, *A Taste of the Real,* was receding, Amanda Feeney-Morin of the *Bugle* tracked down Marilyn Knobbs, the woman whose high school graduation picture was found among the effects of the young man murdered and eaten on that remote island so many years ago. Ms. Knobbs of Beaumont, Texas, no longer young, of course, remembered the boy, saying he was one Richard "Buddy" Waco, also of Beaumont. Well, there was this thing staged on television between the family of the victim and the three gentlemen who, in the name of science, had eaten parts of the boy while participating in a ritual among the Rangu.

There, in front of the whole world, Brauer, Alger Wherry, who is Curator of the MOM's Skull Collection, and Corny Chard all renounced and related with unseemly relish their parts in the sordid affair. Brauer, his head hairless and gleaming like a pale bowling ball, actually hugged the poor old mother, and then the thing degenerated into a regular tearfest. One of the victim's sisters demurred, accusing the men of being murderers, but even that seemed staged, as though there had to be some kind of conflict, some ruffled feathers for the show's hostess, a woman with an iron face and awful voice, to soothe over. The word *tasteless* does not do it justice. While I am no longer quite the old stick in the mud I used to be, thanks largely to Elsbeth's influence, I found the event quite simply *hors concours*.

Now, according to this morning's *Bugle,* a film is in the works, something that will only reignite another media conflagration. The film, I'm sure, will star some Hollywood notables and lots of native women running around in the buff, as we used to say.

Well, I have finally convinced Elsbeth to go to Keller Infirmary for a checkup. She has been feeling poorly for more than a week now. And as ghastly as the food was at the Green Sherpa, surely its effects couldn't persist for that long. So, I must make my way homeward and try to be of some comfort. Concerned as we both are, it seems that she does more reassuring of me than I of her.

4

I met this morning with Rupert Penrood, the Director of the Ponce Research Institute. He's British, with the long face of a royal, and just a bit too well dressed for a research scientist. I mean in his attention to detail, the silk-patterned tie matching the perfectly folded pocket square in his navy blazer. But then a lot of scientists are businessmen these days.

Dr. Penrood had, previous to the meeting, sent me a folder describing all the research projects under way in the lab. It's quite extraordinary what they get up to these days. Dr. Penrood assured me that the time wasn't long off when they would be able to take a cell from your body and alter a few genes to make you smarter or taller or sexier. You then pop the nucleus of that altered cell into an egg cell from which the nucleus has been removed — and *voilà,* you have an embryo that is a new and improved you. I told him I wasn't sure I liked the idea, whatever the improvements, though God knows we could all use some.

I am able to recount in these pages our conversation because I have near-perfect recall, at least in the short term. It's a knack I found useful during three decades as Recording Secretary. Indeed, my memory is very nearly auditory, allowing me to rehear entire conversations in my mind.

Dr. Penrood, for instance, spoke with the ripe, plummy intonations of a British aristocrat, saying, "You understand, Norman, we may be the last generation to die."

"Then we may be luckier than we think," I replied, not

entirely as a witticism. But I didn't smile long. I looked up and said directly, "Dr. Penrood, I have it on good authority that you were present at a somewhat heated argument between Professor Ossmann and another party with what was described as a Minnesota accent not long before Professor Ossmann and Dr. Woodley were found dead in those strange circumstances."

He showed puzzlement, perhaps feigned, and then thoughtfulness. "Yes, I do recall now that you mention it. Yes, Ossmann and Tromstromer, Olof Tromstromer, he's Swedish. They have been working on the final stages of RL . . . ReLease."

"The morning-after pill for tipplers," I said, dissembling that elusive sensation, spinal in its origin, that comes over me when I get a whiff of quarry. Dr. Penrood was hiding something. "What was the bone of contention?"

"Well, as you know, Norman, RL has advanced to human trials. I think it should prove quite lucrative. Pyramed, the pharmaceutical concern, has already started working on the ad campaign. As for Ossmann and Tromstromer, when the breakthrough occurred there was the usual jostling for credit."

I nodded as though satisfied. For all his old-school self-possession — Cambridge, I believe — Dr. Penrood evinced an undeniable edge of *arrière pensée* in his hesitations. But what, if anything, could he be hiding?

We reviewed the principal projects under way at the institute. Dr. Penrood explained how a new version of NuSkalp, the biosynthetic scalp transplant, could be used to replace hair on other parts of the body. "It has enormous potential. There's sure to be a lot more real blonds around." He gave a curious little laugh, and again the double take.

He went on. Chicken without feet; MelSus, the clean transgenic swine; possible therapies for inherited disorders; and deciduous beef.

I raised an eyebrow.

"Oh, yes, very interesting. We're trying to get an Angus to grow an extra set of ribs, one that could be cleaved off with a minimum of blood and trauma, leaving the animal alive to grow another."

"And Mel . . ."

"MelSus. It's a pig that produces virtually no dung. The feed-to-meat ratio approaches one. They produce lots of gas, but that gets harvested and used to heat their pens."

"And these pharmaceuticals?"

"Yes. As you can see, a lot of antibiotics. We're going sub-molecular. It's a war out there. I'm not sure we're going to win it."

Dr. Penrood qualified an attitude of impeccable deference with the remark that, of course, he had gone over all of this with the officers from the Seaboard Police Department.

I admit to being a bit disingenuous in invoking at that point an upcoming meeting with the Oversight Committee, implying that I had to report to a higher authority than even the law.

Penrood appeared to relax, as though academic politics explained everything. He even allowed that, given the range, complexity, and duplication of research conducted in the labs, there could be room for "freelance activity."

I asked if there might be some unobtrusive way to monitor such activity.

"Well, it's all rather difficult, you understand, but we have stepped up our in-house monitoring. I wouldn't exactly call it security, because that is not really the issue, if indeed there is an issue here."

I nodded vaguely, thinking to myself that the "monitoring" could work both ways were something untoward transpiring in the labs.

"Speaking of which," he continued in a tone smacking of the stiff upper lip, "I must protest the changing of the locks in the offices of Professor Ossmann and Dr. Woodley."

"That," I replied, "is official police business. Or, if not quite official, something that can be made so with a phone call. At this point Ms. Stone-Lee is merely making an inventory. Best, right now, to handle it quietly and . . . unofficially."

He agreed, reluctantly. Then, as though taking me into his confidence, he said, "You understand, of course, that Pip . . . Professor Ossmann . . . was not very popular among his colleagues. He liked to poke his nose into things. I'm not saying this had anything to do with his demise, but it's something you should be aware of."

I drew him out about Ossmann's relations with others in the lab while jotting down some notes. At the end of our interview I told Dr. Penrood to stay in touch; I was counting on him to help us in our investigation.

After he left, I spent several moments pondering the man. I could not shake the impression that he had not been candid with me. There is a fine line between professional discretion — the reticence of those in positions where confidentiality is a necessity — and the kind of dissembling that attends efforts to cover up some malfeasance. Perhaps my antennae are too finely tuned, but I concluded that something, somehow, was going on in the Genetics Lab, and I determined to find out exactly what.

In this regard I received another e-mail from Worried.

Dear Mr. Ratour,

I thought you'd be interested in that video of the babe doing the two profs. The guy who has it says he doesn't want to get into trouble for invasion of privates and that sort of thing. He also says it takes a lot of time and he's gotta rent some real hi-tech stuff to do it. Anyway, he says he could probably get you a pretty good copy for about three and half C's. Let me know and I'll tell him to get started. By the way, there was something that happened a couple of months back that you might find interesting. There was a guy in custodial, he's no longer here, and he asked me if I wanted to make an extra hundred bucks. Sure, why not? Here, he said, and gave me a grocery bag. Take this home and bury it in your backyard and don't say anything about it and don't ask any questions. I said, look, I got kids, and I ain't burying nothing in my back-yard until I know what it is. Okay, he says, it's a couple of dead rabbits. Okay, I says, but I want to make sure they don't have dangerous chemicals or radiation in them. No he says, they're clean, you could stew them and eat them if you wanted to, we're just trying to avoid a lot of paper-work. So, I took the dead rabbits home and threw them in the Dumpster where they're taking the asbestos out of the old firehouse. I could probably dig out the guy's name if you wanted to talk to him. Hope this helps.

Worried

Three and a half C's. Strange how Roman numerals have persisted in slang.

It's clumsy and perhaps transparent, but I have sent out another e-mail to the entire list addressed to Worried, saying yes and yes.

On a more positive note, I have just gone through several contact sheets of head-and-shoulder shots of yours truly. From them I must pick an image of myself to bequeath to posterity on the flyleaf of my upcoming book on the history of the MOM. It's a procedure for me that involves a rare and uncomfortable self-consciousness. I mean, how to look authorial but not pretentious, thoughtful but not gloomy, open but not callow; how to evince, in short, the expression of one who leads the examined life but not the overly examined life.

It's an odd sensation, really, gazing at several dozen pictures of yourself, as though there were all of these versions to choose from. The full frontal, I decided, wouldn't do, not with my ears. I have, at Elsbeth's behest, cultivated a rather dignifying, very thin mustache on the lower portion of my somewhat long upper lip. The dear woman says it makes me look as worldly and distinguished as I am.

There is a good three-quarter view in which I am resting my chin on my fisted hand. I like the expression very much; it shows me as open yet reserved, dispassionate but not implacably so. The only problem is that the fist under the chin looks posed, which of course it is, deliberately evading the problem of what might be called the posed unposed look. I took the trouble to white out my hand. The results were encouraging. Thus altered it makes me appear as though I have my nose in the air, but in some ways that does capture the essence.

It certainly goes with the book, *The Past Redeemed: The History of the Museum of Man*. I had wanted to title it *The Solace of Beauty*, but Myra Myrtlebaum, my editor at Wainscott Press, talked me out of it. No matter, you shouldn't judge a book by its title — or by the face of the author, for that matter. To tell you the truth, I am both pleased and not a little doubtful about my first real book. I found it easy enough to encapsulate the museum's remarkable history, its founding by the intrepid Remicks of Remsdale. I devoted a whole chapter to the Skull and the role it played in the founding of the museum. I reveled in describing how those canny Yankee captains scoured the world to collect, no doubt at bargain prices, priceless objects from every known culture. I chronicled the way we have grown, persevered, and kept our independence.

Where I may have failed, I'm afraid, is in my attempts to render for the reader the subtle glory of the treasures we have so carefully collected, curated, and put on display. As of old, when I leave in the evenings, I descend through the galleries that encircle and open onto the atrium, which is lit from above during the day by a domed skylight, a web of wrought-iron tracery worthy of Kew. From the delicate potteries, jade work, and silks of the Far East, to the masks and figurines in our Africa display, from the glories of our Oceanic Collection to case after fabulous case of pre-Columbian Mesoamerican art, I find affirmation that, in our instinct for the beautiful, in our very need for beauty, we partake of the Godhead, that we are not merely creatures, but creators.

Of course it was these kinds of effusions that Ms. Myrtlebaum at the Press kept putting her pencil through. Politely, of course, and with what sounded like good reason. But I do wish I had insisted on one unfettered declaration from the heart, whatever the risk of mawkishness, if only to lighten the darkness that pervades so much of life.

5

Elsbeth is not well. I fussed about this morning, making her breakfast, pampering her, trying to relieve an awful anxiety until she shoved me out the house, telling me I had more important things to do.

Though late in leaving, I walked to work through Thornton Arboretum as has been my custom for decades now. I walked at a pace brisk enough to do my heart and lungs some good. It takes nearly half an hour. Descending Bridge Street, I turn left through the Oakdale section, formerly a patchy area of rundown redbrick housing that has undergone a dramatic revival. *Gentrified,* I believe, is the appropriate term of opprobrium for such improvements. Then, after crossing at the lights on Merchants Row, I ascend through an area of well-lawned affluence to the granite gates of the arboretum.

I have never cared much for the gaudy death bloom of our northeastern autumns. I prefer the aftermath, the subtleties of yellows, golds, and browns, the baring branches, the crunch underfoot, the rustle of wind, the smell of sweet decay. The world was thus this morning, with the sky a forbidding gray rendering the agitated waters of Kettle Pond a dull pewter.

A like agitation stirred my own heart as I walked along, as though more in haste than with the purposeful stride of the health-conscious. The geese paddled the cold water, the crows flew against the palled sky, and the jays called, sounding like augurs of disaster. The very trees, my old friends, might have been watching me, mute, as though in warning. My pulse quickened as I crossed the Lagoon Bridge and saw the museum, its five stories of elegant brick with neo-Gothic and neo-Grecian flourishes, rising into view behind the browning sycamores that line Belmont Avenue. Was that beautiful structure, designed by Hannibal Richards, "the Bernini of Seaboard," harboring another brood of murderers?

Of course, if there is a criminal conspiracy, it's no doubt festering in the Genetics Lab, housed in the bastardized wing that, added later, squats to the left. To the right, appropriately enough, is the new Center for Criminal Justice, all glass and beige bricks, another monument to architectural hubris.

All of this foreboding, of course, is nothing next and no doubt related to the dread that now shadows my life. I am worried sick about poor Elsbeth. We will have the results of her tests the day after tomorrow, and I fear the worst. She has all but stopped eating. Her face is drawn and pale. Her eyes still shine, but it is only her essential goodness showing through. Today, at the first meeting of the Curatorial Ball planning committee, I had an awful premonition that she would not be with us. I shook the notion immediately, of course. She may simply have one of those pernicious viruses that abound these days. Dr. Berns will probably give her a shot or a prescription, and I will have my Elsbeth back in glowing health once again.

I arrived at the office to a waft of a distinct, musk-edged men's cologne. Doreen broke off a giggly phone conversation with one of her friends to tell me that a Mr. Freddie Bain had shown up unannounced and had left behind his card along with his scent.

"Did he say what he wanted?" I asked, trying to recall when I had heard the name before.

"No. Just said he'd be back."

For all my presentiments, I have little to report on the Ossmann-Woodley case. I forwarded the two e-mails I have gotten from Worried to Lieutenant Tracy. He dropped by, and we went over the contents of the Worried missives and what they could import. He agreed with me that it might be very useful to learn the identities of the individuals who were involved in what he termed "the threesome." But more than that, he said he would really like to talk to the person who had asked Worried to bury those rabbits.

I said I had already asked Worried to help us on both of those accounts. I also related to him the essence of my interview with Dr. Penrood, but kept to myself the tincture of suspicion that meeting occasioned in me. I did tell him, however, that I thought it entirely possible that something out of the ordinary might be going on in the Genetics Lab.

The lieutenant sympathized when I told him I was to meet with the University Oversight Committee. In the wake of the Ossmann-Woodley matter, the committee, in all fairness to it, has, through the university administration, come under pressure from a local group calling itself the Coalition Against the Unnatural. He nodded ruefully at the mention of the name. The same group has been lobbying the Mayor's office to have everything in the Genetics Lab opened to general public scrutiny. We live in interesting times, as the Chinese curse has it.

And, I reminded him, it's not just the Ossmann-Woodley strangeness that has attracted undue attention to the lab. Bert, one of our remaining chimps, is back in the news. In a so-called exposé in this morning's *Bugle,* Amanda Feeney-Morin repeated the canard that Bert "was tortured with forced intoxication" during the final stages of animal testing for ReLease, the Ponce's promising new drug. RL, as I may have mentioned, is a morning-after medication for those who have imbibed too much. It combines, among other things, a drug that affects the elasticity of the cardiovascular system, a high dose of vitamin B, and a powerful analgesic. Its commercial potential is said to be enormous.

Ms. Feeney-Morin claims in her article that Bert is now the pongid equivalent of a recovering alcoholic. She claims, erroneously, that Bert has been sent to a program that deals in post-traumatic stress syndrome among animals subjected to "inhumane" experimentation.

I have been over to the Pavilion myself to check on Bert. To be honest, he does appear quite depressed; he has, tinged with self-disgust, that hankering, haunted look in his eyes that many of us can identify with. As Father O'Gould once remarked in another context, there are times when low self-esteem may be a sign of intelligence.

In fact, another chimp, one named Alphus, also took part in the experiment and showed no ill effects whatsoever. But then, Alphus is an exceptionally intelligent member of his species. He apparently succeeded in letting his keeper know that he wanted to participate.

Be that as it may, with this morsel of misinformation Ms. Feeney-Morin has given herself the pretext to rehash yet again the whole so-called controversy revolving around the development of RL. For instance, about six paragraphs into her skein of fabrications, she trots out the "ethical issues" she and others claim attend the development of a "hangover" pill. Given all the other ills of the world, the argument goes, should we really be diverting the time and resources to contrive a medication that encourages people in drinking by ameliorating its more immediate and tangible consequences?

As my good friend Izzy Landes has pointed out, if lovers can have a morning-after pill, why not boozers? Why not, indeed?

Is not the alleviation of suffering, whatever its origins, a noble cause?

In any event Ms. Feeney-Morin has succeeded once again in riling up the animal rights contingent. My phone did not stop ringing this morning for more than ten minutes. One gentleman asked to speak to Dr. Mengele before launching into an abusive tirade. To those making more respectful inquiries, I stated that Bert did in fact undergo a successful detoxification process — admittedly, more like two steps than twelve — and has rejoined his fellow chimps as a functioning member of that community. It's more than you can say for a lot of people out there.

This continuing fuss has made it clear to me that we need to proceed as expeditiously as possible to find places for the animals still on the premises. Back a couple of years ago, we had a sizable population of chimpanzees (*Pan troglodytes,* not *panicus*) that a somewhat demented keeper, one Damon Drex, tried to induce to wax literary. (Mr. Drex, I hear, was recently released from a mental institution and has gone to work for a zoo.)

When I became Director, I decided to close down the Primate Pavilion on the grounds that chimpanzees, whatever their DNA reads out to be, are not human, and have no real place in the Museum of Man. I objected, diplomatically, of course, to the neat paradigm proposed by one or two of the older board members that the Pavilion represented man's distant past, the museum proper his recent past and present, and the Genetics Lab his future.

The Primate Pavilion is now simply known as the Pavilion, although it still contains primates, mostly human, who occupy the same offices built for Damon Drex's typing chimps. We have leased much of the space to Wainscott at a very good rate, thanks to arrangements worked out and insisted on by our new counsel. Indeed, the premises don't look all that different than they did before, what with people in their cubicles bent over computer screens. One big difference, of course, is that there are no droppings on the floor.

But there are still some rhesus cages upstairs, and the old, unconverted part of the ground floor, with its doleful cages and rather pathetic inmates, still exists. *Plus ça change, plus la même chose!* And, under strict supervision, these animals are licensed to the Genetics Lab for experimental uses. Under strict supervision from the appropriate state and federal agencies, I might add.

In other words, we still have in residence a number of troglodytes. To oversee them we appointed Dr. Angela Simone as the Ruddy and Phyllis Stein Keeper of Great Apes, the endowed position Mr. Drex previously occupied. A well-respected primatologist, an attractive young woman with a sympathetic manner, Dr. Simone is devoted to her charges and punctilious when it comes to treating them humanely. She realizes that her duties are to be phased out gradually. (What we will do with the position, I'm not sure. Perhaps we could put the occupant in charge of the personnel department I plan to establish for the museum.)

On the other hand, Dr. Simone may be with us for some time. We have not found it easy to "place" the animals. Some of them have been sold or donated to other institutions. You can't give the creatures away to private citizens because, frankly, they don't make good pets. You don't see sensitive-looking people leading them around the streets the way they do with slow greyhounds. Some of the animals have been habituated back into the wild on an island off the coast of Africa. As an aside, there are times when I think it would be handy if certain humans could be habituated back into some wilderness more suitable to their feral natures. I am thinking about people like Malachy Morin, who might benefit from living in a real state of nature. Though, to give credit where credit is due, he has settled down somewhat since his marriage to Amanda Feeney, the *Bugle* reporter.

The fact remains Mr. Morin does not know how to do anything except hang out with the boys and bluster and bully people around. Or try to. As it stands he has been able, through his cronies, to get himself made a university Vice President with responsibility for museums and other affiliated institutions. He remains my superior on some organizational charts, which are utter fabrications. In reality he is little more than a nuisance.

The fact is, I want to more than hold the line against any university encroachment. For instance, once the chimpanzees are out of the Pavilion, I intend to remove the rest of the primates as well — the people, that is. Well, not entirely. What I want to do is to convert the space in the Pavilion into curatorial areas open to the public. Here, at designated times, people would be allowed to watch as the curators and restorers tease from the matrix of time and rock and neglect some priceless ancient object, reclaiming beauty and restoring to wholeness at least some fragment of our shattered past.

None of this vision would come to pass, I know, if the university were to succeed in getting its bottom-line, budget-obsessed bureaucrats in charge here. That's what I am struggling against. That's why these sudden dark happenings are a threat not just to my institutional survival, but to the fulfillment of a necessary dream.

6

We have had the worst possible news. I went with Elsbeth to the clinic this morning. We knew it wasn't good the moment we entered Dr. Berns's office. I sat next to Elsbeth holding her hand. The good doctor shuffled some papers, took off his glasses, and sighed. "I'm afraid," he said, "the results are not good.

"We've found a tumor in the pancreas. A very aggressive form. The prognosis is not good even with treatment." His words blurred. I clutched her hand thinking only that before long there would be no hand to hold. The doctor said we could try therapy, but he did not recommend it. He said he had some medication that would ease the discomfort and keep the symptoms at bay. "You have perhaps three months, perhaps less. I would try to live them as best you can."

Elsbeth, I must say, took it rather well. After a few moments of quiet shock in which she let the reality of her situation register, she gave me a hug and turned to the doctor to discuss with him several salient points.

"I want to stay home," she said. Then, "I'm staying home regardless. No tubes. No needles. No beeping machines. No endless tests to find out how badly I'm doing." She laughed, inviting us to laugh, such is her generosity of spirit. She said she wanted "killer" drugs for sleeping, "but honestly, I don't want to drowse my way into the next world."

Dr. Berns, a large, bearded presence, said he would have all the tests run again. He wrote out a sheaf of prescriptions. He told her to call him any time of the day or night if she needed him. There was more than a trace of emotion in his voice, and he gave her a big hug when we left.

In the car, in the low-slung parking garage with the bright slabs of autumn light visible in the distance, she broke down and cried and cried in my arms. Then, composing herself, she said she had known about it for some time. Nothing specific, but something going fundamentally wrong. She said it had kindled within her a latent faith, "not so much in a personal God, Norman, but in life itself."

What could I say? Words of comfort failed me. Because there really were none. Reassurances? Of what? *We'll make your death a nice one, Elsbeth, the best money can buy.* Emotions, like words, can seem like clichés. I am devastated, of course, when I am not being incredulous. Life is a habit, after all, and it's always a shock when death, that lurking, monstrous joker, reaches out his inevitable hand.

And what do you do when you have news like this? I feel constrained to call up friends and invite them over for a drink. For a lot of drinks. But we have no ritual response for such announcements. The prognostication of death is, culturally speaking, a recent phenomenon. But surely, we need the comfort of family and friends at these moments, more perhaps than when the body is already cold.

I did call Diantha and Winslow Jr., Elsbeth's daughter and son. Diantha, who has been estranged from Elsbeth for more than a year — some dispute over a boyfriend — broke down and wept. "Let me speak to Mommy," she kept saying. I put Elsbeth on and tiptoed away, leaving them to a tearful, long-distance reconciliation.

Win Jr., a businessman very much like his late father, took the news very much in stride. He consulted his calendar and said he would fly in from New York this coming Sunday. He had been able, just, it seems, to fit his mother into his schedule.

I also called our good friends Izzy and Lotte Landes. They dropped by in the afternoon "for a drink and a good weep." Lotte, who has become a good friend of Elsbeth's over the last couple of years, ran her through a gamut of lifesaving drills. Yes, Berns was a good GP, but Keller Infirmary wasn't called "Killer Infirmary" for nothing. They knew a specialist in Chicago who had come up with an aggressive new therapy that showed lots of promise.

Elsbeth shook her head. "I'm not up for some kind of high-tech torture." But she calmed and comforted them as well. Was her resignation, I wondered, her way of reassuring the rest of us?

Korky Kummerbund came over right away, bringing a big bouquet of lilies. He wept and figuratively, anyway, banged the walls. He is quite literally a sweet man, gay, but not in the least fussy about it. He's of the opinion that people of his predilections should stay in their closets, but make them much bigger, with porches and mountain views, and invite in special friends.

The Reverend Alfie Lopes, Wainscott Minister and Plumtree Professor of Morals (They've dropped the "Christian," I've noticed, in the name of fair play. As long as they don't drop the "Morals," I shan't complain.), said he would come to see both Elsbeth and me whenever we wanted him. I said why not simply come over for dinner and a chat. We made a date. As the years go by, I have come to appreciate Alfie more and more. He refers to himself as an Afro-Saxon and is not shy about being proud of both traditions.

Elsbeth's plight has certainly put matters in perspective for me. I can care for and think of nothing else. Everything else pales to insignificance. Let killers roam the Genetics Lab. Let Wainscott have the museum. Let war begin and the glaciers return. I don't care. I want my Elsbeth restored to her old vibrant self. I feel cursed. It seems I no sooner have Elsbeth in my life, have scarcely sat down at life's feast, when it is all going to be taken away from me. Perhaps I am being selfish in this. I know Elsbeth is the one who must suffer and die in the prime of her life. But I would change with her, take her place, in a moment. Only the result would be the same. My life would be over.

7

It is Friday, the thirteenth of October, and the trees are in their autumn beauty as never before. And though as suspicious as anyone, I no longer fear bad luck. Surely we have had our quotient.

Lieutenant Tracy, an edge of worry to the serious set of his face, came by to make what appears to be in retrospect a curious request. It seems that Police Chief Francis Murphy has been putting the pressure on. I watched attentively as the lieutenant rubbed his hands together. "Of course, Norman, he's only getting heat from the Mayor's office. His Honor is planning to run for Congress and doesn't want a monkey around his neck."

I nodded, indicating my understanding in a general way. Then the lieutenant told me something I had heretofore more felt than realized: It would be better for all concerned if Ossmann-Woodley was a clear-cut murder case; if someone had deliberately dosed them with the intention of having them kill each other in a sexual frenzy.

"People can tolerate evil," he said. "It's the unknown that frightens them. Especially when a genetics lab is involved. We still believe in monsters."

"But Lieutenant, we don't have enough evidence yet to call it murder," I pointed out.

He nodded his agreement. "Would you or the museum mind if we did make it official. I mean as a murder?"

I thought over his request for a moment. "It won't help us

much. Any new hook gives the *Bugle* and others the opportunity to drag the whole thing through the mud again. But I appreciate being asked."

"And it wouldn't be the truth, would it?"

I rebuked myself inwardly for having neglected that most important consideration. But I said, "Perhaps it would be more effective for your purposes if you could announce new evidence at the same time."

He turned thoughtful, then said, "I think you're right. If the ME has anything new from those follow-up tests, we can do it then." He smiled and rose to go. "Norman, thanks. And I'll keep you updated."

I wish I could be as positive about the special meeting of the University Oversight Committee I attended this afternoon, an ordeal by pettiness. There are people who ask me why I bother at all with the committee. Why do I mouth bromides about maintaining cordial relations with the university, why do we want to remain, however independently, a member of the greater Wainscott family? Especially since the museum has become, in their opinion, anyway, the institutional equivalent of the rich eccentric uncle everyone secretly hopes will pop off sooner rather than later and leave them a bundle.

In part it's because I do want to continue the long and fruitful bond between the two institutions, a bond based on mutual respect. Indeed, I would not like it to become well known how highly I regard the faculty at Wainscott. Perhaps it's because I am, at heart, an academic *manqué,* what Elsbeth calls a wannabe. I feel that the involvement of Thad Pilty and even Corny Chard, not to mention Father O'Gould and Izzy Landes, makes us, as an institution, an intellectual force to be reckoned with.

What I want to avoid in the museum is the management style of Wainscott, especially the forces represented by Malachy

Morin. These are the people who would corporatize, to bastard-ize a perfectly innocent word, hell itself. They would bring in their systems, which never quite work, and their regimentation, which renders everything and everyone colorless, all the while basking in the glow of the work done by the scholars.

While independent in fact and in law (the university is chal-lenging us in the courts, but that, we have good reason to believe, will come to nothing), we need Wainscott as a buffer between the outside world and ourselves, especially where the Genetics Lab is concerned. Groups such as the Coalition Against the Unnatural remain under the mistaken impression, which I do little to rectify, that the MOM is part and parcel of Wainscott. I know the public relations apparatus of the university would like to direct such obloquy toward us, but to do so would be to admit our independence. As may be obvious, after a few years of real institutional responsibility, I have turned into something of a Machiavel.

Ah, yes, the committee meeting. We assembled in the Rothko Room, one of those repellent boxy spaces filled with the kind of raw light you find in the upper reaches of modern buildings. It was designed to hold the paintings of the eponymous dauber, but thank God those have been stowed away. It's the kind of place you would expect to find in Grope Tower, that offensive slab of concrete and glass that mars the redbrick gentility of the older Wainscott buildings surrounding it. (Why, I often wonder, has there been, in the long stretch between Gaudí and Gehry, such a paucity of architectural imagination?)

But I digress. The usual suspects, all getting a bit grayer, showed up for the meeting. Professor Thad Pilty, creator of the Diorama of Paleolithic Life that now graces Neanderthal Hall, has stayed on as a member. I don't doubt his intentions, but I believe he's being vigilant — and with good reason. Any changes in the models and the roles of the Neanderdroids, so to speak, still come in for close scrutiny by certain members of the committee.

Constance Brattle, the expert on blame, preened a little in accepting congratulations about the success of her latest book, *Achieving the No-Fault Life*. I'm told it's a sequel to *Effective Apologizing*, her best seller of last year. She remains the somewhat wooden Chair of the committee.

Berthe Schanke, larger than life, no-fault or otherwise, her head perfectly shaven, in studded black jacket over a T-shirt lettered with some slogan about the patriarchy, rootled as usual in the donuts that had been provided. She remains the guiding force behind BITCH, a coalition of groups comprising what Izzy Landes has called "the complaining classes."

Izzy himself, academically respondent in bow tie, his nimbus of white hair swept dramatically back, took a plaudit from Father S.J. O'Gould, S.J., regarding the publication of his latest tome, *The Evolution of Evolution*, successor to *The Nature of Nature* and *The Science of Science*. And while not a best seller, it has been very well received in those quarters where it matters.

Understatedly dignified in Roman collar, Father O'Gould, now best known for *Wonderful Strife: Natural Selection and the Inevitability of Intelligence*, took me aside before the meeting to offer me his sympathy regarding Elsbeth's situation. He said he would like to drop by as a friend to see her. I thanked him and said I was sure Elsbeth would be delighted. I told him I looked forward to hearing him give the first Fessing Lecture.

Corny Chard didn't show up, of course, being down in the Amazon somewhere trying to document people eating other people. Standing in for Corny for the semester was John Murdleston, also a professor of anthropology and Curator of the Ethnocoprolite Collections in the MOM. He recently published an article, "Expressive Flatulence and Male Prerogative in an Evolutionary Context," that created a small stir in those circles devoted to such things.

Professor Randall Athol of the Divinity School arrived late and a little breathless. He apologized and voiced the hope he hadn't missed much. Even he has published recently, something on the nature of divine fairness titled, I believe, *When Good Things Happen to Bad People*.

Ariel Dearth, the Leona Von Beaut Professor of Situational Ethics and Litigation Development at the Law School, sat restlessly, as usual, looking around him as though for the press or for clients. He cranks out books pretty regularly, *Sue Your Mother* being his latest. I'm told there are cases now where children have sued their parents for wrongful birth, bad genes, and all that.

We have a couple of newcomers, chief among them one Luraleena Doveen, a very fetching young woman of color from the President's Office of Outreach. I think she may be the only one not in the toils of publishing something.

A Professor J.J. McNull, who joined the committee last year, smiled on everyone. He strikes me as one of those academicians who, with a bottomless capacity for boredom, sit on committees trying to look sage and saying no. I'm not sure what he's professor of. He glances around a lot, either smiling with approval or glowering with disapproval.

Ms. Brattle opened with a short statement about "what appear to be dark happenings in the Museum of Man again leading to concerns about the administration of that institution." A large woman with the self-obliviousness of a professional professional, so to speak, Ms. Brattle looked over her glasses at me in a manner meant to level blame. She spoke darkly of the need for "a very active subcommittee to monitor the day-to-day operations of the museum, especially the part dealing with the very sensitive area of genetic research." She concluded by reminding us that, as Chair, she reports directly to President Twill himself.

Remaining imperturbed, I responded that the museum's Board of Governors was not likely to allow me to acquiesce in such a step even were I inclined to do so. I informed the committee that the museum is in strict compliance with the Animal Welfare Act and all other local, state, and federal regulations governing the research conducted at the lab. I told them that I was cooperating very closely with the Seaboard Police Department in their ongoing investigation into what had transpired the night that Professor Ossmann and Dr. Woodley died. I reminded them that what happened that night might very well have nothing to do with the lab or with their research there.

Ms. Schanke, in the kind of *non sequitur* to which she is given, stood up and spoke as though reading from a prepared statement. Looking directly at me, she said, "I know that people like you, Mr. Ratour, think that people like me are perverts. But we all know that what's going on in those labs is the real perversion. You people are perverting nature and you're going to f*ck everything up. You pretend to be scientists, but all you're really interested in is the bottom line and how much money you can make . . ." After several more minutes of this kind of diatribe, Ms. Schanke sat down and helped herself to a Chocolate Frosted.

I let the silence at her outburst gather and provide its own rebuttal.

Attorney Dearth bestirred himself. "What Berthe's trying to say —"

Ms. Schanke, standing again, interrupted him. "I'm not *trying* to say anything. I have said what I wanted to say."

In what appeared to be an attempt to strike a moderating note,

Professor Athol opined how "the research into the secrets of life needs a spiritual dimension."

"Yeah, until they find the God gene, and then they'll find a way to market that as well," Ms. Schanke rejoined with some bitterness.

Izzy perked up at that. "Well, judging from what's out there, there must be lots of different God genes. I mean a Methodist God gene, a Catholic God gene, a couple of Jewish God genes, one for the Reformed and one for the Orthodox. And think about the Hindus . . ."

Professor Murdleston, who is hard of hearing, asked, "A Methodist gene?"

"Well, not a Methodist gene *per se* . . ."

"I think Randy is trying to say something important here," Mr. Dearth put in.

And in rare agreement with the attorney, Father O'Gould, the lilt of his native Cork still in his speech, said, "If we are nothing more than our genes, then what are we?"

No one seemed to know.

Mr. Dearth wondered aloud what two people were doing in the lab alone at night.

Izzy asked the learned counsel if he was suggesting there ought to have been chaperones.

"No, I am wondering where the security guard was."

I informed the committee that there were, as usual, two guards on duty in the Genetics Lab building itself, one making rounds, "who can't be in all places at all times," and one watching an array of monitors.

"You mean to say there was no video monitor set up in the lab where this tragedy occurred?" Dearth asked me in his best withering courtroom manner.

"There was a monitor," I replied, "until several of the researchers, led by Professor Ossmann, took the matter to the American Civil Liberties Union and forced us to remove it on the grounds it was an invasion of privacy."

Mr. Dearth subsided.

Izzy waxed philosophical at that point. He noted that we are increasingly taking over our own evolutionary destiny; that, *vide* his latest publication, evolution itself is evolving. Once Crick and Watson let the genie out of the bottle, well, there was no putting it back in.

I agreed. I pointed out that before long we will be raising pigs with genetically altered hearts that can be transplanted into human beings.

Ms. Berthe declared that for most corporate types the genetic modifications wouldn't be necessary.

Thad Pilty weighed in at that moment, saying that "transgenic swine are already old hat." In an attempt to lighten the mood, he added, "Before long, theoretically, anyway, you'll be able to grow yourself a second sex organ."

Not everyone laughed.

Izzy chortled. "I think it's quite enough to manage one."

"Tell me about it," said Ms. Doveen, trying not to giggle.

Ms. Brattle brought us back to the frowning level by recalling the attempts of Dr. S.X. Gottling to produce a new "perfect" human genotype at the lab using chimps as experimental models.

Professor McNull scowled his approval of her disapproval.

The question, Professor Athol stated somewhat pretentiously, "is not what is to become of us, but what are we to become?"

"I see lots of room for improvement," Izzy said.

Ms. Doveen inquired very sensibly if it might be possible for someone to be concocting a potent aphrodisiac in the lab without the knowledge of management.

I told her such a thing was possible but not very probable given the protocols in place for developing and testing such a drug before it would be allowed on the market.

"But you don't know for certain?" Professor Athol spoke in an accusatory tone.

"That's true," I said, "any more than you would know for certain whether one of your deans was downloading pornography into the hard drive of his office computer."

Ariel Dearth revived from an uncharacteristic somnambulence. "But if such a drug were under development in the lab, it would be in your interest to cover it up, wouldn't it?"

"I resent your insinuation," I replied. "And what possible motive could we have for covering up that or any other research?"

Mr. Dearth smiled. "What I mean, Mr. de Ratour, is that should you be experimenting with anything like a powerful aphrodisiac, then the museum could be liable for wrongful deaths."

Izzy gave a snorting "ha!" Then he said, "And what rich postmortem pickings there would be for you, Ariel, and the members of your . . . profession."

It was Father O'Gould who stepped in to point out that we were meeting to offer advice to the Genetics Lab, if it were needed, and not to indulge in accusations based on speculation.

I thought at that point the meeting might be over or move on to something else, perhaps whether the university's health coverage should pay for sex-change operations and that sort of thing. Instead, Professor Athol brought up Bert and the chimp's participation in the development of ReLease, and, with that, the ethical issues surrounding the use of animals in medical experiments.

Father O'Gould, I noticed, leaned forward, evincing a close interest in what I had to say. "Well, first," I began, "we subscribe, as I've noted, to all the provisions of the Animal Welfare Act.

Additionally, we take every measure possible to assure the comfort both physically and psychologically where the latter applies of the organism in any experiment."

Father O'Gould nodded. "The question is one of stewardship. We need always balance the mercy due our fellow creature with the mercy due our fellow man . . ."

"And woman," Ms. Brattle interjected.

Ms. Schanke, visibly agitated, burst forth: "What you're both really saying in fancy language is that it's all right for us so-called human beings to torture other animals, even those that share ninety-eight percent of our DNA, so that booze-swilling men don't have to suffer hangovers . . ."

"Even sinners deserve mercy," Father O'Gould said gently.

". . . and so that big price-gouging companies like Pyramed can make billions in profit . . ."

"We don't torture animals," I replied coolly.

"I think inducing fellow creatures to drink alcohol to excess could be called torture," said Ms. Brattle, the expert on blame.

"What did you give him to drink?" asked Izzy.

"Vodka in orange juice."

"And you don't call that torture?" Ms. Schanke demanded.

Ms. Doveen, an unexpected ally, turned to Ms. Schanke and asked, "How do you know? Maybe he liked getting high. I mean all they do is sit around all day like prisoners."

"Well," I said, correcting her gently, "we do have an exercise yard where they spend considerable time together."

"How do you keep them from breeding?" Professor Athol asked.

"The females are fixed," I replied, without thinking. "With the exception of one or two that are on special medication."

"You spayed them?" Ms. Schanke asked with outraged incredulity.

"Yes."

"Without their permission?"

I shook my head, wondering what Alice in Wonderland realm I had stumbled into.

"Why didn't you fix the males instead?" Ms. Brattle joined in, sensing blood.

"We followed the recommendations of a respected consultant."

"A man, no doubt," said Ms. Schanke.

I ignored her and said something to the effect that the committee might be interested to learn that the museum had had in place for some time a deacquisition program regarding the chimps.

Which opened me up for another round of abuse led by Ms. Schanke. "Right, right. Now that the lab is finished torturing the poor beasts, you're going to get rid of them."

I explained in detail how we were placing and repatriating the chimps in the most humane way possible. What I could not admit to before the committee right then is the fact that I have profound misgivings myself about any kind of experimentation on animals, however humble their rank on the evolutionary ladder. I am privately very embarrassed by what happened to Bert during the trials for ReLease. Indeed the treatment of our animals is one area in the Genetics Lab where I am stickler for protocol.

The fact is that under Elsbeth's gentle suasion, I have become far more sensitive to the rights and sufferings of our fellow creatures. We regularly have several "vegetarian" days a week now. But right then was not the time for a soul-baring confession.

As though sensing my thoughts, Father O'Gould held forth that the time had come in the moral evolution of our species to consider the possibility of moving beyond the use of animals for our food and fiber needs.

Near the end of the meeting Ms. Brattle announced that

early next week there would be an executive session of the Subcommittee on Appropriateness regarding a very sensitive case that had arisen between two employees in Sigmund Library, which serves the Psychology Department. The subcommittee, on which I serve — another gesture of goodwill — investigates and arbitrates on sensitive issues dealing with ethnic, gender, dietary, class, language, olfactory, and sexual orientation conflicts arising among students, faculty, and members of the administration.

The meeting concluded in a muddle of inaction, good intentions, and declarative excess, the way most such meetings end. I simply stopped trying to explain anything. The pall of impending grief that I had held at bay all afternoon descended like a bleak cloud. How trivial everything before me seemed, how like shadows on a stage that had come and would go, leaving no trace. My dear, precious Elsbeth is under sentence of death.

Well, I must call it a day. Or a night. I must go home now and help, as much as I can, Elsbeth into that other, endless night that awaits us all.

8

I am upstairs in my study again. The night is cold, dark, and silent. I am not only staggered with a sadness beyond description, but I am in thrall to new and disturbing thoughts and feelings that I had never expected to contend with.

This afternoon I went out to our sophisticated little airport — it handles smaller passenger jets with alacrity — to pick up Diantha, Elsbeth's daughter. The dear girl could scarcely keep from weeping when she saw me, falling into my arms, clinging to me, her wet face buried in my neck. I was glad to be of comfort and cared not one whit for the stares of passersby. I tried to reassure her as we waited for her luggage — three huge pieces — to come up the conveyer belt as though from Hades and start its clockwise stagger around the oval track of interleaved metal plates. I can tell from my prose that I am already equivocating.

To witness Diantha's shock and pity at seeing her mother in such evident decline opened afresh my own wound. I stood with my eyes damp as mother and daughter embraced and cried and then, not so strangely, started to laugh, as though life, deep down, even at its tragic worst, is comic, the joke of a whimsical creator.

They spoke for hours, it seemed. I served as bartender, cook, waiter, and sommelier, uncorking one, then two bottles of a plangent Graves that Izzy recommended. It went brilliantly with the seafood lasagna that Elsbeth taught me how to make.

(The touch of fennel and rosemary is the secret.) We all got a little tipsy, but I think it helped Elsbeth and Diantha heal any lingering rift between them. They both turned to me on occasion during the course of the evening, each time with something akin to surprise and not a little pleasure in their faces. I like to think they found my presence comforting. It was a great relief not to act as referee, an office I reluctantly undertook during their last meeting and which had earned me, I sensed, Diantha's antipathy.

Now I have the strange, unnerving feeling that a whole new aura has entered the house. In an uncanny way, it's as though Elsbeth's replacement has shown up, a kind of premature reincarnation. Not that I know Diantha that well. She did come to the wedding, but her visit was brief.

We had a chance, doing the dishes together, to chat. "Your mom tells me you're in show business," I said by way of an invitation to her to tell me about herself.

She shrugged. "I've done some acting. Some modeling. I have an agent. I've had gigs and a zillion near misses for the big time. But that's not really what I do."

"What do you do?" I asked, noticing that she stacked the dishwasher exactly the way her mother does.

"I have this knack for sorting out programming problems that confuse people with a lot more smarts than I ever had. It's a kind of idiot savant flair. Even the high-end providers keep making the same mistakes." She laughed at herself. "They pay me lots of money and it leaves me enough time to screw up the rest of my life."

"I'm sure you underestimate yourself." I rinsed off Elsbeth's dish, noticing that she had eaten very little.

"Yeah, so I'm told. It's better than having other people do it for you. Mom says you're working on another murder."

"We're not sure they're murders."

"She says it's juicy stuff. Two people fu . . . did themselves to death."

"Yes. It seems there was . . . intercourse of some violence." In speaking I attempted to maintain the tone of objectivity, however spurious, that allows one to talk of prurient matters without the appearance of indulging in the prurience.

Diantha laughed one of her mother's laughs, a bright, mischievous hiccup. "It sounds like a great way to go."

"It wasn't a pretty scene."

"You were there? Afterward?" Her voice had a touch of awe to it.

"I looked at the crime scene photos. And the crime scene video."

She bent to put a glass in the dishwasher with, I thought, an exaggerated motion. "So you really get into it."

"I'm helping the police with inquiries, as the British put it, but not as a suspect. Not yet anyway."

She beamed at me. "That is so cool."

"That remains to be seen. I could just botch things up for them."

"Now you're the one underestimating yourself."

I smiled. "What did you say before? It's better than having other people do it for you."

As we closed up the kitchen for the night, she took one of my hands in hers. "By the way . . . Dad . . . Do you mind if I call you Dad?"

"I'd be honored."

"I want to thank you for taking such good care of Mom these last couple of years." Her eyes were bright and dark with sincerity, establishing as much as the warmth of her hand the closeness she wanted to have with me.

"She has taken care of me, too, you know. She has made my life . . ." At which point, for the first time all evening, I had to stop and take a deep sigh.

But there remains a jagged, nagging note to this sad and yet curiously jubilant occasion that I have been skirting around throughout this account. In saying good night to Diantha in the hallway upstairs, I leaned down to give her a chaste peck on the cheek only to find myself kissed full on the lips with a sensuality the sensation of which I cannot quite shake. I found myself reeling down the hallway in a kind of sensual time warp, every nerve alive, my imagination full of conjurations, my pulse racing. Though nearly six decades along in life, I find myself still burdened with a persisting virility, as though marriage to Elsbeth has re-endowed me with the manly vigor of youth. I thought the momentary pulse of lust, distressing enough, would pass as I came to my senses. But it lingers and I find myself beset with images and forbidden desires.

It's as though my dear Elsbeth, lying in our bedroom suffering through a drugged, fitful sleep, has become a ghost, replaced in life by Diantha, who is the very embodiment of her mother at a younger age. She has the same full-bodied figure, the same dark glowing eyes, the same pretty if somewhat blunt features, and even, at times, the same dark timbre of voice intimating the essential mischievousness of life.

I may, of course, be reading too much into the incident. For Diantha it was no doubt a kiss that got away. Or perhaps that's the way people in show business comport themselves. Disport themselves more like it. Or perhaps she is needful of an affection that, under the right circumstances, can inflame one to more tangible desires. It may also be that the presence or probability of individual finality stirs us in ways that are only superficially grotesque. As Father O'Gould has reminded us on more than one occasion, it is easy to forget what we are descended from.

Speaking of which, Malachy Morin accosted me in the Club at lunch on Friday and I couldn't get away from him without agreeing to meet with him and "the big-money guys" from the Wainscott Office of Development. I do not consider myself a snob, but it seems to me the Club ought to be one of those places you can go to avoid people like Mr. Morin.

9

Although it is still early in the afternoon, I have closed the door and asked Doreen to hold my calls while I peck at these keys and at a crabmeat salad sandwich we had sent in. I usually don't interrupt my workday to make entries into this subfile. But Lieutenant Tracy came in around eleven accompanied by Dr. P.M. Cutler, the Medical Examiner, and Dr. Arthur ffronche, a forensic endocrinologest from the state crime lab, and I want to record our conversation while it is still fresh in my mind.

Dr. Cutler, as those who read the account of the Cannibal Murders may recall, specializes in analyzing the stomach contents of individuals who have met a suspicious end. A professional gentleman of the old school, Dr. Cutler parts his abundant white hair in the middle, perches his half-moon spectacles on his nose, and wears bow ties bordering on the flamboyant.

Dr. ffronche, a large man of frowning if mischievous mien and extravagant hair in the style of Einstein, spoke English with a noticeable Irish accent.

Dr. Cutler gave us each a copy of his report, and, speaking in one of those Brahmin drawls that go with old silver, he took us through some of the more arcane findings.

"As I reported earlier, the victims, and I think we can safely assume they were victims, more than likely ingested the poison, or the substance that acted as a poison, with what might be called 'snack' amounts of recognizably ethnic Chinese food. These included dim sum, vegetarian spring rolls, and pork strips.

"Further analysis reveals the presence of a potent cocktail of both neurophysiological and biomechanical agents. That is, substances that work on both the brain and the sex organs."

"Unlike Viagra," Lieutenant Tracy put in.

"*Exactement,*" said Dr. ffronche. "This potion must work on the libido and, how do you say, the plumbing." He went on, "Sildenafil citrate, the active ingredient in Viagra, acts, in these prescribed amounts, as a vasodilator in the penis."

The Medical Examiner, raising his calm gray eyes to both of us, said, "Not to bore you with the details, it prevents the break-down of a compound, cyclic guanosine monophosphate, and that, apparently, releases nitrous oxide, which is what causes the smooth muscle cells of the arteries to relax, increasing the flow of blood."

Dr. ffronche nodded his agreement. "That is to say, it enables and prolongs, but does not cause, an erection."

"For that, you would need a psychoactive substance," Dr. Cutler explained.

"Unless the individuals involved were lovers," Dr. ffronché put in. "And in this case that is not the case, yes?"

"Yes," I said, "most emphatically not the case."

"Which leads us to the more problematic part of our report." Dr. Cutler glanced at his colleague as he spoke.

Dr. ffronche knit his brows together. "Absolutely. In this case we have a veritable cocktail, as you say." He picked up his copy of the report. "We have found evidence of cannabis as well as an extract from the herb *Turnera aphrodisiaca,* a shrub of the south said to possess, as its Latin name suggests, aphrodisiac powers. We have also found a significant level of ring-substituted amphet-amines, that is to say, MDMA."

"MDMA?" I asked.

"Methylenedioxymethamphetamine," Dr. Cutler explained.

"Ecstasy," the lieutenant put in. "The drug of choice at raves . . ."

"Raves?"

"Club dances. Users mix it with Viagra or Cialis and call it sextasy."

Dr. ffronche nodded knowingly. "Then there is what we must call ingredient X. I will not speculate on it now. It will take more research and even then we may never be sure. Alas, our resources are limited."

I sighed. "It's very possible then that we have a rogue researcher at large in the lab."

"Or several." Dr. Cutler glanced at his watch. "Assuming the 'cocktail' originated in the lab. As Dr. ffronché has just noted and as the report surmises in its conclusion, there may be one or more unidentified substances that catalyzes the others or acts as a synergizing element, perhaps boosting bioavailability and reducing blood-absorption time."

"And," Dr. ffronche added with an emphatic gesture, "something that stimulates that most important sex organ in the human body — the brain."

We had a few questions for the Medical Examiner and his colleague. In the course of these, he noted that Dr. Woodley, who was taking a nitrate-based prescription for hypertension, died from the consequences of a catastrophic drop in blood pressure. Professor Ossmann died of a heart attack apparently because he had a weak heart to begin with.

When Drs. Cutler and ffronché departed after vigorous handshakes and expressions of appreciation on our part, the lieutenant and I went over the less arcane facts of the case.

I raised an obvious point. "Wouldn't it be wise to check with all the Chinese restaurants in town to see where they might have gotten the snacks they had that night?"

The lieutenant's nod was an indulgent one, the kind a professional gives an amateur. "We've already done that."

"And . . . ?"

"And. None of the thirteen ethnic Chinese restaurants in Seaboard or the surrounding communities reports sending take-out to the lab at that time. They keep very good records, and they all cooperated to the fullest."

"Was it strictly ethnic Chinese food?" I asked, thinking for some reason of the Green Sherpa.

"It was, but we checked all the restaurants that have Chinese-like food, you know, the Thai place downtown."

"And the Green Sherpa?"

The lieutenant reached into his case and withdrew a sheaf of papers. He ruffled through them. "And the Green Sherpa."

"Perhaps one of them brought the food from home. Leftovers."

"Right. Or the stuff you put in a microwave. No go. Mrs. Ossmann, who did not seem particularly bothered by what had happened to her husband, said neither of them knew how to do as much as make boiled rice. And they didn't keep anything like that in the freezer. But yes, they did occasionally go to Chinese restaurants, usually with friends. Ditto for Ms. Woodley's widower, a Walter Gorman. He was very shook up by the whole thing."

"I don't blame him," I said. "But what about the staff refrigerator? Leftovers get left in them all the time."

He nodded, took out his notebook. "I talked to a guy named Baxter. He was down on a list for keeping the refrigerator clean. It was his turn that week, and he's positive that there was no fresh or leftover Chinese food in the refrigerator when he left for home that night. He says he left late, about six forty-five. Woodley signed in at seven eighteen and Ossmann at seven thirty-two."

"So it would be unlikely but not impossible that someone came in and left the food in the refrigerator during that time."

"Possibly. But there's something else."

I waited.

The lieutenant shifted in his seat, the gunmetal eyes in his ruddy face taking on a sudden sharpness as he leaned forward. "At first it didn't seem significant." He paused. "We found no evidence of food wrappers, cartons, plastic forks, or anything like that at the scene. I went over the inventory list myself. I talked to crime scene people. They're good. They would have listed and bagged anything like that in a case like this."

"Perhaps they ate somewhere else."

"The ME's report estimates they ate the Chinese food no more than fifteen or twenty minutes before they . . . did to each other what they did."

"And the sign-in book in the annex shows they were each there at least an hour before they died."

"Right."

The officer rose to go. He put on his trench coat and the sharp trilby that makes him look every inch a detective. "We're going to announce it just before the evening news. That will give you a chance to alert people, control the damage."

"Many thanks, Lieutenant," I said. "It isn't just the bad news that bothers people, it's how they hear it. I'll make a few phone calls."

"Keep your ear to the ground, Norman. This is definitely murder."

Murder, I thought afterward, trying to grasp in my mind what it means to take the life of another. Why was it so prevalent among our species? Murder for hate, for love, for gain, for politics, for its own sake. It brought back last evening when I had what might be called a night out with the boys. Actually, I met

Izzy Landes and Father O'Gould for dinner at the Club. We got into our cups — Izzy came up with a fine Australian Shiraz. We also grew just a bit morbid as the evening wore on. I mentioned Penrood's remark about how we may be the last generation to die. Izzy remarked that perhaps he and S.J. ought to do a book together on the history of death — before people forgot what it was.

We moved into the comfortable common room, and over coffee and a small brandy the good priest confessed how he privately lamented the memorial being erected on the Seaboard Common by the local Irish community to commemorate the Great Famine. "I fear that the Irish in America suffer from a kind of Holocaust envy," he said in his soft Cork accent. "Sure, will it not only add to the spirit of competitive victimization into which we all seem to have fallen. In the end is it not a divisive thing? Does it not keep us apart?"

I was a little surprised to hear Izzy say that he differed very much with Father O'Gould. "I would agree," he said, a world-weary look coming into his kind eyes, "that there is altogether too much made of the Holocaust. To dwell so disproportionately on that catastrophe is to imply that the other millions murdered in the twentieth century are less worthy of our compassion. As a tragedy for the Jews nothing and not enough can be said about the Holocaust. As a tragedy for humankind it needs be put into the context of all the other genocides of the twentieth century. Otherwise there is the danger that it will become a geek show, one that pathologizes the history of the Jews."

"I'm not sure I follow you," I said.

Izzy shook his head slowly. "I mean that the deliberate Nazi extermination of Jews, Gypsies, gays, and others is the singular, most horrific mass murder of the past hundred years. But it is by no means the only mass extermination or the even the largest one.

The Communists murdered tens of millions, perhaps a hundred million in all, in Russia, China, and Cambodia. If we are going to erect memorials to victims of twentieth-century genocides, we need include those victims as well."

"But in that case are we not then pathologizing human history itself?" Father O'Gould asked.

"Perhaps. History is the nightmare from which we are all trying to awake, after all, to quote the conscience of your own race, S.J. We need more, not less, memorials to what we have done to one another."

"To remind ourselves," I said.

"Exactly. Because we like to think it was done in the past by people not like us. But that is a mistake. The genocides have continued, haven't they? In Uganda, in Rwanda, in northern Iraq, in the Balkans, in Darfur. We need to remind ourselves of what humankind is capable of. We need to remember that we are all at risk."

"But are you saying, Izzy, that we should look upon murder, even mass murder, as a natural phenomenon?" asked Father O'Gould, who was still skeptical.

"I'm afraid so."

"The way cancer is natural," I said without thinking.

"Indeed, Norman, the way cancer is natural." And there was a subtle, acknowledging sympathy in Izzy's voice.

The Jesuit reluctantly nodded his understanding. "I suppose you are right, Israel. I mean, in the sense we need to remind ourselves that the natural and the good are not always the same thing."

I wondered if the good priest was referring to his vows of celibacy, but I said nothing.

I walked home rather than accepting a lift from Izzy or calling a cab. I wanted to think, to sort out in my own life the conflict between what is good and what is natural. For me, at the moment, it is more than an abstract conundrum.

The fact is that I have conceived a most powerful amorous longing for Diantha. I trouble these pages with this revelation because, not given to therapeutics, I need to tell someone, even if it is only this mute screen. Imagine my torment. Here is Elsbeth, my beloved wife, visibly shrinking to extinction before my eyes, while I stew myself in concupiscent fantasies for her daughter. I dare not put on paper the details of the scenes with Diantha I have concocted in my fervid imagination, especially after I have had one or two stiff ones and my inner inhibitors have toppled like candlepins.

Though not biologically my child, Diantha is surely my child morally. It doesn't help that she is something of a flirt and, having lived for some time in Southern California, is altogether careless about modesty. The night before last, as an example, she took a shower in the main bathroom and left the door open. I looked right in, right through the transparent shower door, and saw her, a full-bodied naiad oiled with water. And then myself, in the fogged mirror, amid the steam, a peeping old Priapus in a silken gown in the throes of nympholepsy.

There may be relief on the way. Elsbeth tells me that one Sixpak Shakur, Diantha's "on-and-off" boyfriend, whatever that means, is arriving next week for a short stay. "Sixy," as Diantha calls him, is some sort of pop singer.

When I asked Diantha about him, she said, "He's a rapper, Dad."

"Of presents or knuckles?" I asked, not knowing in the least what she was talking about.

It filled her with amused amazement to learn I didn't know

who Sixpak Shakur was, and didn't know or particularly want to know what rap music was. It charmed her when I told her I treasured my ignorance of such things. She gave me a kiss and told me I was like a precious antique.

Still, there are distinct advantages to Diantha's presence. She keeps Elsbeth company during the day. Apparently they watch a lot of soap operas on the television. I don't know what they find in these travesties of normal life, travesties in the sense that they show no moments of repose. Not only does everyone have what looks like steroid-induced complexions, but they continually teeter on the verge of some apocalyptic revelation that, when it comes, turns out to be some predictably banal betrayal about love or money.

But they do occupy dear Elsbeth. She says she no longer has the energy to read murder mysteries, most of which, as she blithely admits, are not very plausible, just another form of pulp fiction, fantasies, really, especially when the protagonist drags in details of his or her personal life, which invariably happens.

We are all growing more concerned about the fate of Corny Chard. At the behest of Jocelyn Chard, I have contacted the State Department and requested that they make some inquiries with the local government agencies in the area Corny was last reported seen. We haven't heard from him in some time. I've had calls from the Department Chair, who persists in believing that the museum funded most of the expedition. He keeps reminding me that Corny is scheduled to teach the second half of the semester in a seminar on the origins of beauty among primitive peoples. I realize Corny's in a place that renders him virtually incommunicado, but surely, with modern communications, such places are becoming exceptional. I do hope the State Department can help us.

And while I remain concerned for Corny's safety, I have a gut feeling that the man would survive almost anything. There's no point in going, after all, unless you can get back to tell the story. I am convinced that the actual doing of something is merely preparation for what is really important in life, which is talking about it afterward.

10

I have received another e-mail from Worried. Again, I will reproduce it in its entirety. I have also redirected it over a secure line to Lieutenant Tracy.

Dear Mr. Ratour:
I think maybe you're right. I think there is something very very fishy going on over here again. Don't ask me what it is, but I get a feeling someone's discovered something and doesn't want anyone to know about it. I don't think it's anything like trying to come up with a new human model like the last time, but something sure is happening. Also, I don't know if this has anything to do with it, but there's a lab assistant here named Celeste. She's got all the straight guys drooling. I mean, you know, long blond hair and hooters big time. It may be she and Dr. Penrood are an item. One of the security guys who works on electronic surveillance showed me this tape of Penrood and Celeste hanging around in one of the offices after hours. Not much happens, but it's pretty clear she's coming on to him and then the body language. Anyway, after a while they get up and leave together. But get this. The security guy tells me it isn't one of the cams they've got hooked into the monitors. So he's put a cam on the cam, trying to figure out who put it there. The whole

thing sounds like a setup to me, but I ain't no expert. I'll let you know if anything turns up. Also, the guy that's working on the threeway tape says it's going to take a while because the guy who has the program he needs is out of town.

Worried

Worried's little missive has revived in me that inexplicable sleuthing instinct, that not-altogether-admirable indulgence in the blood sport of human hunting, even if the prey is a murderer. What, I wondered, is a gorgeous woman doing as a lab assistant? Not that lab assistants are not worthy in their own right. It's simply not an occupation that attracts glamour.

Perhaps I ought to have the security personnel in the lab discreetly interrogated by Lieutenant Tracy. It might also be useful to have Human Resources send me the résumé of this Celeste creature. Of course, it's not that straightforward. Nothing ever is. As an employee of the Ponce, she's not really in our files, though there is an agreement that we can review their personnel files when we want to. But I have to go through the proper channels.

To keep things rolling I made a copy of Dr. Cutler's latest results on the autopsies and gave it, in strictest confidence, of course, to Nicole Stone-Lee, the young graduate student I hired to review the research files of both Professor Ossmann and Dr. Woodley. We met in Ossmann's office and briefly discussed its import. I found talking about erections to a very appealing young lady somewhat disconcerting. It didn't make it easier that she's the kind of young woman to make an older man wish he had it to do all over again. In any event, she took it all with an admirable *sangfroid* and pointed out that, given the nature of Professor Ossmann's specialty, almost any of it could apply to research on what she termed "erectile enhancement." She did ask to hire a specialist in retrieving deleted hard-drive files, and I told her to go ahead and have the bills forwarded to my office.

The fact is I'm starting to feel some pressure quite apart from anything generated by our immediate circumstances. As I foresaw, the announcement by the Seaboard Police Department that it is treating the Ossmann-Woodley case as a murder has stirred things up again. Robert Remick called this morning. He was, as usual, the impeccable gentleman. But he did say that several Board members had voiced to him concerns about "the adverse publicity" that events at the museum have generated of late. With time one gets adept at listening between the lines, so to speak. Remick's call, for all the sincere reassurances that the Board has full confidence in my management, left me far more concerned than all the various ploys the Wainscott satraps have concocted against the museum.

And while I have a normal enough ego when it comes to what might be called my own institutional longevity, I truly believe the MOM's survival as a dynamic, independent museum depends on my continuing as Director. The wrong successor, a few pivotal changes in the makeup of the Board, and we would become a creature of the university. We would cease to be a place where ordinary people can view firsthand the beauty of the ages. We would cease to be what someone has called "the ultimate interpretive center of the human condition."

Speaking of which, we had something of a cursory visit by young Winslow Lowe. He came in on Saturday and left on Sunday. He's remarkably like his late father, as Diantha is like her mother. Strange, the way genes for looks and character get handed around in a family. But then, his attendance, however brief, did cheer up Elsbeth.

On a lighter note, Korky Kummerbund came over yesterday, and I must say we had what very nearly amounted to a celebration. A celebration of what, I keep wondering. But not to cavil. Elsbeth was up and around and, at times, positively jolly as Korky described "a divine new little bistro on Upper Market Street called the Airliner Galley." Korky went on about how the owner, his friend Jeremy, had taken the bottom floor of the old Tweed Building, a narrow leftover at the corner of Morton, and redesigned it in the shape of a jumbo jet interior. "But all first-class."

"I want to go," Elsbeth exclaimed. When I began to frown at the idea, "Oh, God, Norman, I just want to take a break from dying." She took some of the miracle medicine Dr. Berns had prescribed and a handful of vitamins. Korky called ahead, and we set off, Diantha as well.

We were not disappointed. The seats, apparently from a real airliner, were arranged into two rows of snug booths. Each has a porthole through which you look down at a continuous video of landscapes or clouds that you select on a console just beneath the window. Elsbeth pushed the button for clouds. There was a film playing on an overhead screen that you can listen to with earplugs.

A waiter with a drinks trolley took our order. Jeremy came on over the loudspeaker, welcoming us aboard as special guests. He said the seat-belt sign would remain off for the rest of the flight, the weather was clear and calm at our destination, and we were lost, but it didn't make any difference. He then asked one of the cabin staff to please bring him a dry martini, up with a twist.

The food, a parody of airline fare only as far as the plastic accoutrements, proved delicious in an old-fashioned kind of way.

At one point I escorted Elsbeth up to the ladies' room in the back. It had one of those push folding doors, which opened into a roomy vestibule and another door leading to the ladies' room directly. She had to control the laughter of her delight, as it weakens her.

There was one note of . . . well, not exactly discord, but of surprise, at least for me. Diantha, sitting next to me in one of the four-seater booths, in the course of the meal entwined the calf of her leg under and around mine. I would be less than honest if I did not admit to being shocked and aroused. Not to pull away, I knew, was to make myself complicit in the gesture, and yet to draw back struck me as a kind of ungallant rudeness. For once, though, I did something quite natural: I leaned toward her, put my arm around her shoulder, and gave her a kiss on the cheek. Diantha, who had been subdued through the whole course of the meal, broke down and started to cry. Her mother reached over and took her hand, as did Korky. Diantha dried her tears, smiled, and kissed me back on the cheek.

Indeed, with Diantha now living with us, it is as though, through some strange alchemy of being and becoming, she and Elsbeth are merging into one. There are times when, in my heart, I cannot separate them.

Perhaps Diantha is sad not only because of her mother's decline, but also because Sixy left a message, which I could barely decipher, dude this and cool that, telling her he would be a few days late. In solving her problem, I'm hoping it will solve mine, which persists like some alluring danger to us all.

Well, I must get back to work on the uncorrected proofs of my magnum opus. Why does it all seem so much in vain? Another dusty book to sit on remote shelves, mute to all save the occasional scholar looking for stones to add to his own little monument of words. But I can't just put it aside. Ms. Myrtlebaum wants it back next week.

11

It's been one of those days — a lot of motion and no movement. Or that's the way it feels.

In following up on a suggestion of Lieutenant Tracy's, I called Professor Olof Tromstromer, a well-known pteridologist who came to molecular biology through his research into the medicinal properties of ferns. Tromstromer readily, perhaps too readily, agreed to meet with me and tell me what he knew regarding Professor Ossmann and the unfortunate way he had died. One of those hearty Swedes, well fleshed if not plump, with bright blue eyes, ruddy complexion, and shaggy blond hair, he welcomed me with a laugh and dispelled any notion that he might be mixed up in foul play. I walked over to his office, a virtual greenhouse in the Tetley Herbarium. He asked me to sit down and join him in a glass of herbal tea.

I said yes, and he began answering my questions before I asked them as he fussed with a contraption that hissed and steamed and released a stream of colored liquid. "Well, of course, I had my disagreements with Pip. Everyone did. He was a very poor astronomer."

"What do you mean?"

"He had curious notions as to where the sun shines." He laughed, his face reddening. "Sugar?"

"A little. Thank you. What did you disagree about?"

"Everything. Pip would dispute the time of day if you gave him a chance."

"Do you know if he was working on any kind of substance that could be considered an aphrodisiac?"

The professor made an extravagant gesture meant to be a shrug. He struck me as a large troll, an outsized garden ornament amid the collection of potted ferns, some of them huge, others extravagantly feathered, that surrounded his desk. "It wouldn't surprise me. Pip liked to imagine himself a ladies man, how would you say it . . . a kind of sexual gourmet. He saw himself as a great scientist. He wanted to be rich and famous. Last October I put on a real Swedish accent, ya, and called him at a meeting where they had a speaker phone. I told him I was calling on behalf of the Swedish Academy and that he had won the Nobel Prize for Medicine. I mentioned some piffling little thing he did years ago. He fell for it hook and line, and . . ."

"Sinker."

"Ya, sinker." Professor Tromstromer laughed, obviously blessed with the gift of self-amusement. "He never forgave me for that."

"Do you know anyone who might have wanted to murder him?"

The big shrug again. "Ya, anyone who worked with him. He disputed everything. He sat on all the important committees and used his position in the administration to bully his colleagues. He stole ideas. We all started telling him things. We set little traps. We sent him chasing wild swans."

"Could the research you and Professor Ossmann were doing for ReLease be used on a Viagra-like compound?"

"Sure."

"Can you elaborate?"

He gave a half smile. "That's what you came here to really ask me, ya?"

"Ya."

His smile vanished. "Do you want to know if I helped concoct the sex potion that killed Ossmann and Clem?"

"Did you?"

Though only a fraction of a second long, his double take made me think that might have been the case. Or that he knew something he didn't want me to know. I listened then, trying to decode the cipher of any evasions and half-truths he might resort to.

"Mr. . . ."

"De Ratour."

"Mr. de Ratour, things happen in every research laboratory that might be considered . . . anomalous. People have pet projects they work on after hours. People spy on what other people are doing. People discover things and keep them to themselves. People use themselves as guinea pigs. People are people. Ya, ya, sure. RL is a vasodilator, and Viagra prolongs vasodilation. But they are very different. You'll be able to get RL off the shelf because its side effects are minimal. Believe me, it relies very much on the placebo effect. Did Pip concoct a love potion and try it out on Clem, who wouldn't sleep with him? Sure. Why not? Life is short."

"Do you know anything for sure?"

"No, but there were rumors."

"Rumors?"

"Ya, ya. Rumors that Pip had something that made rabbits and mice screw themselves crazy. For a while there were a lot of missing animals that got blamed on the cleaning ladies, but I never believed it."

"Do you have any idea what Professor Ossmann's substance might be?"

"I don't know for sure he had a substance."

I didn't believe him. But I had neither the interrogation skills nor enough technical background to question him further to any effect. I thanked him for the time and the tea and took my leave. In walking to my office through the leaf fall and brilliant light, it struck me that Professor Tromstromer, behind his evident bonhomie, was not the jolly fellow he pretended to be. Not that any of us are. I did not list him as a suspect, but I felt sure he was hiding something.

On the other hand, I may only be projecting my own melancholy, which burns the deeper with the beauty of the day. I will be losing Elsbeth, it's true, however much I hope against hope. But she will be losing all this, the air, the light, the sounds, the beauty. I think it was the Russian writer Vasily Grossman who pointed out that each death is the death of a universe.

I have received another e-mail from Worried, one that confirms what Professor Tromstromer told me about missing research animals.

Dear Mr. Ratour:
I found out what happened to the guy that asked me to bury the rabbits. He's still around town and I'd give you his name but then he'd tell you who I was and I don't want to get involved in this thing any more than I already am. So I called this guy and asked him about what was going on. And I think he's telling the truth because I told him I was getting pressure from the cops and that if he didn't come clean with me he'd have to deal with them. Anyway, he tells me that the rabbits weren't part of any experiment, just a couple left over from a thing they were doing on hair grooming. So one morning he comes into work and there are the two rabbits, a male and a female, dead in a cage together. He says it looked like they had been fighting. He says

there's some kind of state regs that make you find out what happened when an animal dies for no reason even when they're not part of some experiment. He says it's a pain in the ass. You got to have them examined. You got to do paperwork. You got to file the thing in triplicate. So he cleans out the cage, puts the things in a bag, and gives them to me. Anyone asks questions it's hey, maybe the Haitians took them. I mean that's the joke around here with the cleaning ladies. When anything's missing, rats, mice, anything, the Haitians took them, you know, for lunch, for voodoo, for whatever. Anyway, I think the guy's telling me the truth. I'll let you know if I hear anything else.

Worried

I think tomorrow I'll print out a copy of this and take it over myself to Nicole Stone-Lee. She might find it useful. Perhaps I'm being overcautious, but you can't be too careful about these things falling into the wrong hands.

Speaking of which, despite my initial reservations, the meeting I had this afternoon with Malachy Morin and two gentlemen from the University Office of Development left me quite enlightened. I say "gentlemen" advisedly, as they struck me as the lodge-member types, full of that heartiness that's always ready for a good laugh. Indeed, the individuals involved, taking their cue from Malachy Morin, carried on in an underlying tone of risibility that I find puzzling and disturbing in retrospect. Perhaps it's just that I find the annoyance of it all distracting and am in much need of distraction.

We met in the offices of the Wainscott Next Millennium Fund, which are located in the upper reaches of Grope Tower, that architectural wart that . . . but you've heard me on that topic already.

"We're here, Norm, to help you and the museum," Mr. Morin began portentously. "We're here, Norm, to make you a player in the Fund. We're here to make you an offer you can't refuse." To which his two colleagues supplied what sounded to me like canned laughter.

One of them, a Mr. Jeff Sherkin, a short plump young man with black mustache, fresh complexion, and nervous blue eyes, professed amazement that the museum did not have a development program of its own. This, for some reason, got a frown from Mr. Morin.

"I'm not sure we need one," I said. "We have income adequate to our purposes."

"Development isn't just about raising money," put in the other, a Mr. Peter Flaler, his voice condescending. The Mutt of this duo, Mr. Flaler was thin, tall, and apparently unable to relieve his narrow face of a supercilious smirk. He went on to explain in the manner of one speaking to a dullard, "People of substance like to and want to give to worthy institutions."

"Yes, and to receive due recognition, of course," chimed in Sherkin.

"You don't just ask for money," said Mr. Flaler with his smirk. "Who wants to give millions for paper clips and staff dental coverage? No, you give them something they can put their name on."

"Right," said the Jeff. "A building. A center. A professorship. A library. A gate."

"A gate?"

"Of course. Your main gate, for instance. You could, for a reasonable bequest, name it, say, the Bill Gates Gate." They all smiled. "All it would entail is a little plaque stating that the doorway was given in memory of Bill Gates."

"But the gate wasn't given by Mr. Gates. The gate's been there for more than a hundred years. People aren't stupid." I was now playing their game, playing as dumb as they thought I was.

"Of course. It's only a convention. Mr. Latour, we all want in some small way to be immortal."

"Do living people really have doors named for them?"

"You wouldn't believe the things people have named for them. We have one benefactor, a couple actually, who have an elevator named for them. It's over in the Medical School. The Waldo and Rose Grosbeak Elevator."

"Amazing."

"Oh, yeah. Waldo's Class of 'Sixty-one. Founded Grosbeak Camping Gear. Deep pockets in those hiking pants, ha, ha. Of course, a named elevator isn't really like a named chair. I mean it doesn't get endowed as such."

"It wouldn't have an occupant," explained Mr. Sherkin, his face contorted with suppressed laughter. "That is to say, no one would hold the elevator except in the sense of keeping the door open."

"Where do you put the plaque?" I asked.

"On the inside. Right next to the municipal inspection notice. In fact, the Grosbeaks would probably pay to have that old elevator I noticed over in your place redone as something far more efficient and safe."

"Amazing."

"Hey, it happens every day. And what's really hot is the last-name deal."

"The last-name deal?"

"Okay, it goes like this. Instead of the plaque on, say, a reception desk, stating THIS DESK GIVEN THROUGH THE GENEROSITY OF DICK AND DOTTY DICKHEAD, it just has a nice brass plate that says DICKHEAD. Because if you put up all that other stuff, it looks like someone just coughed up the bucks to get their name there. But if it just says DICKHEAD, it makes you stop for a minute and think, yeah, that *Dickhead*."

"I see."

"Isn't that what Walter J. Annenberg did at Harvard?" Mr. Morin put in.

"Exactly. He gave several million dollars to Harvard just to have a dining hall named for him."

"A dining hall?" I repeated with not entirely feigned incredulity.

"A freshman dining hall at that."

"Amazing."

"Well, it is a Harvard dining hall."

"But a dining hall nonetheless."

"Yes."

"I mean a place where people eat."

"Not really people, students. But eating is very important."

All three were now openly tittering as Mr. Flaler went on. "Exactly."

"Well, Mr. Annenberg must be very rich and very humble to do such a generous thing."

"Rich and generous but not necessarily humble."

"What do you mean?"

"Well, he has his name, just his last name, and the word *Hall* incised in great gold letters like they've been there forever just outside the dining hall in a hall that has until now been reserved for small marble plaques bearing the names of those sons of Harvard who were killed in the Civil War."

"Really? Annenberg's name stands out among the fallen heroes of Harvard?"

"Sure."

"Isn't that a little . . . louche?"

"Oh, no, Mr. de Ratour. It merely exemplifies what benefactors want in return for their money."

"But those are heroes . . ."

"Yeah, but they only gave their lives . . ."

"And not for Harvard, either."

"Do people give their lives for Harvard?"

"They'd rather have your money."

I shook my head. "I really don't see the point of trying to be remembered by people who don't know who you are or what you were."

Mr. Morin snorted. "Maybe that's because the people they knew wouldn't want to remember them."

Mr. Sherkin then turned on what he must have taken for charm, telling me, "Your museum, Mr. Ratour, is virgin territory. I took a walk through it the other day. It was disorienting to find hardly anything named for a hit . . . I mean a benefactor."

I nodded and dissembled a quiet excitement as a plan began to form in my mind. I asked, "What's the actual mechanism for getting people to make really big contributions?"

Mr. Flaler inhaled sagely. "The approach. Asking for money is like asking for love. You have to do it right. Mostly, you get the rich to ask the rich. People with a lot of money need reassuring."

"You have to schmooze them," Mr. Morin put in.

"Schmooze?"

"Give them drinks and praise. Glad-hand and glad-mouth them. Talk up the vision thing."

"Like we said, people like to see their names chiseled on buildings."

"Yeah, it's like the whole thing becomes their tombstone. Only it's not in the cemetery."

"Right. And buildings need names."

I shook my head. "We have a policy at the museum. All gifts must be anonymous and with no strings attached. We are willing to consider naming a room or gallery or library for someone whose achievements in his or her field — Mason Twitchell's, for instance — merit such consideration."

Mr. Sherkin frowned. "Any gifts to the university need to be channeled through the Development Office."

I grimaced a smile at the man and said nothing.

Mr. Morin cleared his throat. "Look, Norm, we're making you an exceptional offer. Everyone wants a piece of the New Millennium action, but the deal is strictly limited."

"And what does the Museum of Man have to do in return for this privilege?"

"Simple. You get your Board to agree to a closer association with the university. Then we can cut out all this crap in the courts."

"I might even bring it up with the Board. And now, gentlemen, you'll have to excuse me. I have a museum to run."

It took me a while to extricate myself. Thanking them each graciously and shaking their hands, I picked up the impressively designed three-ring binder titled "Development Goals for the Museum of Man in the New Millennium." It could well serve as the basis of a fund drive of our own.

But I must be careful. What I sense at Wainscott, what I don't want to happen at the MOM, is the philistinism that can result when an institution becomes too consciously institutional and loses sight of its original purpose.

12

It is late evening and I sit under the eaves in an attic study I have had knocked together and fitted out with shelves for books and an old couch for dozing. It is a veritable eyrie and overlooks the backyard of the Dolores family, the nubile young girls of which sun themselves like semi-aquatic creatures next to the aquamarine pool during the sunnier months. (My father's old study down on the first floor that I resorted to of yore has been turned into the entertainment center with the big television.)

It is nigh on Halloween, and I sit in this perch typing into my little tabletop — I've never had the thing on my lap once. From far below, in the fieldstone foundation, I can hear the syncopated *thump thump* of some infernal electronic noisemaker reverberating through the house as though it had been possessed by some mad demon of the aural. It's only Sixpak Shakur, King of the Redneck Rappers, lead singer of Cool White Fudge, or that's what was stenciled all over the van in which he arrived yesterday. I suppose we're lucky that they all didn't decide to camp here, four or five other young men, that is. They speak a gibberish among themselves that I take to be a kind of English.

Well, at least Diantha is happy. She positively flung herself at the young man, wrapping her legs around his midsection and carrying on in such a fashion that I feared for a moment they would attempt congress right there in the hallway. I should be relieved that she now has someone to assuage her too palpable needs. But I find myself just a bit envious, perhaps of their youth, their vigor, their sense of utter irresponsibility, as though the world is some great machine that will tick over by itself forever regardless of what they do. And perhaps they are right.

We sat down to dinner, the four of us, with lobsters, salad, the very last of this year's corn, as well as a piquant little Sauvignon Blanc. Sixy, as Diantha calls him, slurring it into "Sexy," wore only a T-shirt with some sort of message on it and jeans, seemingly impervious to anything like the temperature. He is a big fellow, with a bland, blunt, sensual face, and sports, if that is the term, a polished shaved head and more rings in his ears that a Papuan native. It took me some time to realize that he was speaking English. When he saw the lobsters he launched into something like, "Oh, wow, man, real bugs, too rad." Then, to me, glancing around, "Man, you are some kind of cool dude. I mean look at this crib, man, it's right off the set."

Later, when we were alone, he extended his sympathy regarding Elsbeth. "Di told me about your old lady, man. I mean bummer big time. I mean like too soon, man, for the big nap." I took this to be an expression of sympathy and confess to being oddly touched inasmuch as he appeared utterly sincere in his sentiments. Still, I do wonder betimes what planet I am living on.

Poor Elsbeth couldn't really manage to eat much of the dinner. She did seem happy that Diantha's friend had arrived. She told me not to fuss with her, but I excused myself from the table as well. I asked her if she wanted to take some of her pain medication, and she shook her head. "I'd rather bear anything than have my head muddled," she said.

We spent some time together, she lying in the bed we've arranged for her in the alcove off the living room, me sitting beside her holding her hand, now all skin and bones and ligaments. What frail vessels we are, finally.

But Elsbeth appeared at peace with herself. Alfie Lopes, the minister in Swift Chapel, our friend who married us, came by today for something halfway between a pastoral visit and a crying fest. We held hands while Alfie improvised a little prayer about how we need to remember that each of us will be called. It is only a matter of time. And time, he intoned, quoting the much-underappreciated Delmore Schwartz, is the fire we burn in.

Perhaps not that strangely, Elsbeth comforted Alfie as much as he did her. But then my dear wife always has been strong in that way. She told me that early on she had decided not to cheat death by dying by her own hand when it dawned on her as a young girl the finality that life entailed. "Dying is not what you think," she said as we sat together in the near dark, hearing the sounds Diantha and Sixy were making down in the basement setting up his equipment. "It's frightening, yes. It's too damn final. I'd rather postpone it. But it's not strange or horrific or even malignant. It just is. And having you here is all that matters right now."

So that I wept, but quietly, and then lay out on the narrow bed beside her, taking her in my arms and holding her, as if, like that, I might keep her forever.

Later, when the ruckus started from below, I made to go down to quell it. But Elsbeth forestalled me. "It's okay," she said. "I kind of like it. It's alive."

When she finally drifted off, I quietly got up, pulled the drape over the alcove, and made my way here.

We haven't heard from Korky in a few days, but that's not unusual. I know he isn't one of those fair-weather friends who abandons you the moment the going gets rough.

I did have a run-in today with Maria Cowe, who is in charge of Human Resources for Affiliated Institutions, what used to be called Personnel. She demanded to know why I wanted the file of Celeste Tangent, the lab assistant Worried referred to in one of his e-mails. I told her it was an administrative matter, and that surely it was only routine for directors such as myself to ask to see employee files and for her office to comply.

She responded that, because Ms. Tangent was really an employee of the Ponce Institute and not of Wainscott, I would have to fill out forms to make an official request.

I became quite angry. I told her that if Ms. Tangent's file was not on my desk when I arrived the next morning, she would be hearing from the museum's legal department.

Indeed, the first thing I did upon returning to my office was phone Felix Skinnerman. I told him that I wanted the museum to establish its own human resources department sooner rather than later, in fact immediately. I told him I wanted it called the Personnel Department. I told him I wanted him to subpoena from Ms. Cowe the records or copies of the records of anyone who works either directly or indirectly for the museum.

Well, Felix, as usual, calmed me down. He said this was an area where we had to go cautiously while our case was still in the courts. To raise this issue now, he said, would be to call attention to a very strong de facto link between the two institutions, strengthening the case of the university. He suggested I do what all administrators do — go over her head.

I told him that meant going to Malachy Morin, which was something, on principle, I simply would not do.

"Why do you need the file?" he finally asked me.

"It may have something to do with the Ossmann-Woodley case," I said.

"Oh, then. Why don't you contact your friend in the SPD and have him obtain it through the courts? It might take a while, but you'll have it."

I thanked him effusively and called Lieutenant Tracy. He wasn't in, but he called back a short time later. I admit I felt a bit foolish telling him that I could not, as a matter of routine, obtain the file of someone working, however indirectly, for the museum.

But the lieutenant put a different spin on it. "Perhaps," he said, "they're trying to hide something."

"Yes," I said, "that's a possibility." And while using that, so to speak, as a cover for my managerial impotence, I seriously wondered, thinking back to my confrontation with Ms. Cowe, if there might be something to his suggestion.

The lieutenant took down the particulars and said he would get right on it. And now I can't get it out of my head that Malachy Morin and Maria Cowe are all mixed up in this together.

But that may be just a measure of how desperate I'm getting, clutching at straws and strawmen. For instance, I received a personal and confidential memorandum today regarding the matter pending before the Subcommittee on Appropriateness that has me perplexed. It's a strange affair, to say the least. As Professor Athol, the Chair of the subcommittee, outlines it, both parties are accusing the other of date rape. The matter is further complicated by the facts that the woman is an outspoken lesbian activist involved in social issues while the man is an African American born-again Christian confined to a wheelchair. To avoid an expensive and prolonged legal wrangle, the two individuals have agreed to appear before the subcommittee to present his-and-hers sides of the story and to abide by any findings we make.

Now, we have dealt in the past with situations of nearly intractable sensitivity, but nothing, I daresay, approaches what we have before us now. And I feel tempted to "vent" (a word I've picked up from Diantha) my usual indignant homiletics about modern mores: If young people cannot be trusted to act civilly while alone in one another's company, then we need to bring back chaperones and all that entails.

Athol's memorandum has triggered in me an awareness of something both anomalous and at the same time integral to an emerging, still nebulous larger scheme. Could this incident have anything to do with the Ossmann-Woodley case? I don't know. But I am nearly tempted to jump the gun and go interview these two individuals by myself. On the other hand . . .

Well, the thumping from the nether regions of the house has finally subsided. Though it won't surprise me if a different kind of thumping starts up down the hall from my own, now monastic bed.

13

There has been a shocking development. Bert and Betti, two of our remaining chimpanzees, were found dead in a cage this morning under circumstances remarkably similar to those of the Ossmann-Woodley case, only worse. They were discovered by Dr. Angela Simone, the very responsible young woman who took over from Damon Drex as Keeper of Great Apes. The poor woman was in a state of considerable shock when she phoned me at home just after eight this morning to tell me the news.

I came over immediately in a cab and secured the area as a crime scene before calling in the Seaboard Police Department.

Dr. Simone took a moment to compose herself. But she is a tough professional, and she soon related to me the simple facts. Upon her arrival she sensed immediately that things were amiss. Lights, normally dimmed, were on full. Doors normally closed were open. The other animals were in a state of considerable agitation. Then she discovered Bert and Betti dead in the cage.

We went into the area, and I can tell you it was not a pretty sight. I forced myself to look at it carefully and take mental notes. Betti lay sprawled in one corner of one of our larger cages, most of her left ear missing, one eye hanging from its socket. From her bloodied mouth protruded what might have been the genitals of Bert, who lay facedown in the opposite corner, his hands clutched at his crotch. In their struggle they had wrecked the exercise tree and tipped over the water bowl. There were blood and feces everywhere.

"What about Mort?" I asked, referring to the security guard who has kept watch over the Pavilion and the museum proper since before I came on board more than thirty years ago.

"I haven't seen him," she said, alarm making her eyes go large. "I hope he's okay."

We were just about to go down the spiral staircase to the basement where Mort has his office when Lieutenant Tracy arrived with his crime scene crew. We left the crew in charge and clattered down the steps with the lieutenant to the enclosure equipped with an array of television monitors that Mort watches when he's not out making his rounds.

He was slumped in his chair, his old graying head back, his mouth wide open. I feared the worst. "Mort," I said, shaking his arm. "Mort, wake up." As the lieutenant and I stood over him, he opened first one and then the other eye. He sat forward, his disorientation obvious as he moaned and put his hands over his eyes.

"We should call an ambulance," Lieutenant Tracy said.

Mort shook his head. "No ambulance. No hospital. No doctors. I'm fine."

Dr. Simone disappeared for a moment and came back with a cup of black coffee. Mort sipped the coffee, rubbed his eyes and the back of his neck, and answered our questions.

We determined that Mort, who came on duty at midnight to work a twelve-hour shift, as is his preference, found everything normal as of 2:30 AM when he went to the staff room for the lunch he had brought with him. There, in a refrigerator used by the staff, he had left a sandwich and a large bottle of Coke with his name taped to it. He said he warmed his sandwich, a cheese and tomato, in the microwave, poured himself a paper cup full of Coke, and brought it back down here. He ate the sandwich and drank the soda and that's the last thing he remembers.

I asked him if he'd noticed then that the monitor covering the area of the cages had gone blank. He replied that he was certain all the monitors were in working order when he started his meal.

After directing one of the crime scene officers to secure the Coke bottle in the staff refrigerator, and after seeing that Mort had a ride home, Lieutenant Tracy and I went with Dr. Simone into her office.

Taking notes, the lieutenant with firm gentleness took Dr. Simone through what she had found upon arriving at work. I must say I admired again the thoroughness of his questioning. However, I was able to make one important contribution. I asked if Bert had been in the larger cage alone when she had left in the evening.

Dr. Simone nodded. "He still gets moody, and at night we usually put him in that cage by himself."

"How would someone have enticed Betti to leave her cage and go into Bert's?"

"They may have used M&M's."

"M&M's?" the lieutenant asked.

"M&M's were used in the writing program that was in place before I came here," Dr. Simone explained. "Betti participated in that program and, like the others, developed a craving for them. We still use them as little bribes to get the animals to do things."

"Who would have known about that?" I asked.

She made a shrugging gesture with her hands. "Anyone who worked with the chimps. I mean people in the lab."

"Could you possibly get us a list of names?" the lieutenant asked.

"I'll try," she said. "It might not be complete."

The lieutenant thanked her in leaving and paused to commiserate with her, letting her know in a subtle way that he realized her charges were something more to her than mere animals.

We stopped by the crime scene again so that the lieutenant could tell one of the crew to keep an eye out for M&M's.

"We've already found some," the officer said, and indicated a clear plastic bag with some of the candies in it along with a distinctive brown smear.

Next we met with Hank, the technician in charge of audio-video security. He indicated the camera, an unobtrusive black device with a short lens that covered the cage area. As he showed us, the cable from the camera to the monitor and the digital recorder had been not only cut but also reconnected to a router programmed to a device attached to the pay phone in the booth next to the visitor cloakroom. A sign on the booth said OUT OF ORDER. The thing was wired into the phone in a way that made Hank, a burly fellow with an engaging face, shake his head. "Whoever did this knew what they were doing."

"What do you mean?" Lieutenant Tracy asked.

"I'd say, when they wanted to see what was going on and to tape it at the same time, all they had to do was dial this number."

"Wouldn't the phone company have a record?" I asked.

He shrugged. "You could try them, but I doubt it. They probably phoned from another booth. There's other ways around it as well." He attached a small video screen to the device on the telephone and showed us how the video camera had been adjusted to take in just the cage where Bert and Betti were found.

The lieutenant and I finally went up to my office. Doreen brought us coffee. I could not sit still. I paced diagonally corner-to-corner while the lieutenant watched me pensively.

"The two cases are obviously related," I said, stating the obvious.

"But not really the same."

"Yes." But for the moment I was too agitated with anger and

frustration to think straight. I sat down and took a couple of deep breaths.

Lieutenant Tracy went on. "The Ossmann-Woodley case could be murder. This looks more like an accident."

"Yes, yes, but a kind of deliberate accident."

The lieutenant's frown eased as he picked up on my meaning. "The way accidents occur when someone is testing something."

"Exactly. They may be trying to calculate exact doses or ratios of that mix Cutler described for us. Which is what may have happened to Ossmann and Woodley. But . . . if both cases were deliberate and made to look like accidents, experiments gone wrong . . ." I paused, and the lieutenant waited. "Then what exactly would the motive be unless . . . unless it is part of some grotesque scheme to get me out of the museum."

"How realistic is that?"

"I don't know. They want the lab and the revenue it brings in. The university itself would never sanction such means, but there's a cabal doing everything it can to discredit me. But you're right, Lieutenant, it's a stretch. At the same time, you might want to question Malachy Morin . . ."

"The fat guy involved in the death of Elsa Pringle?'

"The very man."

"We'll bring him in."

"Good. And have someone leak the timing of his arrival to the television newspeople."

He gave one of his rare smiles. We spoke about what to do next. I called one of the mammalian specialists in the Biology Department and asked him to assist Dr. Cutler in a postmortem.

With the lieutenant's assistance I dictated a news release to Doreen setting out the facts as tersely as possible. We checked it over and had her fax it to our priority list. The phone started ringing immediately. Amanda Feeney-Morin, in that peremptory tone of hers, demanded to know every last detail. I told her the matter was under investigation and that I would keep her and others up to date with any developments. She persisted, asking a lot of insinuating questions designed to make it seem we are covering things up.

The lieutenant agreed with me that, given the implications of what had happened and the intense media interest, it would be best to hold a press conference. Accordingly, I secured Margaret Mead Auditorium for one in the afternoon and had Doreen contact our list with that information. Lieutenant Tracy, after talking to Chief Murphy of the SPD, agreed to conduct the conference with me. As best we could, we went over probable questions and arrived at responses we deemed as candid as we could make them.

In the midst of these preparations, Malachy Morin called to ask me why I was conducting a press conference without his authorization. I'm afraid I lost my temper. I told the man that he was a poor deluded wretch to think that he had any authority over anything that happened at the Museum of Man. I told him he was perfectly welcome to call a press conference of his own and share his considerable ignorance with anyone so feeble-minded as to take seriously anything he would have to say about anything. I then gently hung up the receiver.

Now, I want to go on record as saying that, in the course of my career in dealing with the press, I have met many thoughtful, diligent, intelligent, and responsible journalists. And it is clear that a democracy cannot function without an active Fourth Estate. But even in a community as small as Seaboard, there appear to be hordes of them. And so many of them are benighted beyond redemption, crude beyond credibility, and so openly hostile as to be comic. One young man, after making a dramatic entrance in a long, swirling overcoat that looked like a bathrobe, asked me in a challenging manner some long unintelligible question with the phrase "sex torture" thrown in. I simply shook my head and said I didn't know what he was talking about.

Another, wearing raked-back hair and those squinty little glasses you see in photographs of W.B. Yeats, asked me if Bert and Betti were a "breeding pair."

I answered that we no longer had a breeding program at the Pavilion and that the two chimps had been placed together in a single cage by persons unknown and without any authorization.

"If the chimps are not allowed to breed, how do they take care of their sexual needs?"

When I responded facetiously that we did not disclose details about the sex lives of our chimpanzees out of respect for their privacy, I was taken entirely seriously.

"Was Bert still in a program for recovering alcoholics?" someone else asked.

"No. Bert completed that program and had been sober for more than three months at the time of his death."

Amanda Feeney-Morin sat right up front, poised, I knew, to make slurs disguised as questions. Right on cue, she stood up. "Given what's been happening at the Museum of Man over the past few months, Mr. de Ratour, are you going to resign as Director?"

"Absolutely not."

"Have you considered, given what's been happening, turning over administration of the museum to the university?"

"Absolutely not."

To be fair, the journalists did ask some pointed, pertinent questions that it was our responsibility to answer. One of the network reporters, who had flown from Boston, asked the lieutenant if the deaths of the chimps confirmed his suspicions concerning the Ossmann-Woodley case.

The officer nodded. "The similarities are obvious and, of course, we're exploring any links it might have to this case."

"Is the Genetics Lab as vulnerable to break-ins as the Pavilion?" one sharp young woman asked me.

I indicated that her question was a good one before reassuring the public, through the press, that the lab had its own highly sophisticated and independent security system.

I was starting to feel a little complacent when the same reporter asked, "If that's the case, what happened to Professor Ossmann and Dr. Woodley?"

I responded as honestly as I could: "We don't know. There was no detectable break-in. That's the mystery we're trying to solve."

When a reporter asked me what possible motive could anyone have to be wreaking such havoc in the constituent parts of the museum, I had to bite my tongue. I wanted to say that perhaps it was part of a conspiracy to discredit me and the museum so that the university could take us over. Instead, I shook my head with what could have been wise sadness or sad wisdom and said I didn't have a clue.

After more than an hour of taking abuse and providing some useful information to the public, I closed off the questions. Afterward, outside, in front of the museum, I could see the television reporters in front of cameras, reading from notes, sawing the air with their hands, and pausing to glance away, as though in thoughtfulness, before resuming their narratives for the evening news.

I spent most of the afternoon answering press calls. It is an exhausting, nerve-racking exercise in trying to balance candor with discretion as you talk to people who, basically, have given themselves the right to insult you with impunity.

The one bright spot was a call from Elsbeth, who told me I looked absolutely dashing during the news conference. She said that a reporter on the midafternoon news summary had labeled the death of the chimps the latest of "The Love Potion Murders in the Museum of Man." I told her it sounded like a title for a murder mystery and heard her give that good old chortle of hers.

Sometime well after six I was able to leave for home. In the relative darkness of the Arboretum, as I strode along, I nearly fainted at the sight of a chimpanzee coming up the path toward me. I was about to start back to the museum and spread the alarm when the chimp was joined by a gorilla, a nun in full regalia, a football player in helmet and pads, a ballerina, and a fairy godmother. I had forgotten it was Halloween.

14

I feel like Job, stretched on a rack of torments, afflicted with the Seven Plagues, if I may be allowed to conflate a couple of tales from the Good Book. I sometimes think we invented God because we need someone to complain to.

The press simply has not let up on the Bert-Betti tragedy. Indeed it has drawn far more coverage, if that is the word, than the deaths of Professor Ossmann and Dr. Woodley. The tabloids are publishing outright lies, talking about "a new, deadly aphrodisiac" and "the Tristan and Isolde pill" and that sort of rot.

I have been besieged with calls from what are called news shows for interviews and camera access to those parts of the Pavilion that still house chimpanzees. I did agree, under the prompting of Felix Skinnerman, to allow a camera crew in for a "pool" shoot, whatever that means. I have agreed to submit to taped interviews on the condition that I be guaranteed final editing approval with elaborate safeguards including a one-million-dollar performance bond. That has gotten me much outrage over the telephone and no takers.

Felix also urged me to open the Pavilion and allow Dr. Simone to give a few "backgrounder" interviews. It appears some animal rights firebrand has filed a bill in the state legislature to set up a committee to investigate the lab and its treatment of the animals used in its experiments. I explained to Felix that while we had to do something, I did not want to use the panoply of lobbyists the university keeps on staff to influence legislation in both Washington and the state capital.

He explained in his calming voice that we didn't have to. "We can use the same private firm they use when they really need help. It will cost a few bucks. I'll look into it and get back to you."

What, I wonder, would I do without that young man.

The fact is, I haven't really had much to report to anyone in terms of "breaking" news. I did receive a call from Lieutenant Tracy. He said Dr. Cutler had phoned to tell him that the M&M's ingested by Bert and Betti had been dipped in soy sauce. Soy sauce had also been present in significant amounts in the food eaten by Ossmann and Woodley not long before they tore into each other. "Soy sauce, it seems," the lieutenant said, "is the vector of choice."

"An interesting little clue," I responded, "but for the moment it doesn't ring any bells."

As though I didn't have enough on my hands, I received just after lunch a most noisome call from a gentleman named Custer or Castor representing a company called Urgent Productions. He chewed my ear for a full half hour with one of those awful grasping voices, trying alternately to cajole me and to threaten me to let them use the museum for filming parts of *A Taste of the Real,* based on the book by the same name. It would drag the museum into the grotesque hoopla surrounding Raul Brauer's account of the ritual cannibalizing of that young man on Loa Hoa.

Mr. Castor took it for granted, I think, that I would accede with groveling gratitude to the request to "borrow the authenticity" of the museum for a "serious film" that will "explore a profound human experience with an edgy but sensitive treatment."

When I demurred, implying that the museum's authenticity derives in part from eschewing participation in such ventures, he said that the studio would be willing to pay a "site fee" in the form of a considerable contribution. He mentioned a generous sum and added that they would give the museum "priceless, worldwide publicity."

I demurred again. Mr. Castor increased the amount of the "donation." I said no, thank you. He offered to hire me as a "consulting museum expert" and named a considerable sum.

When I said no again, he said, "Mr. de Ratour, I am a serious producer making you and your museum a serious offer to have you help us make a serious film."

I told him I was a serious museum director who had just made a serious refusal. I told him I had read Professor Brauer's book and found it to be full of half-truths, gratuitous sensationalism, and self-promotion. I said I expected the movie to be no less exploitive of an event that involved the tragic death of a hapless young man.

Mr. Castor's voice took on a tone that I presume he meant to be quietly threatening. "I'm going to give you a couple of days to consider our offer. If the answer is still no, then we are prepared to go over your head big time."

I told him that, given most of the world was over my head, he was welcome to it.

On the pretext of a managerial inspection, but mostly to satisfy my curiosity about the apparently fabulous Celeste Tangent, I took a stroll through the Genetics Lab in the afternoon, dropping by departments and saying hello. I wasn't more than twenty minutes on my little excursion when Dr. Penrood approached rather breathlessly, a thin smile more revealing than concealing his annoyance, asking me if he could be of assistance.

By that time I had been into the area where Ms. Tangent works amid banks of complicated machines attached to computers that dice and splice bits of DNA from various sources. We were introduced, and I can still feel the unmistakable frisson of that women's erotic aura. Worried is right. She is a strikingly attractive woman and about as plausible as a laboratory assistant as I would be a sumo wrestler. And, though I can't prove it, I am quite certain that she is the woman involved in the three-way sexual congress caught on video by the surveillance camera.

In fact, Dr. Penrood's agitation rather pleased me. Had he been just a little more officious, I might have thought he had nothing to hide except for a possible sexual peccadillo with his most attractive employee. Because Ms. Tangent has more than looks. She has the confidence of her sensuality: She is the kind of woman who can lead a man on, turn him down while sympathizing with him, and make him her slave. And I suspect now that the man in the three-way engagement with his back to the camera is indeed Dr. Penrood.

Moreover, given the incongruity, as I see it, of these three individuals involved in that kind of congress, I can't help but speculate that some sort of powerful aphrodisiac was involved. Professor Tromstromer's words come back to me: Researchers are not above experimenting on themselves. This may be the break we're looking for. I'll have to push Worried on getting us that enhanced version of the surveillance tape.

Perhaps I should be excited. Perhaps I should call Lieutenant Tracy and tell him there's been a "development." But frankly, all of this pales to insignificance when I think on my dear wonderful Elsbeth, who grows more wan and weak with each passing day. The unrelieved impulse is to get her help, to take her to hospital. But there is no help. And she doesn't want to go to hospital. She wants to die here, in our home, surrounded by friends.

At least she doesn't object to my having help brought in for her. I've never been very good with bedpans and that sort of thing. We have a couple of unobtrusive ladies from a hospice outreach program. Estelle is the thinner one and Mildred is the plump one. They've been coming only a week and they already dote on Elsbeth, who spoils them.

Elsbeth did have a very good meeting yesterday with Father O'Gould. Though she is anything but Catholic, she told me afterward that what he said to her made her feel doubly that her life had not been in vain; that there was a purpose. "He made me feel that I and every living creature is part of a larger, ultimately beautiful scheme in which we all have a role to play. He made me believe that everything we do has meaning."

I nodded, having heard the good priest expatiate on the moral implications of evolution, how it fits in and accounts for everyone and everything in the universe, even those who think they have gotten only scraps from life's feast.

She was telling me about it this evening as we sat in the more formal living room, each of us with a glass of wine. Elsbeth was holding my hand, reading my eyes, comforting me, saying, "I used to look at old family pictures, not just mine, but those of other people, and I would have to fight a sense of desolation. They are all dead, I would tell myself, and how sad, how futile it all seemed. But I was forgetting that they and countless others had lived, had loved, had gotten joy and satisfaction out of life. And so have I, even married to poor Winslow and pining every day for you, dear Norman."

Then I tried to comfort her, holding her hand in both of mine, bringing it to my lips, blinking back tears at the sight of hers.

But I must confess that beneath my pity and pain and concern for Elsbeth, I feel a strange, familiar anger. Elsbeth is leaving me again, as she left me so many years ago for Winslow Lowe. Now she is leaving me for God, and how can I be jealous of God, who, truth be told, I feel has gone on sabbatical. It doesn't matter. My

Elsbeth is going away again, going somewhere beyond my reach.

At the same time, these petty resentments leave me with nothing but shame. And worse. My dreams are full of Elsbeth and Diantha, each merging into the other as they recede smiling beyond my reach. Then I find, upon awakening, that I am being left stranded by creeping death and by this bumptious, oblivious creature who daily consorts with Diantha in a way that I, in my darkest heart, yearn to do.

And I swear, I will use my father's revolver if I hear once more, "Yo, Mr. Dude Man, you got your groove slidin'." It's bad enough to hear the endless thumping in the cellar and the seemingly endless thumping down the hallway upstairs with the unrestrained sound effects and the smell of what I am sure is marijuana wafting from under the door. What makes it worse is that young man doesn't seem to have a mean bone in his body. "Oh, Norman, he adores you," Diantha tells me. "He thinks you are one classic dude, you know, like one of those worldly men you see in old movies who knows all about culture and wine and stuff like that."

Indeed, I am so ensconced in the young man's good graces that he deigned last night to play me a new "song" he is working on. I was taken down into the basement where he has, in a section paneled back in the thirties, if I'm not mistaken, set up what he calls his synthesizer. He had me read the lyrics from something titled "Gettin' Rough in You Muff," that he had scrawled while he fingered away on a keyboard-like contraption hooked up to Nuremberg-sized loudspeakers. Then, in a kind of stylized chant, he sang,

> *I'm gettin' rough*
> *I'm gettin' rough in you muff*

I'm gettin' tough
I'm gettin' tough in you fluff
I'm gettin' down
I'm getting down where you brown
'Cause you
'Cause you got the butt
You got the butt of no joke
I'm gettin' rough
I'm gettin' rough in you muff

And over and over.

I repeat these "lyrics" in the hope my good reader might make more sense of them than I could. Indeed, I have not the slightest idea what the words mean. Perhaps, I thought, as I nodded my appreciation, they weren't supposed to mean anything. Or perhaps they were avant garde, like a lot of modern poetry, which reads, or used to read, like something written for academics to write about, the verbal equivalent of abstract art. I did mention, as an attempt to make polite conversation, that the cadence of his "music" bore some resemblance to rhythm patterns in early English verse. I cited *Beowulf* as an example.

"Yeah, cool, man. Beowulf. I dig where you're coming from. They're one grooving group, man. Punky funk with some real heavy tunes."

It would be so much easier if we simply despised each other.

The fact is that I have larger concerns than accommodating Sixpak Shakur or placating people like Mr. Castor. And it's not only Ossmann and Woodley, Bert and Betti, Elsbeth and Diantha. I have as well a gnawing unease about the fate of Korky Kummerbund. It's simply not in the young man's character to go away for this long a time without telling Elsbeth and his other friends.

At the same time, as though at another remove, I wonder what's happening to Corny Chard. People joke that he's probably been eaten by the tribe in whose purity and cannibalism he puts such faith, but it's scarcely a laughing matter.

15

Not long after I arrived at the office this morning, I received an unannounced visit from Mr. Freddie Bain that turned out to be disquieting and not a little bizarre. He is, it turns out, the proprietor of both the Green Sherpa and an art, gift, and spice emporium called the Nepalese Realm. I say disquieting because in the aftermath of his visit — the lingering musk of his cologne among other things — I had the distinct impression that he had been sizing me up.

A man as tall as myself but ruggedly built with closely barbered blond hair, a handsome, feral face, and an annoying passive-aggressive manner, he waxed fake obsequious as he placed his card on the edge of my desk. "I won't take much of your time, Mr. de Ratour," he said, declining the chair I offered with a gesture. Instead, he walked around the office inspecting the items on display. He wore a tailor-cut hacking jacket of green-brown tweed with leather at the elbows. "Nice. Very good, yes," he murmured in his strange British English.

I waited a polite amount of time before I asked, "What can I do for you, Mr. Bain?"

He turned on me an enigmatic smile shaded with cynicism. "The question, Mr. de Ratour, is what can I do for you?"

I regarded him steadily, resisted a glance at my watch, and said, "You have me at a loss, sir."

His smile vanished. "I have a considerable private collection of Nepalese art. It includes, for instance, an ancient, wonderfully wrought *kirtmukha cheppu*. Someday I will have to find a home, a more permanent home for what I have."

I nodded noncommittedly and dissembled a sudden wariness. It is true that museums and like institutions become cravenly acquisitive when there is some extraordinary piece or collection up for grabs. Especially if it comes with a generous endowment. But more often than not, people in my position are faced with a bereaved widow relating how, above all else, her late husband wanted his collection of Mexican dolls or Siamese elephant miniatures or genuine antique primitive African art to go to the musuem.

Or there are those gentlemen looking for a massive tax write-off for the Japanese swords or hand-sewn quilts they find in the attic that some "expert" has described as "priceless."

Or there are those instances when the donor wants to super-vise the care and display of his or her gift. Just last week I had to patch up yet another dispute between Feidhlimidh de Buitliér, the curator of our small but exquisite Greco-Roman Collection, and Heinrich von Grümh, the Honorary Curator of the Greco-Roman Coin Collection he donated. Von Grümh bullied and charmed me into naming him to that position, a decision I have regretted ever since.

So, when presented with well-intentioned individuals bear-ing gifts and expecting gratitude, my office in most cases is to explain, as tactfully as I can, that the MOM must move slowly on acquisitions given the limitations on storage space, display space, curatorial time, preservation, insurance, and the like.

When I began to make this clear to Mr. Bain, he failed to hide a flash of angry incredulity. "I can assure you, Mr. de Ratour, that I have collected the best there is on my journeys to that elevated nation." Then he relented. "But that is in the future. I understand your position. You must play keeper of the goal."

I said nothing. And when he responded with a like silence, I made a point of looking at my watch. He gave me a dismissive smile. He said, "You have quite an operation here, Mr. de Ratour. I mean the museum, of course, but also the laboratories and the Pavilion . . ." He paused. "I'm acquainted with Professor Chard. We have friends in common . . ."

"Indeed," I said, bemused now.

"I understand he is on a trip somewhere in South America . . ."

"As a matter of fact, he's up at the headwaters of the Rio Sangre, a tributary to the Amazon. I just had a communication from him."

"Indeed. And he is well?"

"Well enough, I gather."

"I understand it's dangerous territory . . ."

I nodded. Was this the purpose of his visit? I wondered. "Yes, but he reports everything is going well. And let's hope it stays that way . . ."

"Excellent. Excellent." As he spoke his smile appeared like a change of masks. He stood up. "I won't take any more of your time, Mr. Ratour."

I rose and took his extended hand, which was large and powerful. "Not at all," I said.

"And please, if you would oblige me by letting me know when you hear from Professor Chard again. We are all most concerned for his welfare."

He left me musing. But I decided not to dwell on the man or his visit. Corny attracts all sorts of strange individuals, as, indeed, does the museum.

In fact I have had other matters on my mind. I have been frustrated in attempts to learn anything really pertinent about the parties involved in the date rape case that came up this afternoon at the hearing before the Subcommittee on Appropriateness. At the same time, details came to light that lead me to believe it has a bearing on the Ossmann-Woodley murders.

We met in one of those of those soul-less little rooms that honeycomb Grope Tower. A platter of donuts was set on the largish square table around which, with our coffees, we exchanged pleasantries awaiting what Izzy Landes has deemed "official exercises in prurience."

That began when a side door opened and the two disputants, followed by Ms. Maria Cowe of Human Resources and her assistant, came into the room. Ms. Bobette Spronger and Mr. Moses Jones sat well apart but facing each other. Ms. Cowe thanked the subcommittee on behalf of the department and made introductions. We in turn introduced ourselves.

I had some difficulty at first imagining the couple engaged in any kind of sexual activity together. Mr. Jones, who pivoted around in his wheelchair with a certain amount of flair, is a man of medium size, quite dark in complexion, with a rectangular face and handsome African features. He wore chino trousers and a plaid shirt with the cuffs neatly folded back, and I could not help but notice his well-muscled arms and shoulders. Ms. Spronger, decidedly plump, with cropped hair emphasizing the roundness of her face, looked to be one of those unfortunate creatures who are attracted to the low pay and opportunities for moral posturing that universities provide.

I was surprised to notice that they appeared to be fond of each other. Ms. Spronger's glances at Mr. Jones might be described as possessive in a maternal kind of way. He regarded her in turn with that healthy if somewhat naive enthusiasm of the born-again.

Ms. Luraleena Doveen of the President's Office of Outreach presented "the facts agreed upon." According to this account, during lunchtime on Thursday, September 28, Ms. Bobette

Spronger and Mr. Moses Matthews Jones accompanied each other to a supply closet located in the basement of Sigmund Library for the purposes of having sexual intercourse.

Ms. Doveen, reading from a prepared statement, said that while both parties had "an active talking relationship," neither had at any time previously contemplated anything like intimate relations with the other. These conversations, often intense, apparently involved attempts on the part of Ms. Spronger to convince Mr. Jones to see himself as an exploited member of "a racist patriarchal system that kept him in an ideological wheelchair." For his part, Mr. Jones tried to convince Ms. Spronger that sex between women was unnatural and "a perversion of the love Our Lord Jesus has for every living soul."

"All of a sudden," they both agree, "they felt a sharp and inexplicable need to have sex with each other." Upon arriving at the supply closet in question, they closed the door and immediately, "with considerable urgency," prepared to have sex.

Needless to say, with that statement, the light heretofore flickering in the back of my mind turned painfully bright. Two people of utterly disparate backgrounds and inclinations in matters amatory suddenly suffer a compulsion to have sex with each other. I took the pad thoughtfully provided in front of me and started making notes.

To quote Ms. Doveen again: "The couple began intercourse with Ms. Spronger, divested of her lower undergarments, easing herself onto the lap and erect penis of Mr. Jones while he remained seated in his wheelchair with the wheels locked so as to provide stability."

At that point the written statement concludes. Their accounts of what happened after that diverge. Ms. Doveen lowered the document in her hand and sat down. The verbal testimony began. By prior arrangement, it was Ms. Spronger who would go first, giving her account of what happened next.

A little nervous (who wouldn't be?), Ms. Spronger described herself as "a virgin where like the male sex is involved." In one of those modern accents often heard among young women these days, she continued, "Well, like I've never gotten it on with a guy. Some of my sister friends tell me it's okay but not really that interesting. I mean like it's over before it begins.

"So when we were sitting there like having lunch and Mosy looks at me and says, 'You want to go down to the book ends,' I said sure. I mean I was just thinking about the same thing. I was like horny and all that but I thought maybe it would help him get through this Jesus thing he's going through."

"What is the book ends?" Izzy asked.

"It's like this big storage room in the basement where people sometimes go for privacy. It's got a combination key on the outside and you can like shut it with a bolt on the inside."

She glanced significantly at Mr. Jones and continued. "So when we got there we both like pulled down our pants. Mosy was very ready and I was, too. He showed me how to like sit down on him and took care of the details. And we started doing it."

She seemed to have run out of things to say. I wanted to ask her what they had for lunch, but thought it best to wait.

"Then what happened?" someone prompted gently.

"Then, I don't know. It was kind of like vigorous motion. Then I felt this feeling go through my whole body, right into my bones. It made me feel strange to myself. When I came to my senses, I said, 'Please, Mosy, please stop, please.' But Moses wouldn't like let me get up."

Mr. Jones, shaking his head and smiling self-consciously, interrupted. "You kept saying stop but you wouldn't get off me."

"You wouldn't let me."

"Please, Mr. Jones," Professor Athol admonished. "You'll have your turn. Ms. Spronger, please continue."

"I mean he's like a wheelchair marathoner and he's got these powerful arms and he just like kept me in place and I gave up trying to stop."

After a moment of silence, during which time it was more or less established that she had completed her version of things, Professor Athol, who is chair of the subcommittee, asked, "How sure are you that Mr. Jones understood your request to stop?"

"He had to. He was like right there. I mean you can't get any closer."

"Were you facing him or did you have your back to him?" Izzy asked.

"I had my back to him."

"Could you tell me what you had for lunch?" I asked, drawing puzzled stares and frowns from the other members of the subcommittee.

Ms. Spronger shrugged. "I had rice."

"From a restaurant?"

"No, I made it myself."

"Is this really pertinent?" Ariel Dearth asked.

"It could be very pertinent." But glancing around at a majority of puzzled frowns, I realized the morass of skepticism I would have to slog through to get to the facts. I decided to interview them privately as soon as I could. Like a cross-examining attorney, I shook my head. "No more questions."

Mr. Jones spoke next. His account accorded pretty much with what Ms. Spronger had to say except for his motivation and who would or would not desist during their congress. While admitting, like her, to a sudden, inexplicable impulse to have sex, he added a note of righteousness, saying, "I thought if I could show her what she was missing by messing around with other women, I would be doing the work of the Lord."

He said that while he did hear Ms. Spronger use the word *stop*, he was unable to lift her considerable bulk off his lap, especially as she continued "to squirm around like she was really into it." He continued, "Then I really shot my wad. I mean I had an ejaculation like man . . ." He was shaking his head.

"Then I told Bobbers okay. I mean she should get off, I mean off of me. I said I'd had enough. I tried to push her, but she had grabbed the arms of the wheelchair and wouldn't let go."

"That's not true, Mosy, and you know it."

"Please, Ms. Spronger, allow Mr. Jones to continue," said Professor Athol. "Mr. Jones . . ."

"Then, I don't know. I never did lose my woody, so we were into it again. You know what I'm saying. I think she was coming again."

From the rest of his account, events apparently continued in that fashion for some time before the couple, sexually exhausted and horrified at what had happened, were able to separate and make themselves presentable.

"What made you stop finally?" Ms. Brattle asked.

Mr. Jones shrugged. "I lost my woody."

"If the arms of the wheelchair were lowered," Izzy asked, "how did Ms. Spronger manage to stay in place?"

"I only lowered them halfway down."

By this time I was in an agony of interrogative anticipation. I had a dozen questions I could have asked them. What did they have to eat? Where did their lunch come from? How long after they started eating did this strange and sudden passion come over them? What was the exact nature of this passion? I did ask Mr. Jones, "Had you ever felt any sexual attraction to Ms. Spronger prior to this encounter?"

"No way. I mean she digs other chicks. That's not my scene. I am one with the Lord on this."

When there appeared to be no more questions, Professor Athol thanked the disputants. They in turn thanked the committee and, in the company of Ms. Cowe and her assistant, withdrew.

The subcommittee at this point entered the deliberation phase preparatory to making a preliminary finding. By degrees and perhaps inevitably, the discussion turned to the nature of erections.

Ms. Schanke, working on the Lemon Filled, stated with some force that "Erections are a social construct devised by males to punish women and keep them subservient."

Ms. Doveen gave her an eye-rolling glance. "Speak for yourself, darling."

Thad Pilty stepped into the fray, spelling out the matter in simplified biological terms. He said that from a physiological point of view, both the advent and maintenance of an erection is not entirely a voluntary act and becomes less so in the throes of intercourse. "Erections occur," he said, "when hormones cause the blood vessels leading to the penis to relax and those leading away to constrict, causing the member to become engorged with up to eleven times the amount of blood it has when flaccid."

Izzy opined somewhat wistfully that for gentlemen of a certain age natural erections are something of a gift.

"Is there a female equivalent?" someone asked.

Professor Pilty responded that there was obviously no real equivalent. "In a state of sexual arousal, a woman's nipples, her clitoris, and her vaginal labia become engorged, and there's usually a concomitant secretion of lubricating moisture on the walls of the vagina."

"What's it called?" Professor Athol asked.

Thad shook his head. "I'm not sure the phenomenon has a term."

"Perhaps we should create one," someone said.

Professor Pilty shrugged his shoulders. "How does *lubrition* sound? In the sense that a man has an erection and a woman has a lubrition?"

"Sounds good to me," Ms. Doveen said as the rest of us passed.

Izzy shook his head, holding back a laugh. "Good enough to cause vagina envy."

"I'm not sure it's within the purview of the committee to decide medical terminology," Ms. Brattle stated. "I think —"

"There are possible legal consequences," Mr. Dearth interrupted.

"Or consequential legal possibilities," I muttered.

Mr. Dearth's eyebrows raised. "Yes. Yes."

"We could certainly suggest the term to the appropriate authorities," Professor Athol put in.

"I think women and women alone should decide what to call it." Ms. Schanke spoke with considerable vehemence.

"By that standard only the elderly should be allowed to coin terms for geriatric medicine."

"Surely there must be a committee on nomenclature within the medical establishment that the issue could be referred to."

"The real question is whether this body is authorized, as an official act, to suggest nomenclature to any such entity."

"It doesn't have to be an official act."

"What's the point if it's not official?"

"What do we mean when we say 'official'?"

"It means with the stamp of office."

"But we don't have an office."

"No, but we perform an office."

"That's right. An office as an official function."

"What's the etymology of the word, anyway?"

"I'm not sure. Probably from *facio,* Latin 'to make or do.' You find it the root of such words as *factory, manufacture, effect, efficient, fact . . .*"

Ms. Brattle's gavel came down with a bang. "Please. We were discussing erections."

Thad Pilty remarked as to how there was something called the IIEF, the International Index of Erectile Function.

"Thank God," said Izzy. "For a moment I thought you were referring to *L Institute International d Études Françaises.*"

"But does it define an erection?" Professor Athol asked.

"Not as such. I think the accepted definition is a penis sufficiently rigid for unassisted penetration of the vagina."

"I think it's like the judge said," Ms. Doveen put in. "I can't define it, but I know one when I see one."

"Can we all agree on Professor Pilty's definition?" Professor Athol asked.

"Why do we have to agree?" someone said. "It's been established that Mr. Jones had an erection."

"I think definitions are important," Professor Athol retorted. "Without the presence of an erection, rape is impossible."

"That's not true. Men rape women mentally and culturally all the time," Ms. Schanke put in. "So-called civilization is one long rape."

Ariel Dearth, assiduously taking notes and uncharacteristically quiet, declared that "erections *per se* have no standing in law, as far as I know. I doubt there is a legal definition of an erection as such, but there's considerable case law as to what constitutes penetration."

"More to the point," Thad Pilty asserted, "if Mr. Jones is

accusing Ms. Spronger of rape then we have to establish that not only was there an erection involved but that under the circumstances its presence was involuntary."

During a tedious back-and-forth that ensued, the issue arose as to exactly how far into the act of heterosexual intercourse in which the genitals of both partners are "in deep contact" can a woman legitimately change her mind and ask her partner to withdraw.

Professor Pilty cleared his throat and opined that once there had been "consensual penetration without any obvious trauma," it seemed unreasonable to ask the male to withdraw. Certainly, he continued, "once ejaculation has begun, it's unrealistic to think that a man can just stop and pull out."

"That's total bullshit," Ms. Berthe Schanke proclaimed. "Rape is rape and nothing you say changes that."

Constance Brattle reminded the subcommittee that *coitus interruptus* had been practiced since ancient times and was considered a legitimate part of the sexual repertoire. She wondered aloud why Mr. Jones, if he had wanted to end the intercourse, did not simply detumesce?

I'm afraid some of the men smirked.

Ms. Brattle, noticing that response, said, "What I'm saying is that he could have thought of something to distract himself."

"Such as?"

"I don't know . . . preparing his income tax . . ."

"Or sleet falling on nettles."

"Or battery acid."

"Or having a root canal."

"Or his wife."

"Please, gentlemen, this is a serious matter."

Izzy Landes sensibly argued that perhaps Mr. Jones was not in a position to withdraw given Ms. Spronger's considerable weight.

"If a man is expected to desist at any point along the way, then certainly women should be expected to do the same."

Ms. Doveen, in what seemed to me an attempt to keep up sexually, so to speak, with the Joneses from a gender point of view, retorted that "when a lady gets her groove going, there is nothing going to stop her."

Somewhat surprisingly, I was asked by Professor Athol for my opinion before I had a chance to proffer it.

I stated that whether a man is responsible or not for his erections, surely he remains responsible for what he does with them. I also remarked that I was starting to understand more and more why those so-called old fuddy-duddies of yore insisted on both high standards of conduct and their enforcement, through chaperones if necessary. Certainly if that young woman in the White House had been more closely supervised, there would not have been that encounter with the former President and the disgrace it brought to his exalted office.

No actual finding was made as to the merits of the case. We took the matter under advisement while recommending that both parties seek counseling and that they avoid having lunch together unless others were present.

I was not long back from this meeting when Mr. Castor accosted me by phone again. He asked me if I had any questions about the contract he had sent by overnight mail some days before. I told him I had no questions insofar as I had not read and did not intend to read the contract he had sent me and that my first answer was my final answer. When he tried to engage me in conversation I put him on hold long enough for him to hang up.

It should not have surprised me, but Malachy Morin lumbered into my office not long after lunch with the florid face of the freshly boozed. He lost no time in blustering on about Urgent

Productions and the need to go ahead with "Brauer's project."

I told him he was wasting his time, something I have a feeling he is very good at. "I will not have the museum turned into a setting for sensationalism."

"Norm," he said, in that fake congeniality of his that makes me clench my teeth, "we live in a new age. Any public perception is better than none. People are gonna flock here."

I told him I did not approve of flocking people.

He stood and pulled himself up to his full six foot five or six, a grandeur compromised somewhat by a rather rotund middle and an agitation that showed itself in the color of his ears. "I'm afraid I'm going to have to overrule you, Norm."

"You don't have the authority to overrule me, Mr. Morin. The university has no warrant here that's in any way enforceable. We are establishing that in court. If Mr. Castor or any of his minions as much as sets foot on museum property, I will contact the Seaboard Police Department and have him arrested on criminal trespass."

Mr. Morin shook his head with the assumed grimace of the worldly-wise and turned to go. At the door, just as in a certain kind of movie, he stopped and looked back. "You just don't get it, do you Norm. You just don't get it."

"What don't I get, Mr. Morin?"

"Mr. Morin, Mr. f*cking Morin. You know how to make it sound like a put-down. Well you ought to know, Bow Tie, that there's some serious and tough, very tough money behind this thing. I'm not talking about a couple of Hollywood fags, either, that want to make some kind of feel-good movie . . ."

"What are you trying to say?"

"I ain't going to say any more. Just remember what I told you."

"It will take an effort."

At which point he stormed out.

There still has been no word from Korky. I finally got up the courage yesterday to tell Elsbeth he had gone missing. I was forced to, really. Not only has Korky been officially listed as missing by the Seaboard Police Department, but the *Bugle* is to run a front-page story tomorrow with an account of his disappearance. A goodly sum has been collected as a reward to anyone coming forward with information as to his whereabouts. But as time passes, hope dims.

She took it well, as though, in facing her own death she already knew all she needed to know about disappearing. "I hope he's all right," she said. "But if he has gone to that great restaurant in the sky, I'm sure he's telling the head chef what he thinks of the ambrosia."

Lieutenant Tracy called me this afternoon as a courtesy to fill me in on some new developments. He told me Korky was last reported seen at the White Trash Grill, which opened some months ago at the old truck stop out on the bypass. According to the lieutenant, it is a hangout for a pretty tough bunch of what he called biker and trucker guys. He said prostitutes of various persuasions cruise the trucks pulled up for the night, and this attracts other unsavory types. Korky's editor at the *Bugle* said he may have gone out there to do a review of the restaurant, but he didn't know for sure. As for suspects in any possible foul play, I told Lieutenant Tracy he might want to check Korky's clips at the *Bugle* morgue. I daresay there are lots of restaurateurs out there who would love to see him choke on some indelicate morsel. At the same time, I don't know why, I cannot get out of my mind that Korky's disappearance has something to do with the Ossmann-Woodley case.

Speaking of which, I informed the lieutenant what I had learned at the meeting of the Subcommittee on Appropriateness.

We agreed the best course right now would be for me to contact the parties involved and try to find out quietly if what happened that afternoon in the storage closet at Sigmund Library has any bearing on the Ossmann-Woodley case. He told me to get back to him were I to run into any real obstacles.

Well, I think I'll wend my way home. I only hope that Sixy and Diantha will be going out tonight. The thought of listening to all that thumping dispirits me.

16

Every person, I think, questions his own courage from time to time. And for me that time is right now. I have on the desk, not far from where my hands address the keyboard, a videocassette. My responsibility is clear: I must take this cassette to the Twitchell Room, insert it into the VCR, and watch it.

But I cannot bring myself to do it.

Perhaps I should start at the beginning. As many people know by now, Corny Chard has been on an expedition to one of the very remote tributaries of the Amazon to witness the rituals of the Yomama tribe. Still "anthropologically untainted," according to Corny, the Yomamas are reportedly the last group in the world still practicing cannibalism. Concern has been mounting, both here at the museum and among his family, because no one, until today, has heard anything in weeks. (As to his family, I think his daughters are more concerned than is his wife, the merry Jocelyn, who keeps saying that Corny will come to a bad end.)

This afternoon, just as I was about to descend to the Twitchell Room for the annual meeting of the Visiting Committee to the Skull Collection, a likable young man by the name of Henderson appeared in my doorway. I surmised that he brought me news of Professor Chard inasmuch as he wore the garments of a field scientist or nature guide — loose-fitting chino jacket, matching trousers with a lot of pockets, and a well-worn leather hat with a wide brim. He also carried a canvas duffel betokening rough usage in rough places.

He came in at my invitation, apologizing for not having phoned ahead, but indicating that the purpose of his visit might justify the forgoing of such civilities. I glanced at my watch and told him I had a meeting to attend, but could spare him a couple of minutes. He nodded and sat down in a manner that betrayed the diffidence of one still not at ease with the amenities of civilization.

"I've just flown in from Manaus," he announced, as though apologizing for the state of his clothes. "I just came out of the bush."

"And you have news of Corny?" I wondered aloud. "Professor Cornelius Chard?"

He smiled uncertainly. "I think so but I'm not sure. I was given a package by a man I know from the Rio Sangre area. The man's Christian name is Fernando. He works as a jack-of-all-trades, you know, between the local tribes and the prospectors, loggers, anthropologists, and missionaries that make it into the area. He had this package for me. He kept saying, "Very important, very important. For Mr. Norman at museum." Then he paused as though trying to think of how to word something. "He seemed very upset, scared even. He was very happy to be rid of it."

He produced from one of his capacious jacket pockets a rectangular package roughly wrapped in brown paper and tied with string. "He said a Professor Chard promised him two hundred and fifty dollars if he could get it to you in America." He handed the package across the desk to me.

"And you paid him?"

"I did."

"I'll make sure you get compensated," I said, feeling the slight weight of the package with a premonition of excitement and dread.

He nodded his thanks.

"You have no idea what's in it?"

He shook his head. "It might be a videotape of some kind."

My hands just a little uncertain, I took scissors and snipped away the string and then carefully cut away a bit of what looked like duct tape. Young Henderson was right: Nestled in several layers of paper was a cassette from a video camera in wide use.

I called Doreen and asked her to get Mr. Henderson a check for $250. I glanced at the time. With relief I realized I couldn't watch it then because of the meeting in the Twitchell Room. The equivocation of avoidance had begun. It deepened as, in assembling my papers for the committee meeting, I chatted with Henderson, learning about conditions in the region of the Rio Sangre. It did little to assuage my misgivings when he told me that the unrest there had turned violent with murders, maimings, and mutilations.

I asked about the Yomamas. He shook his head. "Those are bad hombres from what I've been told. It's hard to get porters even to go near the area. They joke about being eaten, though most people think the talk about cannibalism is a lot of nonsense."

Reluctantly, shaking his hand, I left him in the good care of Doreen who, despite her new boyfriend, appeared quite taken with the young man.

All through the meeting with the committee my thoughts kept turning to the package, which I had brought along, determined to play the tape once the room was clear. I kept thinking of questions I should have asked. Where had he met this man Fernando? What else had the man said? I wondered why Corny himself hadn't turned over the tape to Henderson. Why hadn't he put my name and address on it? As I sat there listening to Alger Wherry detail his usual problems and some new ones that had developed over the past year, I was in the awful quandary of wanting to know what it was I really didn't want to look at.

I did, however, manage to impersonate an attentive museum director deeply engrossed in the problems of acquiring, curating, and storing human skulls. It turns out there is something of a crisis in the collection. In his subdued but pithy way, Alger reported that, because of space limitations, you would have at present a better chance of winning a Nobel Prize than of getting your skull into the collection.

The members of the visiting committee listened attentively. The committee is little more than a holdover from the days when the university was tightening its grip on the museum. I added a few new members on my own, an action that prompted a rebuke from the university's Committee on Visiting Committees, which I ignored.

Morgan Marsden, Professor of Divinity Emeritus, an expert on the afterlife and a longtime member of the committee, scratched the back of his own fine skull and said that surely, with the repatriation of skulls to various American Indian tribes, there must be a lot more room for new specimens.

Alger, his head bones prominent, his complexion unnaturally sallow from spending a life virtually underground, reported that in fact the repatriation program had bogged down because of intertribal squabbles as to what skulls belonged to whom.

Why not just move some of the less valuable skulls into a "deacquisition" program, asked Hermione Cabot, the doyenne of curators at the Frock, Wainscott's small but well-endowed art museum.

Alger shrugged. "It's not that easy. They are human remains, and we'd have to bury them in a cemetery with all that entails. Crematoriums won't touch them without a death certificate. I mean you can't just load them into a Dumpster and have them taken to a landfill. Although, I suppose you could."

Alger also reported that the problem of bone mold, a pernicious form of which has afflicted our well-known Forensic Collection, is worse than initially estimated. He said they were running dehumidifiers around the clock, but it's been a wet summer and part of the basement sits right on top of an old streambed.

We went down to the basement for our usual tour of the collection, row upon row of grinning death. We examined a few serious cases of bone mold and looked at some new acquisitions for the Curiosities Cabinet.

When we passed the room with the door of green baize behind which the *Sociéte de Cochon Long* used to hold its secret meetings, I tried the brass knob and found it locked. "What's this used for?" I asked Alger.

"Oh, we're thinking about it for storage," he said in a way that made me wonder.

The meeting finally ended with resolutions to pursue funding for warehousing off-premises "marginal specimens" as well as those contested by Native American tribes. A subcommittee was formed to look into the bone mold problem and report back to both Alger and me.

When the meeting concluded, I remained in the Twitchell Room, thinking I would pop in the cassette and simply watch it. I have to confess I was relieved again to be told the room had been scheduled for a meeting of the museum's Subcommittee on Signage.

Before returning to my office, I dropped in on Alger and said I would like to take a look at the room with the green baize door.

He stalled me. He said something about not having the key. I mentioned that Mort would have one. Most reluctantly he produced one, and we made our way over there. I don't know why. I found nothing there out of the ordinary. Except, perhaps, for the barest whiff of a scent vaguely familiar and disturbing to me.

"So why not just store your overload in here?" I said to Alger.

"It doesn't have the proper climate controls," he said.

"But if they're all surplus skulls, who cares what happens to them?"

He nodded as though in agreement, but still with an odd reluctance.

Returning to my office, I learned that Lieutenant Tracy was on his way over to see me. Doreen offered to fetch coffee, and I sat down pondering what news the Seaboard constabulary had come up with that could not be trusted to the telephone. All the while, I was conscious of Corny's tape lying on my desk like an accusation.

The coffee served, the door closed, the lieutenant got right down to business. The preliminary analysis of blood and tissue from Bert and Betti indicate that they ingested compounds similar if not identical to those found in Ossmann and Woodley.

"Dr. Cutler called you?" I asked.

"Right. He says the dosage may have been different, but he can't really tell."

It does not reflect well on me, I know, but my real concern upon hearing this news involved the media. I did not want another circus. The lieutenant understood when I voiced my misgivings, agreeing that it was important not to have the information released until we had it all and until we had decided how best to handle it.

He then asked me about my follow-up to the incident in the library involving the two employees and their accusations of mutual date rape. I told him I had drawn a blank so far. I recounted how, despite my initial resolve, I had, like any dutiful citizen of the institution, asked permission from Professor Athol to interview the disputants privately. He said he would have to refer the request to University Office of General Counsel, a veritable law firm, before taking any action.

We discussed as well Celeste Tangent and the slow progress we were both having in obtaining her CV. It was then I realized something I already knew: Lieutenant Tracy had other cases, lots of them. Indeed, he told me then of a body they had just found behind a derelict gas station in Seaboard's Old Town, a dicey sort of area.

"Not Korky Kummerbund's?"

"I doubt it. A middle-aged man. Been there too long. We've called in Strom Weedly from the Herbarium."

"The forensic botanist."

"Right. He's looking at ground cover, root invasion, fungal growths. Competent guy."

He got up to go, his coffee scarcely touched. An altogether decent man, I thought, considering how much of his life is spent dealing with the dark side of human existence.

So here I am, with the cursor blinking at me, as though my words had a heartbeat. The tape and keys to the Twitchell Room are in the drawer. My responsibility to the museum and to the Chard family is to go downstairs, put the tape in the VCR, and watch the damn thing. But courage takes energy, and right now I am utterly drained. I scarcely have the wherewithal to go home. It seems that everywhere I turn death has come or death awaits and I suffer the awful realization that in life the only escape from death is death itself.

17

My quandary regarding the Corny Chard tape is worse than ever. I came in this afternoon with the express purpose of taking the tape to the Twitchell Room, putting it in the VCR, turning it on, and watching it. Which, indeed, is what I did. To a point.

But not without stalling for a while, I have to admit. I joined the public for a stroll through the Diorama of Paleolithic Life in Neanderthal Hall, the space on the ground floor that undercuts the galleries in the atrium above. What a superb job young Edwards, our Director of Exhibits, and Thad Pilty have done. Many of the sensitive issues were sorted out finally. The individual Neanderthals look racially homogeneous; women are shown in positions of respect and authority; the children are all engaged in environmentally sound forms of play; all the hides and furs are clearly labeled as synthetic. (There is a courtship ritual of sorts that to me looks like some kind of lowlife making a pass at a woman in a bar, but all can't be perfect.)

How simple things must have been back then. Food, clothing, mating, and shelter. Although, I'm sure, back in some cave or other, on some ledge near where the rock face was being used as a canvas, someone had started a collection of discarded, nicely carved spearheads and bear claw jewelry, just for display. And someone had to curate it.

But to the matter at hand. I cannot be too hard on myself. I finally left the public area, let myself into the Twitchell Room, found the right niche for the tape, inserted it, turned it on, and watched.

As expected, the first few minutes of the tape were scarcely exceptional: shots of a dense jungle trail and smallish natives naked except for thongs around their waists and under their buttocks carrying what appeared to be blowguns and bows with great long arrows. The camera bobs a bit even in clear stretches, throwing out of sync the rhythmic walking movements of the all but naked haunches of the natives up ahead. It is clear that for much of the time they are climbing a fairly steep incline.

They stop finally at a small clearing where, through a break in the dense canopy, the camera scans over a great, green, riverine forest. Corny's voice comes over from the side in a breathlessness reminiscent of that Englishman who narrates nature programs. "Down below to the left you can see where they have clear-cut several hundred hectares, destroying habitat for both man and nature."

The picture jostles, goes blank. Then we see Corny standing on a log, slouch hat pulled over his balding, cropped pate, face blistered by the sun, stance defiant, every inch the fearless anthropologist of yore. "A lot of the tribespeople are noticeably hostile to outsiders now. I had difficulty recruiting what porters and guides I have with me here. As you can see ahead, even getting into Yomama territory is difficult. There are no permanent trails, and we will now have to cut our way with machetes through dense vegetation that reasserts itself very quickly.

"Ahead of us, in a hidden upland valley, is the sacred village of the Yomamas, where no outsiders have been before, not even Ferdie, who's been everywhere around these parts. Melvin Bricklesby made it as far as our base camp in 1957 but turned back when his porters wouldn't go any farther. His account of *Osunki,* the anthropophagic ritual of the Yomamas, is, as he freely admits, based largely on hearsay. And now our escorts, from one of the small tribes along the tributary, refuse to go any farther. They've been getting more and more nervous. They've been making jokes, pointing at one another, rubbing their stomachs and laughing.

"Ferdie yesterday made contact with a member of the tribe, and he tells me that the headman has agreed to let me witness and videotape *Osunki* in exchange, believe it or not, for the video camera taking this footage. An important Yomama I met down at the base camp thought it sheer magic that we could capture the living world in this box. Well, I'm not about to say no to a deal like that. So, at the risk of pomposity, let me say I am setting forth to record the conscience of my fellow humans, to refute once and for all the cannibalism deniers, that legion of the misguided who think the human species too good for the natural behavior of which it is capable.

"Whew. We've been climbing along this trail now for several hours and we've only now come to the rough part. I've have never been in an area so remote in all my life."

For a while there is no voice-over, only the sound of birds in the canopy, Corny's heavy breathing, and the slash of machetes as they cut their way through the dense understory of the jungle. The screen goes blank. When it comes back on it's obviously some time later, though nothing seems to have changed. They are still moving slowly upward, the men ahead hacking away at the vegetation.

The screen goes blank again. But when the picture returns, it shows them in a large, nearly paradisical setting, a green clearing spaced with conical grass huts with steep, heavily wooded hills all around.

Corny, his voice with a distinct edge of excitement, his breathing strained, is saying, "We have arrived at Yama-beri, the sacred village of the Yomamas. As you can see, it is not exceptional from the other villages we have seen in this region. What's different are these elaborately carved spit poles called *issingi,* yes, right Ferdie, that's what the Yomamas call them." The camera closes in on two forked poles embedded in the ground, the tips of which had been worked into knob shapes suggestively phallic. The camera shows several of these spaced around a large cleared space at one end of the village. There, lots of natives mill around, virtually naked from what I could see. "This is the *issingi,*" Corny continues, directing the camera at a gallows-like affair with two stout logs buried in the ground and a crossbar lashed to the top of it with rope woven from the inner bark of trees.

A drumroll of sorts sounds from a hollow log beaten with sticks. The camera swings around to catch an imposing older man in loincloth and monkey skins, his face elaborately painted, as he approaches. Accompanying him are three nearly naked women, one quite heavy, and a fierce-looking younger man who shakes a gourd.

Off camera, in a near whisper, Corny can be heard saying, "Here comes the chief and his three wives. The young man is his first son by his first wife."

The chief stops and, after an elaborate bow, makes a long speech as his son shakes the rattle all around Corny's person. There is a sudden commotion on the screen. When the picture comes back on, Corny is being held and his limbs bound by several muscular-looking natives to the four corners of the gallows-like affair he mentioned earlier. He is looking into the camera, somewhat breathless, and saying, "Keep the tape rolling, Ferdie. I don't know what they're going to do, but let's not miss any of it."

Corny shows, surprisingly, little obvious fear, more a kind of breathless exhilaration. He says, wincing as they strip off his clothes and bind him with what look like pieces of grass rope, "If being killed and eaten by a lion could be called the ultimate wildlife experience, I suppose that being killed and eaten by cannibals is an anthropologist's ultimate contribution to research. It appears that I am no longer merely the observer, but have become the observed. Keep the camera steady, Ferdie."

The screen went blank for a moment. I fervently hoped it was the end of it. Then Corny appears again. One native is holding a slender hollow tube, perhaps five feet long, up to one of his nostrils, while another blows something through from the other end. Corny retches, but bends his head down for another dose of whatever it is they're blowing up his nose. Finally, still retching but smiling, Corny is again talking into the camera, sounding even more like that hard-breathing Englishman.

"That was tremendous, probably one of a class of hallucinogens used in these parts to induce trances. I should shortly be seeing visions. I am, of course, terrified. But I am also exalted. I only regret that I am not able to take notes, except verbally. My fervent hope is that whatever happens, that researchers will study this and do papers on it. I am scared but I am also excited. Both emotions, no doubt, will affect my objectivity as I am reduced in anthropological terms to ultimate subjectivity. Ferdie, pan to the right for a moment."

The camera pans to the right, and Corny can be heard in a voice-over. "There are the sacred cooking spits on which specific parts of the victim are slow-cooked, according to Bricklesby's account. He relates that the body parts are consumed according to rank. The chief, seated over to the left, close on him, Ferdie, will get my heart. My genitals will go to his oldest son by his first wife. I'm quoting what I remember of Bricklesby's report. I may get to witness the event depending on what they start on first. If

Bricklesby has it right. My liver will go to the portly woman to the right of the chief. His first wife. The brain, strangely enough, is considered refuse and discarded. Perhaps it's an example of primitive dietary laws. Oh, my God, here comes the chief and all his retinue. Ferdie, make sure you get this all down."

Ferdie pans back, showing a group of the natives coming over to kneel in front of Corny. They make placatory, almost devotional sounds. A figure in mask and loincloth shakes ashes over Corny's head. "This is the purification ceremony. Those are the ashes, Bricklesby tells us, of the last celebrant as they call the victim. Notice that there is no animosity here. They consider it a great honor. I am about to become a part of the tribe. The Yomama word for 'initiation' is very close to the one used for this ceremony. Ferdie! Ferdie! It's about to start . . ."

A figure in an elaborate headdress dances to the pounding log drum and appears in front of Corny, who is spread naked like the universal human figure by Leonardo. "Ferdie, keep the camera on the shaman in the cockade of red macaw feathers. Oh, God, I think he's doing the cleansing dance right now."

The camera keeps to the man in the brilliant headdress and painted, near-naked torso dancing around and bending over an object on the ground. As Corny again comes into view a harsh, familiar sound is heard off camera. Corny gasps. "Oh, God. That's a chain saw. Bricklesby said nothing about that. It's not in the tradition. Oh, God. Or am I hallucinating?"

Poor Corny is not hallucinating. The shaman figure comes into view holding what looks like an old chain saw. It's sputtering and emitting great clouds of blue smoke as the figure approaches Corny.

At which point I pressed the OFF button. I simply could not watch any more of it.

Am I a coward? Perhaps. But as ambivalent as I may feel about

Corny sometimes, he is still a member of the museum community. He is still one of us. And I dread, absolutely dread, having to watch him being sacrificed on the altar of anthropological research. More than that, I dread having to go to Jocelyn and explain to her what has happened to her husband.

18

No, I have not yet viewed the rest of the Corny Chard tape. I have dreamed about it. I obsess about it during my waking hours. The very drawer in which I have placed the tape seems haunted. Several times now I have taken it in hand, gone down to the Twitchell Room, and, at the last minute, pavid and pale, lost my nerve.

Of course I have my excuses. I have been spending a good deal of time at home with Elsbeth. She has finally agreed to have an oxygen apparatus available to use when she has trouble breathing. I think she did it to relieve the anxiety Diantha and I experience when she starts gasping for breath like a fish out of water.

Perhaps, at some unconscious level, I have conflated what awaits me on the tape and what awaits Elsbeth. Both are unimaginable and yet as real as the ground and the sky. I wonder if we find death a mockery because life, after all, is all we've got.

To more mundane matters. I have received at long last the curriculum vitae of Ms. Celeste Tangent. Indeed, I have received two copies, one from a young man in Human Resources with a note apologizing for the delay, and one from Lieutenant Tracy. The woman appears to have had, if I do say so, a rather checkered career to have ended up as a laboratory assistant in a genetics lab.

Born twenty-seven years ago in Norman, Oklahoma, Ms. Tangent claims a degree in business administration from a correspondence school associated with Oral Roberts University. She next lists herself as an assistant supervisor at the Caucasian Escort Service, Brooklyn, New York. In that capacity, she "recruited, trained, and directed young women in the etiquette of an upmarket escorting service patronized by a distinguished and discreet clientele."

After several years of plying this trade, she accounts for a gap of some seven months to conduct research into the leisure patterns of successful entrepreneurs in vacation spots in Mexico, Rio, and the Caribbean. Upon returning to New York, she assumed the position of maître d at the Crazy Russian. This is an establishment in the Brighton Beach section of Brooklyn that she describes as a pricey, after-hours bistro for a discerning clientele interested in seeing a side of New York few tourists know about.

She lists another hiatus devoted to research in exotic realms, including, of all places, Nepal, where she studied spirituality. And for the past six months she has been working as a laboratory assistant for the Ponce Institute, "helping the best scientists in the world make really great discoveries."

I put in a call to the lieutenant. He wasn't available, but he called back a few minutes later.

"Ms. Tangent's CV," he said as a greeting.

"Thanks for sending it along. Tell me, Richard, do we have any background on the organizations she's been associated with?"

"Not a whole lot. My sources in New York say there's a good chance that both the escort service and the restaurant were mob-connected. But it will take them some time digging to find out exactly what mob because both of those establishments are out of business now."

We discussed the obvious incongruence of Ms. Tangent's current employment given her background. "But if she's a plant," I said, not entirely comfortable with the jargon, "it implies there is something going on in the lab that's of interest to organized crime."

The lieutenant smiled. "Elementary, dear Watson."

"Too elementary, perhaps," I conceded. "But how would 'the mob' know enough for them to want to infiltrate the lab? The research really is quite sophisticated, and the bureaucracy formidable. I mean it all seems a bit far-fetched."

"You're right, Norman, to a point. But people talk. They get a few drinks on board. They brag. They exaggerate. Someone down the line or up the line hears about it. Criminals are businessmen, they're opportunistic. They do some checking. The scam gets rolling. I've decided to make Ms. Tangent the object of some light surveillance. Find out where she hangs out and who she hangs out with, that sort of thing."

I said I thought that was a good idea and then brought the lieutenant up to date on the Sigmund Library incident. I told him that after waiting several days and finally deciding that the proper channels were clogged — as usual — I called Ms. Spronger and Mr. Jones directly. It seems both have retained lawyers. They said they would get back to me. "One wonders, Lieutenant," I said, "what the world did before lawyers insinuated themselves into every aspect of our lives."

The lieutenant said to give him a call if lawyers continued to get in the way. "I have to admit I was somewhat dubious at first. But I think what happened there is strange enough to warrant closer investigation."

We chatted awhile longer and ended agreeing that, while we had nothing definite to go on, there were some promising leads opening up.

I may be mistaken, but I think I detect strains in the Diantha-Sixy arrangement. It was noticeable on Friday when she brought him by to show him the museum. I was in the midst of evaluating and commenting on the quarterly reports of the curatorial staff when they appeared in the doorway, seemingly disoriented by a wholly new milieu. I was delighted, of course, to see Diantha. She is so demonstrative, coming around the desk to give me one of those full-length hugs I find so unnerving, especially when they come with a big kiss on the lips.

Mr. Shakur, as usual, didn't just shake my hand, but went through a whole routine after a "gimme five, bro." Then, instead of sitting down like an ordinary person, he paced around like a caged cat with a bald head and earrings, jabbering away in that argot of his. "Too f*cking, spanking real, man. I mean real like ozone, out there, man, orbit. I didn't know they had places like this, man. I mean cool with a capital *K*. That African gear downstairs is right over the edge, man. I mean off the freaking planet Earth. What you say, Di, we do a shoot here, like with all of our faces morphing in and out of those, like masks and shit, and I do my black honky cut?"

"He's saying, Dad, that he would like to do a music video in the museum." Diantha spoke with an apologetic edge to her voice, as though embarrassed, as though, perhaps for the first time, seeing her paramour through my eyes.

I smiled indulgently. "Getting permission would be a problem, I'm afraid."

The Rapper King turned a chair around and sat in it facing the desk, his chin propped on top of the back. "But you the top dog, Mr. Dude. I mean you bark and the others, man, they shit. You know what I'm saying?"

"It doesn't quite work that way, Sixy. The curators have a very large say about what goes on in their collections, and I know what they'll say." My response didn't seem to faze him in the least.

"I'm mellow with that, man." He shook his gleaming skull.

"This crib is totally killer, man. I mean cool with double *K*'s."

It went on like this for a while longer until they finally took their leave. Diantha gave me another one of those kisses that stay on the lips. I'm not going to bring it up with her, of course, but I do think it would be for the best if she and Mr. Shakur were to part company. She deserves so much better. But I confess I would feel a proprietary sense regardless of whom she associated with.

At the same time, Mr. Shakur's effect on me borders on disorientation. I felt I had been in touch with a different kind of consciousness, not necessarily lower, but off to the side, like off the edge, man. If I'm not careful, I'll end up speaking like him.

Mr. Shakur's productions came up later that afternoon when I went over to the Pavilion to drop in on a party for Marge Littlefield, who is retiring as comptroller of the MOM. She's taking early retirement, because, she told me, she and Bill don't need the income and she has grandchildren to enjoy.

Anyway, in the course of this little affair, held in what used to be the "rec room" for Damon Drex's literary chimps, I ended up talking about Anglo-Saxon poetry with Maria Cowe's assistant, a comely young woman with nervous eyes from Human Resources. She said she had just read a translation of *Beowulf* by the Irish poet . . . whose name escapes me now (a senior moment, Izzy would say). I remarked that I thought there were similarities between rap music, so called, and the rhythmic scheme in Anglo-Saxon poetry. As a demonstration, I proceeded to quote to her some of the lyrics Sixpak had shown me.

I was amazed to see this young woman blush quite red, stammer something, and on the flimsiest of pretexts turn from me and pretend to listen to people in another conversation. But then, I've come to accept that manners among young people and a lot of others aren't what they used to be.

19

It's been one of those days. I sit here in my perch at home like some old gangly bird full of hankerings more suitable to a man half my years. My unseemly yearnings stem in part from the "enhanced" video I received from Worried this morning showing the three people having sex in an office at the Genetics Lab. Worried e-mailed me last night, telling me I would find the tape in a bag labeled TOXIC next to the recycling area on the second floor. I was to remove the tape and replace it with an envelope containing $350, which I did, no questions asked.

I played the tape alone in the audiovisual room. You can imagine my surprise when I was able to identify the gentleman being fellated as none other than Professor Ossmann. What I found interesting was the manner in which he contorts his face as though in pain or from pleasure bordering on pain as he holds on to the back of the woman's bobbing head. She had, as far as I could tell — it is a black-and-white print — thick blond hair done in a braid that fell to one side of her neck. The woman is, I'm willing to bet now, Celeste Tangent.

The gentleman behind her is tall, more slender than thin, with dark hair and very white buttocks, which twink, as buttocks are wont to do, with his thrusting motions. I have a distinct feeling the unknown man is Dr. Penrood, but I can't be sure as I have not been privileged to see him in that situation before. His face does appear in profile, but only for an instant. When their various culminations are reached, to judge from their motions, parts are disengaged and they move off into shadow and darkness.

I immediately supervised the making of a copy — keeping the screen blank throughout — and sent the original to Lieutenant Tracy by special courier. In an accompanying note I identified Ossmann, but I also wondered aloud, so to speak, about how useful, at this point in the investigation, the information really was. Had Ossmann and the other two been working on some kind of love potion and decided to give it a try? Had he tried again with Dr. Woodley and gotten the dose wrong? Or was the effect of a lethal dose known and for some reason used against Ossmann and Woodley? If so, why experiment on Bert and Betti?

Speaking of whom, the spotlight of unseemly publicity has once again been turned on the Museum of Man. Amanda Feeney-Morin wrote a front-page story in yesterday's *Bugle* disclosing details from the autopsies of Bert and Betti. She revealed that the biochemical analysis turned up compounds identical to those found in Ossmann and Woodley. Ms. Feeney quoted an unidentified source within the SPD to the effect that the compounds constitute "a blockbuster aphrodisiac." It sounds like my friend Sergeant Lemure is at it again.

Then Ms. Feeney got to the real point of her story. "Norman de Ratour, Director of the museum, did not return calls." Of course the woman called me. She calls every day to ask me if I beat my wife or molest donkeys. So of course I don't return her calls. But that's not the kind of thing I can include in the press releases I put out stating that no research on aphrodisiacs is taking place in the Genetics Lab. It would get twisted around until it sounded like an evasion.

Which reminds me, I have yet to look at the rest of Corny's tape. *Why me?* I complain to the air. Why not send it to Murdleston or Brauer? Because Murdleston's too foggy and Brauer, who has his own geek show in progress, can't be trusted.

But none of the above, I must confess, is what has me dithered like a teenager. Sixpak Shakur has moved out, lock, stock, and amplifiers, and while a measure of peace reigns here at home I find myself beset again with the worst kind of temptation.

More accurately, the King of the Redneck Rappers was thrown out by Diantha, for whom I feel heartfelt sympathy, genuine love, and a low, cunning, opportunistic lust. Even when I try to be high-minded, when I lift my head and straighten my shoulders and think, yes, indeed, the breakup will be the best thing for her in the long run, I find myself in the equation. I find my imagination flaring, conflating with images from the video so that I am behind her, in front of her, on top of her . . . Which is shameful beyond words because the dear girl is, for the nonce, very upset.

Diantha, in fact, was close to hysterics when I came in around seven thirty this evening. She met me at the door, her eyes fetchingly pink from weeping. She fell into my arms, sobbing again.

"Elsbeth?" I asked in alarm, fearing and expecting the worst.

"No, no, no," she moaned. "It's Sixy. He's gone. Sixy's gone."

"You poor girl," I said, taking her in my arms, my relief at the man's departure mixing with my commiseration for her all-too-evident distress.

"But I still have you, don't I, Norman," she sniffled and gave me a big wet kiss on the lips, which I can still feel imprinted, like a stain I want to keep.

I decorously disentangled myself. "Gone," I said, trying to dissemble the sense of giddy release that kept arriving like pleasant shocks as I hung up my topcoat in the hall closet. "Diantha," I said firmly, putting my arm around her shoulder. "Tell me what happened. But first, how is your mother doing?"

Diantha nodded, my indirect rebuke and its implied perspective calming her. "Mom's okay. She's still sleeping. Do you want a drink?"

"A martini would do the trick." I rootled around the drinks cabinet and made myself a strong one. Diantha poured herself a glass of white wine. For a strange moment it seemed we were an old established couple going through the routine of homecoming.

"So tell me what happened," I urged her as gently as I could.

She sat demurely on the couch, one shapely knee pertly crossed over the other, and took a sip of her wine. "I threw him out. I told him to get out before I called the police."

She began to grow tense again. I went over and sat beside her and put my arm around her shoulders. "It will be all right," I said.

She put her face into my chest and snuffled. "I came in from shopping around four and found him screwing that little slut Candy Dolores from next door. Right in my own bed. In our own bed."

"Oh, dear."

"They didn't even stop when I came into the room and started screaming at them. And her little sister, Shirleen, the one with the braces, she was standing there watching them. She was probably in line."

"I'm not surprised, frankly," I said, saying, I'm sure, the wrong thing. "It's happened before, hasn't it?"

She snuggled closer, and I felt the fullness of her breast nudging into my ribs. Oh, to find out what a loathsome, crawling monster one is! To find out that pity can be as much allied with lust as with contempt! Or is it just natural? To want to transform those sobs and sighs of hurt into moans of pleasure? Or is it all a matter of self-sophistry? Because right then I wanted nothing more than to take her in my arms, kiss her tear-wetted lips, and roger her silly, as the English say. And, indeed, she did pull even closer, her hips against mine, and kiss me full on the lips. How in that moment I kept my hands to myself I simply cannot explain.

But resist I did. Diantha suffered another outbreak. "I mean, Dad, they were both buck naked and f*cking like fiends. And no apology. He just got off the bed, steaming from that little slut, and telling me to 'chill out, baby, chill out. I was just helping the chick find her groove.'"

I stayed with her, sensing that her tears and the flood of angry words gave her some release, a kind of purgation. I don't remember what I said, nothing, really, just comforting noises disguised as words.

Until finally she calmed, wiped her eyes, beamed at me with a most endearing smile, very much like her mother's, and said, "Go wake up Mom. I'm going to make us all one fabulous dinner."

So that, despite everything, a new spirit descended on the house. I certainly felt liberated. And Elsbeth, poor dear, waking from her drugged sleep, caught something of the mood. I helped her to the bathroom. I helped her wash. It is painful to see how Elsbeth is wasting away. But what spirit. What courage! I helped her into what she calls her "frolic" clothes, a smart turtleneck jersey and a wraparound skirt. We chatted. Yes, she had heard the commotion. "Frankly, I'm glad he's gone. The poor boy had begun to believe in his own wigger fantasies, as Di says."

"Wigger?" I asked.

"It's a Di word. She said we wouldn't understand."

Elsbeth shrugged, took another of her pain pills, and I helped her into the dining room.

Diantha served up a delectable seafood dish and a salad of fresh greens that we had with a deal of wine, a robust California Zinfandel Izzy had recommended. When we had finished, she excused herself to go upstairs and "hit the RESTART button on a whole new life."

Elsbeth and I, mostly I, finished off the second bottle. And as I rinsed the dishes for the dishwasher — I must say I am enjoying the new kitchen very much despite my hesitations — Elsbeth said plainly and simply, "I want you to take care of Diantha after I'm gone."

When I started in about how she still had a fighting chance, she repeated what she had said.

"But, of course, darling, I'll take care of Diantha. She's my daughter, after all."

"I didn't mean as a daughter."

I told her straight out that I would hear no more of that kind of talk. At the same time, I suffered from such a sense of possibilities that I was left dizzy with a kind of experiential vertigo. And while I wanted to ascribe Elsbeth's amazing statement to fatigue and perhaps even a low-grade delirium brought on by the medications for her illness, I could tell from her smile that she knows I fight the fiends within me when it comes to her daughter.

20

I still cannot quite believe what I witnessed earlier this evening, but the proof is there, in stark, horrific images. Yes, I have finally found the courage to watch the rest of the Corny Chard tape. It wasn't easy, but I fortified myself for it.

First, I left work early to be with Elsbeth for a while. She is so appreciative of the time I give her, even if it was spent mostly watching soap operas that, for me, blend one into the other, with the same people saying the same things to one another again and again. (Perhaps they are more realistic than I give them credit for.)

Then, deliberately, almost self-indulgently, giving myself plenty of time, I dressed in a tuxedo in preparation for Father O'Gould's presentation of the first Fessing Memorial Lecture and the dinner to follow. I kissed Elsbeth good-bye and drove over to the museum. From a bottle of good Scotch that I keep in the office closet, I poured myself a healthy double. I took the Scotch and Corny's video down through the deserted exhibitions to the Twitchell Room.

I think being dressed in a tuxedo and sipping neat Scotch definitely helped as I inserted the tape and pressed the button and rewound it just a bit, a final delaying action. I saw again the figure in an elaborate headdress dancing to the pounding log drum and then appearing in front of Corny, who has had his clothes cut away. I hear Corny say, "Ferdie, keep the camera on the shaman in the cockade of red macaw feathers. Oh, God, I think he's doing the cleansing dance right now."

Then we see the man in the brilliant headdress and painted near-naked torso dancing around and bending over an object on the ground. Corny comes into view again and a harsh, familiar sound is heard off camera. Corny gasps. "Oh, God. That's a chain saw. Bricklesby said nothing about that. It's not in the tradition. Oh, God. Or am I hallucinating?"

I held my breath and resisted the impulse to hit the STOP button as the shaman appears with the old chain saw. It sputters and spews smoke. And I forced myself to watch as in one horrific motion, the saw is brought up under Corny's outstretched left arm. Corny screams as the whirring blade slices off the arm through the biceps, spewing blood and bits of bone. I turn away.

Incredibly, it is Corny I hear next. "Follow the arm, Ferdie," he says, his voice weak and choking. "Get a close-up on the ceremony. I think . . . I think it's going to the ceremonial grill."

As I watched, amazed and horrified, the camera closes to where the severed arm is being sanctified before being placed over the sacred fire. Corny is heard again. "Ferdie. Keep the camera on the ceremony. They're going to keep . . . chopping me up. Get as much as . . . you can. Especially when they come for my heart. Try to . . . get it down . . . especially the cutting ceremony . . ."

The camera swings back to Corny. One native has successfully tied a tourniquet of leather thong around the stump of Corny's severed arm, while another paints the bloody stump with a thick dark paste from a gourd.

Corny keeps talking, more breathless than ever. "I'm not really in any great pain. I know they are taking me in parts. They want to keep me alive as long as possible. It's only death. I'm . . . I'm . . . like the center of the universe now. Their universe. This is a true honor. Groundbreaking. I smell my own flesh cooking. I know I couldn't eat any. Not that auto-anthropophagy is unknown."

Ferdie pans back with the camera. The shaman is dancing around again with the chain saw. It's turned off. As though part of the ritual, he pulls the cord. It doesn't work. He pulls again, and the infernal thing roars to life with a great belch of smoke. The camera swings back to focus on Corny again. He's breathing in gasps. "God, I hurt. And this is just the beginning. But this has got to be the first for an anthropologist. Norman, don't let Joss see this. Promise me. Here comes the shaman for more of me." Corny screams again as the shaman, not as neatly this time, saws off his right leg halfway up the thigh with another spewing of blood, bone, and flesh.

I have to cover my eyes. I knock back the Scotch. The drumming reaches a fever pitch. There are whoops. Incredibly, Corny speaks again. "I'm still okay. Ferdie get the, get the . . ." Like his arm, the stump of his leg is tied off again and anointed with the dark paste. "Bricklesby will have to be revised. They don't start with the genitals and the . . . How . . . how could they, and keep the sacrifice alive? My God. This is a amazing."

Mercifully, right then, Corny passes out. He sags in the crude stanchion, horrific and yes, strangely glorious, stirring within me some atavistic recognition of what we are. A few minutes later he manages to open his eyes and say, quite clearly, "Norman, no copyright." And while the shaman is dancing around the chain saw and trying to start it, the tape goes blank.

I ran it for a while longer, but there was no more on it. I couldn't have gone on watching it anyway. I was in shock. I felt half crazed. Is this the heart of darkness? Who is worse, those savages or Corny himself, making himself complicit in their debauchery? What are we?

I have no real idea what to do with this truly incredible piece of documentation. I suppose I should make a copy and then clear its legal status through our attorney. I mean, while the MOM did not contribute very much to underwriting the trip, is it possible that Jocelyn and their children will be able to sue the museum for wrongful death or some such thing. Strange how, in our lawyer-infested society, the first thing you need think about in a situation like this is liability.

On the other hand it is a kind of evidence of a heroic if unwise exploration of the heart of our species. Perhaps I will consult the Reverend Alfie Lopes. The matter involved here is moral as well as legal. I would not want this footage to fall into the wrong hands. There are parties that would exploit it for its sensationalism. There are enemies of the museum who would use it as a pretext to attack us. At the same time, it is a remarkable piece of anthropological fieldwork. And our allegiance must be to the high purposes to which the founders dedicated it: to explore the phenomenon of man in its many manifestations.

In a kind of daze I rewound the tape and made my way over to Margaret Mead Auditorium. I thought of stopping the introductory proceedings at some point to announce what I had just witnessed. But of course, that would have been utterly inappropriate.

On the other hand, I could not help having the tape color my appreciation of Father O'Gould's address. In his lecture, "Why Is There No Tuna-Safe Dolphin," the good priest gave us a taste of his upcoming book, *Paragon of Animals,* taking a bead on a question he has been grappling with all his professional life.

Everyone knows, of course, that S.J., as we all call him, holds the recently created Teilhard de Chardin Chair in Evolution and Cosmology. In his lecture S.J. went right into the teeth of prevailing notions, contending that there is indeed a *scala naturae,* and that mankind is at the very top of it. He said that to claim that there are no normative standards that can be used to rank species is arrant nonsense. The very professors making these claims, and he named a few who are vociferous on the subject, "are themselves part of a well-defined hierarchy, one that carefully grades people, especially fellow academics seeking to join their departments. They rank very precisely who is or is not good enough to be a colleague. Yet they maintain that *Homo sapiens* as a whole is no better or worse than any other living species. No better than, say, a turnip. Sure now, would Professor Dawkins of Oxford, for instance, consider a turnip worthy of a professorship? On the contrary, most of these thinkers would think nothing of uprooting a perfectly innocent turnip, skinning it alive, boiling it, mashing it with salt, pepper, and perhaps a little butter, and then eating it. Would they consider doing the same thing to a colleague? I doubt it very much. Yet they claim that we are no better or worse than a turnip."

Needless to say, Father O'Gould's talk at that point had provoked more than a few laughs. But I kept wondering what he would think were I to show him the tape I had just watched. Are we the paragon of animals? Or just animals?

He shortly turned serious, and a hush fell over the standing-room-only audience — many of them students, I was pleased to note. Father O'Gould declared that unless we recognize and accept our position at what he called "the transcendent apex of the chain of being," i.e., our superiority relative to other species, then we undercut what little moral authority we have left "in an age when the God of our fathers has retreated into myth and history . . . To say that we are no better than bacteria or turnips or rabbits is to give ourselves license, like them, to submit blindly to natural processes, to overrun the planet, to indulge in mass exterminations, indeed, to act any way we want to."

The good priest went on to point out that the denial of any

rank in creation was pushing the rationality of the laboratory to absurd lengths. "Is it not a philistine notion that truth is only to be found in a test tube or under a microscope? Simply because the position of mankind at the top of creation is not a verifiable hypothesis does not render it invalid. Because neither can you prove that Mendelssohn's Octet in E is beautiful. Those who declare that all species are equal are assuming a stance that, in its apparent disinterested objectivity, is fraught with more pernicious hubris than to simply admit that we are, as human beings, on top, and with all that means in terms of responsibility.

"I do not mean superior in any aesthetic sense. At least as depicted by Freud — Lucien, that is, not Sigmund — we suffer in comparison with the beauty of the hyacinth macaw or to that of *Panthera tigris altaica*. We certainly are not morally superior, though there is the potential for that. But we are clearly superior in intellect and technology, and that translates into power. With that power comes an awesome responsibility.

"Indeed, it is this position at the top of creation that ought to provoke in each of us the moral anxiety to proceed with scrupulous care in our stewardship. Make no mistake about it. We are the wardens and we must attend our duties in a manner befitting superior beings. Otherwise, we will answer to history as surely as the despots and dictators that have gone before us."

Father O'Gould concluded that real humility was nothing less than the acceptance of reality. "The incumbent responsibility that comes with our place in the universe is the gift of natural selection, the basis on which we must become our own necessary gods."

It was, in all, a moving and provocative occasion. Father O'Gould's inspiring talk, along with some help from the dinner wine, restored a good measure of my faith in humankind. But not entirely. Images of Corny's cruel demise haunt my inner vision. I recoil, of course. I deplore what happened. Yet something atavistic in me assents to the sacrifice. There is nearly a kind of comfort in it, a comfort I resist. Is human sacrifice, in its myriad forms, an attempt, however grotesque, to give meaning to death?

21

The plot is thickening like one of those soups you throw things into without being quite sure how it's going to turn out. I finally worked up the courage this morning to undertake a most delicate and sad task: I called Jocelyn Chard, Corny's widow, and told her I needed to come by and see her.

"You've heard from Corny?" she asked, an excited hope in her voice.

"Yes, but I'd rather . . . come over."

There was one of those silences. "He's dead, isn't he?"

"Yes, I'm afraid so, but I'd like to come see you anyway, Jocelyn."

After another silence, she said, "Yes, of course. I'll call the children in the meanwhile."

I drove over to their home on Wordsworth Avenue, a tree-shaded neighborhood of commodious but not ostentatious houses known as Professors Row. Jocelyn let me in as she spoke into one of those walkaround phones. "Yes, dear. I'm fine. He's just arrived. Yes, I'll call you right back."

A nearly tangible aura pervaded the house as Jocelyn led me into the bow-fronted living room. I could feel that dark sense of expectancy that the news of death brings, especially the death of someone close. I think we expect a kind of revelation, when in fact it's only death, the end. With bright nervous eyes, the Widow Chard bade me take a seat in an armchair adjacent the sofa. I couldn't help but notice, as I had on happier occasions (though I seldom socialized much with the Chards until Elsbeth came along), that the things on the walls, the masks and the bark-cloth hangings, were of museum quality. And, I wondered in a shameful sort of way, had Corny left any of them to the museum?

A slight, enthusiastic woman, Jocelyn effects more than a touch of the Bohemian. Her long graying hair braided down her back was of a piece with the necklace of heavy ebony figurines and the layered dark clothing she always wears. She put a hand on my forearm. "Tell me, Norman, tell me what's happened. We can have coffee later."

"Of course, of course," I expostulated. To think that the routine gestures of hospitality still pertained under the circumstances. I took a deep breath. "He was killed by natives. By members of a tribe whose traditions he went to document."

"Oh, dear." She placed her hand over her mouth. She held on to my forearm again, as though to steady herself. "Did they . . . did they eat him?"

"I'm afraid they did."

"Oh, my, my." She held her hand to her mouth again for a moment. Her face twitched. She gave a short, hysterical laugh. "I think it was what he always wanted." Then, with utter composure, she asked, "How did you find out?"

"A tape was made."

"Of the . . ."

"Yes."

Her self-possession wavered for a moment. "I don't want to see it. I don't want the children to see it. I want it kept private."

"Of course. I can see to that. For estate purposes, I will have to show it to whatever authorities need to see it." I cravenly avoided the word *attorney*. I could envision some lawyer convincing her to sue the university or even the museum for wrongful death.

"Was it . . . gruesome?"

"By my standards. By anyone's standards, I would think."

"It shows him being killed?"

"Yes."

"Was he terrified?"

"Only partly. I think he was exalted in a way. They had administered a drug to him, a hallucinogen, before they really started."

"They stabbed him?"

"No."

"How did they . . . ?"

"They cut him up."

"Alive?"

"I'm afraid so."

"With . . . ?"

"A chain saw."

"Oh, my poor Corny." Her attractive gray eyes went awry for a moment, and she held her hands to her breast. "I don't want anyone else to see it."

"I understand."

"These things have a way of getting around . . ."

"You and I are the only people who know about it other than a young prospector who brought it to me. And the cameraman, of course, as well as members of the tribe. The cameraman is a kind of go-between. He gave the tape to the mining geologist who delivered it to me personally."

The widow was nodding, looking around the room, as though it were now strange territory, its trappings those of a man, a husband, who no longer existed.

"Jocelyn," I began, "I don't know what kind of legal consequences there might be in terms of prosecution for murder. I doubt very much that the long arm of American law can reach into such remote parts. I have a feeling that the State Department will say, in a very nice way, of course, that Corny should have known better."

"He did know better. He knew it was very dangerous."

"We all knew it was risky. It's one of the reasons, frankly, that I refused to fund any part of the expedition. Except for medical supplies and insurance for medical evacuation."

"I know. Corny understood that. He was very appreciative of what you did."

I cleared my throat. "But what I would like to know, Jocelyn, is who did fund his trip."

She hesitated for a moment and then threw up her hands. "Oh, I don't suppose it makes any difference now. Corny swore me to secrecy, but he's dead now, isn't he. Dead and really gone." She held onto to my forearm again, the tears welled but didn't spill. I admired her for that.

"Who was it, Jocelyn?" I pressed.

"Oh, someone in that pig society he was always going to."

"Pig society?"

"*Le Société de Cochon Long,*" she said with a disdainful exaggeration of a French accent.

"*Really?*" I exclaimed, just managing to conceal the extent of my surprise and that nearly vaporous sensation, vertebral in its origin, that comes over me when I feel I have somehow uncovered a piece of the larger puzzle. Though in the mundanity of things, I couldn't see how Corny's death in a far-off jungle had anything to do with the murders of Ossmann and Woodley. "I didn't know it still existed," I said, trying to sound casual.

"Oh, God, all that publicity around the cannibal killing trial brought in every screwball you could imagine. There's a lot more of them out there than you might suspect."

I nodded. "Who belongs to the society today?"

"The usual people. Raul is very active, as is Alger from down in the Skull Collection. And some newcomers. Corny didn't talk about it much. It was, after all, supposed to be a secret society."

Of course, I thought, determined now to go back to the room with the green baize door and take a much closer look around. I remained awhile longer, going over arrangements I would need to make with the university about an official notice of death and an obituary. I told her I would speak to the dean and to Alfie Lopes about a memorial service if she wanted me to.

"Thank you, Norman, that would be a great help." She was visibly rallying, doing what had to be done. "I know Alfie well. I'll call him myself. I'll need his comfort. He's so good at times like this."

As I was leaving, she took one of my hands in both of hers, and her face had a contrite expression. "I'm sorry, Norman, but I forgot to ask, but how is Elsbeth?"

"Not well," I said, realizing with a wave of empathy that I would be in her shoes before long.

"Oh, I'm so sorry." But the Widow Chard was also looking me over, I swear, as a man who would soon be single again.

I went back to the museum and spent a good deal of time and effort contacting the list of people I thought should know of Corny's demise while also penning a suitably ambiguous account of how the news arrived, to the effect: "Though a final confirmation has yet to be made, reliable sources report that Professor Chard died at the hands of a remote tribe on which he was conducting ethnographic research."

I found on my office phone another recorded communication from Urgent Productions. Mr. Castor's voice reached out of the little speaker on the phone in a squawk as he apologized a bit too profusely for "losing his cool" during our last conversation.

He said he had been under intense pressure from the film's backers to have "respectful use" of the museum for "the authenticity of the project." This time I did not find his call a nuisance. On the contrary, it gave me an idea regarding Corny's fate that I intend to pursue.

While there, I decided to take a look at the room with the baize door in the Skull Collection. Luckily, Mort, back to his usual form, was on duty. He fished out his ring of keys, and we made our way down into the kingdom of grinning death. At first Mort couldn't open the door. He said the key had been changed. The master wouldn't fit. But Mort is a man of many resources. He took out of his pocket something that looked like burglar's tool, pried around for a while, and *voilà*, the door opened.

Again, there seemed nothing out of place. The table and chairs were as they had been. And just the merest whiff of that distinctive odor I could not place. Until, in making a thorough search of everything in the room, I came across evidence that it had recently been a venue for a meeting. In the wastebasket I found eleven folded pieces of paper marked with *Y*'s and *N*'s, evidence of a vote. Someone had also thrown away a withdrawal slip from one of those automated money-dispensing machines with an early-November date.

Mort said nothing when I told him I wanted to leave the room exactly the way we had found it. He nodded knowingly when I said we were to tell no one about what we had uncovered. Driving home I entertained little fantasies of placing a hidden camera or a microphone in the room, though I had little idea of what I might learn thereby.

22

I received a call today from Mr. Freddie Bain, the restaurateur. He was in quite a state about the news of Corny's death, which appeared in the *Bugle* this morning. When I tried to fob him off on the Wainscott public relations people, he turned peevish. "Mr. de Ratour, they are the ones who told me to call you. Please, can you tell me who told you of Professor Chard's death?"

I told him about Henderson's visit and his contact with Fernando and that the State Department had received reports to the same effect.

Who was this Henderson? Where might he be contacted? Was he reliable? I answered as best I could. I gave the man a post office box number for Henderson in Manaus and told him that was all I had.

"Are you sure there was no documentation?" he asked, his voice edged with insinuation.

I replied ambiguously, saying that final confirmation was awaited, but that it seemed the worst had happened. I hung up finally in bemusement. It was almost as though the man knew about the tape Corny had sent back. I made a mental note to call Jocelyn to tell her not to let anyone else know about it.

Prejudice, as the Reverend Lopes has remarked, is like excrement: We tend to think of our own as less offensive than that of others. I try to keep Alfie's dictum in mind when it comes to my feelings regarding members of the legal profession. Not all lawyers, to be sure. When I catch myself wanting to send the whole lot of them to the wall, I stop and recall the good ones I have known. Not many, actually, but a few. I tell myself that it may be something genetic, something over which they have little or no control. I remind myself that in the past members of the de Ratour family have married lawyers or even gone to law school. But that was at a time when it was considered something of an honor to join the profession.

I bring this up because of what happened today when I finally met with the principals of the date rape case that came before the Subcommittee on Appropriateness. After several futile calls, I informed them each that I was assisting the Seaboard Police Department in a matter that their case could have a bearing on, and that our conversations would be off the record and strictly confidential. Pulling one of my own teeth would have been easier.

Ms. Spronger told me they would have to consult "their" attorney, a use of the plural possessive I didn't pick up on immediately. I increased the pressure at that point, letting them know my requests to see them sprang from the Ossmann-Woodley case, now considered a murder investigation, and involved some urgency.

My action constitutes a transgression of the rules of the subcommittee. Indeed, the whole point of that body is to avoid involvement with the police or the legal system unless absolutely necessary in conflicts between members of the community. I didn't really cavil with myself on the point. If these young people had been exposed, however inadvertently, to some kind of potion being concocted in the lab, then we needed to find out about it. Still, I was somewhat surprised to learn that a lawyer had become involved; that the rules had already been bent if not broken.

It perplexed me even more that they insisted on meeting me

together. For my purposes it made little difference except that important information can be garnered from the differences that inevitably arise in separate accounts of the same incident.

At the appointed time, I made my way over to Sigmund Library, a modern, faceless building of gray granite that exudes an air of futility. We met in the Rex Room, named for a donor, I'm sure, as there seemed to be donor plaques on everything. The room is one of those small, nondescript spaces that all libraries seem to provide and which few people seem to use.

You can imagine my surprise when Mr. Jones and Ms. Spronger arrived in the company of Ariel Dearth. I could not completely conceal my chagrin at seeing the ubiquitous lawyer, but I dissembled my reaction enough to get through the obligatory introductions and handshakes. Mr. Jones wore chinos and a short-sleeved, open-collared jersey, and I could not but note again the musculature of his arms and shoulders. Ms. Spronger sported denim overalls, and for a moment I thought she might be a member of the maintenance staff. Mr. Dearth wore a contentious expression and one of those tweed hunting jackets with a leather patch at the shoulder, fitting attire for a predator, when you think about it.

"Are you their counsel?" I asked after we, the mobile, had sat down at a stark table and Mr. Jones had pulled his wheelchair up to it.

He appeared to think my question over, perhaps consulting the lawyer within. "I am," he said.

"In what capacity?"

"We're suing the university," Ms. Spronger announced.

"Bobba . . . ," Mr. Dearth started.

She bridled. "Just because we've hired you doesn't mean I've like given up my First Amendment rights."

Mr. Dearth nodded perfunctorily and turned to me. "I want

to know, Mr. de Ratour, what gives you the right to threaten my clients with a police investigation?"

"Because, Mr. Dearth, it's a fact, not a threat."

"And you know it's strictly against the rule of the subcommittee for any member to contact disputants privately without the consent of the Chair."

I had to suppress a laugh. "You mean you had the consent of the Chair to solicit these good people as clients?"

"That's privileged information."

"I'm sure it is." I turned to the disputants. "Are the grounds on which you plan to sue the university also privileged information?"

"We —" Mr. Jones started.

"That's privileged," Mr. Dearth said.

"We're victims of an institution that like created a working atmosphere in which people like want to rape one another." Ms. Spronger spoke with what seemed like pride.

"Ms. Spronger . . ." Mr. Dearth twitched his nose in frustration.

"How much are you suing the university for?" I asked.

"We haven't settled on an amount," the learned counsel said emphatically.

"We're not concerned with the money part of it," Ms. Spronger added with a touch of indignation. "It's a way of like sending a message."

"How much is the message going to cost the university?"

"Is this germane to your interests?" Mr. Dearth asked.

"Five big ones." A large smile lit up Mr. Jones's handsome face.

"Five million dollars!" I repeated, incredulous.

"Five big ones each." Mr. Jones seemed to be enjoying his freedom of speech.

"Have you settled on a contingency fee?"

"I advise against answering that question."

"Is it thirty percent? Forty? *Fifty?*"

The disputants were nodding.

I turned to Mr. Dearth. "Have you no shame, sir?"

He shrugged. "It is a long shot."

"It's a way of like effecting social change," Ms. Spronger said, as though in defense of her attorney.

"I suppose making lawyers rich through this kind of extortion is a form of social change," I said.

Mr. Jones leaned back and laughed. "Makes lots of change, anyway."

"What have we got to do with what happened to those professors?" Ms. Spronger began immediately, speaking as though she had been accused of something.

"Perhaps nothing," I said, Investigator de Ratour now, professional to my fingertips. I paused for effect. "And perhaps everything."

Sitting across the table from me, she in a chair and he in his wheelchair, they exchanged glances at my words then looked to their attorney.

I thought this curious, as curious as their insistence that they meet with me together.

"What are you saying?" asked Mr. Jones.

I shook my head. "I don't want to prejudice any answers you might have to my questions."

"They are not prepared to answer any questions until they know what they are." Mr. Dearth spoke with great solemnity.

I kept the obvious rejoinder to myself, as I know Lieutenant Tracy would have. I nodded sagely. "It's quite simple," I said. "First, as you stated in your statement to the subcommittee, you ate lunch together on the day of the incident."

"You don't need to answer that," Mr. Dearth put in.

"That's true," I said, "since it has already been established. "What I need to know is what food or drink you shared just prior to the incident that you brought before the Subcommittee on Appropriateness."

"You don't need to answer that," Mr. Dearth said.

I started to gather up my notes, making as though to rise. "In that case, I am turning the entire matter over to the police." I turned to the disputants. "That, of course, will be to Mr. Dearth's advantage as he will be able to bill you for the hours of interrogation that are sure to ensue and at which he will insist on being present. And that may well adversely affect your quote unquote case against the university."

They glanced at each other. "We shared your rice, Bobba," Mr. Jones said.

"As your attorney . . . ," Mr. Dearth began.

Ms. Spronger waved him off with a frown. "I don't see what harm there is in the truth." She turned to me. "I'm like on a whole-rice diet. I had plenty for both of us."

"And you had a half of one of my tuna fish sandwiches," the wheelchair marathoner said.

"That's right. My diet allows for like a small amount of wheat gluten."

"Did you cook the rice yourself, Ms. Spronger?"

"Oh, yes. I use only organic rice."

"And none of it came from a Chinese restaurant, from a take-out place?"

"No."

"And the tuna fish sandwich?" I asked, turning to Mr. Jones.

"Ditto. My wife made them for me. Right out of the can." He shrugged. "I mean with mayo, salt, pepper, and some chopped chard."

I winced. I had begun to get the empty feeling of drawing a blank. I took one last stab. "In your preparation of your respective lunches, did you at any time leave them unattended?"

Ms. Spronger shrugged. "I like put my rice in the microwave. But I wasn't gone more than a few minutes."

"And there were other people in the area?"

"Lots of them."

"Any strangers?"

"None that I recognized."

I frowned. "You mean you saw no one you didn't recognize."

"Yes."

"And what did you have to drink?"

"I got a Coke from the machine in the staff room," Mr. Jones said.

"And I like have my water." Ms. Spronger held up the quart-sized bottle I had seen her drinking from at the subcommittee meeting. Apparently she's one of those people who carries a nippled container with her everywhere, like a child still on the bottle.

"How soon after you shared your lunch did the incident occur?" I asked.

"Actually, we hadn't quite finished," Ms. Spronger replied.

"But almost."

"Mr. de Ratour," Mr. Dearth said with an ominous voice, "I am going to report your behavior to the university authorities."

"Feel welcome to, sir," I responded and turned back to the library employees. "Can you tell me exactly how the feeling came over both of you?"

They were both clearly embarrassed. "It just came over us," Mr. Jones said. "Big time."

"Me, too," Ms. Spronger said. "It was like a compulsion."

"Who first suggested that you retire to the closet?"

"You really don't have to answer that question. In fact, I advise against it very strongly." Mr. Dearth had grown visibly agitated during this time.

For my part, my irritation at what Mr. Dearth was attempting to do with these two young people had grown to indignation. But I kept my voice calm. "Actually, that's not really a question pertinent to my purposes. What's really important is that I ascertain that the only food you ate during that shared lunch came from home."

They both nodded. Mr. Jones asked, "What are your purposes?"

"Very good question," I said. "It's one your attorney should have brought up at the beginning." I paused to let that register. "It's possible that somehow, somewhere, you ate food that had been doctored with a very powerful aphrodisiac. We're not sure, but it may have been a mild form of whatever it was that killed Professor Ossmann and Dr. Woodley."

Ms. Spronger grew pensive. "Actually . . ."

"We doubt very much anything like that happened," Mr. Dearth said forcefully.

"Because that would exculpate the university." I turned to Ms. Spronger. "You were about to say something?"

She glanced this time at her counsel. "Nothing. Really."

"Are you sure?" I persisted. "This is very important. Other lives may be at stake."

But Mr. Dearth had them back under his control. He kept advising them not to say anything. He said, "Mr. de Ratour has no standing legal authority in this case."

I regarded Ms. Spronger and then Mr. Jones. I said, "If either of you changes your mind about anything, please give me a call. Anything you tell me will be kept private."

When we all, except Mr. Jones, rose to go, I asked to speak to

Mr. Dearth in private. The principals left to wait in the hall, and I closed the door. I did not sit down. I leaned across the table on my fisted hands. I looked Mr. Dearth straight in the face. I told him I could scarcely believe what he was doing.

"I am defending my clients' rights to a safe working environment," he responded.

"You mean to tell me that the university is responsible for the private consensual actions of these two adults?"

"We are contending that in the particular case of Sigmund Library, the university wittingly or unwittingly allowed an environment of sexual exploitation to exist of which these two young people are the very evident victims."

"What exactly, could you tell me, Mr. Dearth, should the university have done differently?"

"That is up to the deans in the administration to decide. But the very existence of a large securable closet and the ends to which everyone knows it was used indicates substantial grounds for complaint. The principle of undue temptation applies here."

"Undue temptation?"

"A concept I developed. It recognizes the limits of human virtue."

I shook my head in wonder and disgust.

"There's considerable case law in this area," the lawyer continued. "*Morin versus Museum of Man* established a good many of the points now being used in current cases."

I told him what he was doing was unconscionable even by the farcical ethics of the legal profession. I paraphrased for him a quote from Izzy Landes to the effect that an organism's worst parasites are usually indigenous to it. As in the case of Mr. Morin, I accused him of making a travesty of the law. "You, Mr. Dearth, and people like you in the legal profession are consciously and for your own selfish ends deconstructing a great and noble American institution."

"Are you calling me a parasite?" he demanded to know.

"That's exactly what I'm calling you, Mr. Dearth. You and your ilk do not help society in the least. You merely find and feed on its vulnerabilities, all the while perverting the law as you go."

I told him that, as a member of the Subcommittee on Appropriateness, I was writing to the state bar association demanding that he be disciplined in a most decisive way.

It was some small gratification to see Mr. Dearth dumbfounded for once in his garrulous life. Leaving him there I turned and walked from the room, ignoring the two pathetic individuals he had suborned into a suit against the university.

I'm afraid I spent valuable time and a deal of spirit making good on my threats. Not only did I send a detailed and indignant letter to the members of the subcommittee with copies to President Twill and the Wainscott Board of Regents, but I filed a complaint with the state bar association. Not that I have much faith in that latter organization, despite its impressive-looking code of ethics. The lawyers handling the estate of my late aunt, Harriet Heathering, all but looted its substance, leaving the sole heir, a nephew, with a pittance. When he took the matter to the state bar, they sat on it for a year and finally did nothing. As Izzy says, we live increasingly under a rule of lawyers, not law.

And such is life and death that none of this really means a damn to me; it is nothing more than a tempest in a tosspot next to the daily unraveling of my beloved Elsbeth. She is now insisting that we spend Thanksgiving out at the cottage, but the poor dear is scarcely able to get out of bed.

23

I received this morning a most extraordinary document. It indicates — the good news — that Korky Kummerbund may still be alive. It also indicates — the bad news — that he is under considerable distress and possibly in great danger. I'll let the document, which is carefully handwritten and which came via ordinary mail in a standard number 10 envelope, speak for itself.

Dear Norman:

The following article must appear in the Bugle as soon as possible under my byline if I am to have any chance of being seen alive again. It must be word-for-word or I will be starved to death. As it is, until the meal described below, I had not had anything to eat for more than a week. I am allowed to tell you that I am under extreme duress from lack of food and noise on a loop, but that is all.

Your trusting friend,
Korky

A Unique Repast
by Korky Kummerbund

It is not difficult to describe the decor at this new eatery, which opened recently to a very select clientele. It is strictly no-frills, a setting informed by a radical minimalism that announces an anti-aesthetic so total it defines a whole new aesthetic.

Suffice it to say, the surroundings achieved a congruity with the food and service to a remarkable degree. The walls are . . . well, walls, unfinished gray chalkboard. The floor, of concrete, is covered with a thin carpet of gray-beige, and the ceiling matches the walls. The toilet facilities, over in the corner, are rudimentary but adequate. The food is served through a hinged pet flap in the bottom of a sturdy door of solid wood.

To start this memorable dining experience, I had what the simple but elegant, hand-printed menu called *bouillon aux bons morceaux de papier journal*. It was in fact a transparently thin bouillon with florets of newsprint cut from one of my food columns in the *Bugle*. I was unable to discern which particular column. The bouillon came in a tin bowl with a ring attached to the rim for hanging. Along with the white plastic soup spoon, which had a slightly flaring handle, the bowl made for a fittingly Spartan vessel for the dish, especially when arrayed against the scarred Formica top of the table and the simple and effective lighting, a naked 75-watt bulb hanging from a standard ceiling fixture, dirty white against dirty white.

Appetite truly being the best relish, it takes an effort to describe how delicious the bouillon and the bouillon-soaked newsprint tasted. The first sip of the nearly clear liquid is like a revelation, an epiphany of the senses, as the tongue and the esophagus surrender to its essential minerality, satisfying a primordial craving for salt in a way hard to describe with mere words. (It brought to mind the remark by A.J. Denny that food gives the tongue a voice beyond language.) The florets of news-print, cut into simple, almost child-like patterns, added body to the fluid and, when properly chewed, proved not all that difficult to swallow.

It was, in any event, the perfect prelude to the fish, or should I say amphibian, course. The menu lists *les petites tranches de crapaud grillées avec des allumettes*. The toad came under the door on a small, stark cutting board complete with a box of wooden matches, plas-tic fork, and X-Acto knife. To my great delight, it was accompanied by a pint of Thunderbird, a sweetish little wine with no pretensions to complexity whatsoever.

If anything, the bouillon and newsprint had whetted my appetite, and I tore into this delicacy with a gusto I usually reserve for more prepossessing dishes. The truth: I found every morsel of the thing delectable, especially after I had gotten the hang of cutting off an appropri-ately sized piece and skewering it on the tip of the X-Acto knife where, with one or two matches, I could crisp it nicely. The sulfur from the matches added its own distinct resonance to a taste hard to limn with mere words. The essence was that of a paludal origin, not quite fetid, but definitely smacking of the swamp. The bones were sufficiently pliable not to be crunchable unless properly singed, but alas, I ran out of matches before quite finish-ing. Actually, raw toad isn't that bad, either.

Again, after the perfect interval, I was served the main course, which, according to the simple but beautifully wrought bill of fare, consisted of *Tartare d'écureuil écrasé dans la rue sur un lit de glands gratinés*.

But I do not complain. Again simplicity added an undeniable elegance to the presentation. The rodent had been skinned and flensed. The meat and, from what I could gather, the rest of the soft parts had been ground medium-coarse then served in the cavity of the pelt, artfully splayed on its back, legs outspread and tail in full fluff curling upward and over toward the turned little head.

It was delicious. I never thought acorns could be so tasty. They added the exact right textural counterpart to the chewy meat and the shredded newsprint, the flavors combining with a gustatorial synergy little short of wondrous. I was ingesting nothing less than the essence of oak, at first hand in the muted yet subtle woodiness of the acorns, and then, at one remove, in the nutty echoes alive in the flesh of the little creature that feeds on these underappreciated delicacies.

The service was truly excellent, the dishes being slid on the floor through the door flap after just the right interval between courses, as you would expect in any well-run establishment.

As well as food, I was served food for thought. It is seldom in life that a meal serves both the body and the spirit, if only with a lesson in the true meaning of hunger and humility.

It was only after I had read this document through twice that I realized it constituted evidence of a kidnapping case and of a sick, deranged mind. Holding it by the edges, I forthwith placed letter and envelope in a plastic bag and phoned Lieutenant Tracy.

He arrived at my office less than half an hour later. Donning white gloves, he examined the letter in detail. He shook his head in disbelief. "What is this? Fresh roadkill squirrel? What kind of sicko . . . ? Is this serious or some kind of joke?"

I nodded. "Both, I'm afraid."

He shook his head again. "Where do you find fresh toad this time of year?"

"Maybe it wasn't fresh."

Lieutenant Tracy started to laugh, something I had never seen him do before. It was an attractive, revealing laugh that had him shaking his head and wiping tears from his eyes. Then, like a squall, it stopped as abruptly as it started. He wiped his eyes and apologized. I said I understood.

I told him it was, as far as I could determine, Korky's hand-writing. Over the past two years he had sent numerous notes and cards to Elsbeth and me. I said I could easily provide a sample, but I thought the editor of the *Bugle* should be informed imme-diately as to what had transpired.

Donald Patcher, the editor of the *Bugle,* responded with a sense of concern for Korky's welfare when we contacted him. There was no bluster about the inviolability of the press and that sort of thing. He said he would run it the next morning just as though it were Korky's regular column.

In part because it can't be avoided — I'm sure she would read the column in tomorrow's *Bugle* or one of her friends is sure to mention it to her — I called Elsbeth and let her know what had happened without going into details. She took it well, saying it would be good to read his column again whatever it said. I've told her about Corny's death as well, again without going into details. Truth in these matters is always the best policy.

Robert Remick has called again. He was his gentlemanly self, but news of the Bert-and-Betti fiasco had reached him, as I knew it would. I sensed a note of exasperation in his tone as he told me that he and the rest of the board had full confidence in my ability "to clean up this latest mess" at the museum.

I had his call very much in mind when I summoned Alger

Wherry up for a meeting. Closing the door and having Doreen poised with her pen and steno pad did not have much effect on the man. He refused to answer any questions I had about the use of the empty room in the Skull Collections. "Good," I said, "you're fired. Effective immediately. Please collect your personal effects and remove them."

He turned surly. "There are procedures . . ."

"We are no longer part of the university in that way, Alger. Appeal all you want to Human Resources, it won't do you any good. In fact I'm looking for a good excuse to get rid of Maria Cowe and her inefficient staff."

"The Long Piggers have been using the room."

"You mean they never stopped using the room."

"Right."

"Who are the members?"

"I honestly don't know."

"You don't really expect me to believe that."

"I don't know most of the new members. Everyone has a code name. I don't know who they are. I don't really care."

"Who does have the names?"

"Brauer. And Corny did."

I believed him if only because I could tell from his air of defeat, which was more pronounced than usual, that he didn't care enough to lie. He left, agreeing to clean out the room and start using it for storing skulls.

Word of Corny's demise has spread far and wide. I have arranged for the Chards' family attorney and an officer of the Middling County Probate Court to witness the tape. I can only hope they don't start telling others about it afterward.

24

It's evening and we are back from a couple of days out at the cottage. Elsbeth, weak and frail as she is, asked several times to spend Thanksgiving at the lake. I remonstrated with her, saying what if something happened? What if there was an emergency?

She smiled and took my hand. "Norman, dear, it's already happened. I'm beyond emergencies."

"But . . ."

"What's the worst that could happen? That I die out there. I'd love to die out there." She laughed her wonderful laugh, even if it were only a slight echo of itself. "You could build a bonfire on the lakeshore and cremate me right there like they did Byron. And then have an orgy."

It turned out to be, despite everything, a wonderful time, of the kind that haunts you afterward. We all knew, of course, that this would be the last time Elsbeth would make the journey, taking the same roads, the same turns, winding our way through the needle-carpeted evergreen forest until we come to the fork in the road that I always used to miss. I think we fear death because we think we will miss all the things we do again and again in life.

It hasn't changed much over the years. We've cleared back the hemlock saplings encroaching on the drive that leads to the cottage. We've had the rotting sills replaced, a new well dug, and some new wiring installed. But otherwise it's not a lot different than it used to be all those years ago. We packed an extra space heater, because Elsbeth does suffer from the cold.

Upon arrival, I plugged in an electric blanket for Elsbeth on the wicker sofa in front of the fireplace. I lit the fire while Diantha started the turkey breast in the oven. She said it looked like something that had been given thalidomide, what with the stumps where the legs had been. But we had all the fixings — stuffing, cranberry sauce, creamed onions, gravy and mashed potatoes, three kinds of squash, a decent white wine, and pumpkin pie. We toasted our lives and we said a prayer of thanks and asked that Korky be returned safe and sound to us.

While there was still light, Diantha and I took a walk along the lakeshore to the pines on the point that reaches like a widow's peak into the mirroring water. Why, I wondered, is there consolation in the beauty of dying nature? All around, the light of the setting sun touched to gold the browns and yellows of the trees, shrubs, and withered grass. I could hear the blue jays of my youth and the chiding of chickadees. I wanted to weep out of sheer poignancy.

Perhaps sensing my mood, Diantha looped her arm in mine, as though to remind me that life goes on. Her gesture both deepened and sweetened my melancholia, because it was exactly the way, over the past couple of years, Elsbeth and I had walked these paths — in a communing bliss so complete we were as one with each other and with everything we could see and hear.

Later, as it darkened and the wind came up, we made Elsbeth comfortable on a bed we had moved into a small room downstairs. Then we sat together on the same wicker sofa Elsbeth and I had courted on when we were young. The sensation for me was not so much of *déjà vu* as of temporal collapse, as though time had contracted and vanished, as though back then and right now were one and the same.

"Do you miss Sixy?" I asked as Diantha sipped an iced Pernod and I toyed with a dry sherry.

She laughed and shook her head, pleased, I think, that I was that interested in her personal life. "Naw. I was outgrowing him, anyway. I can't believe I ever took that stuff he calls music seriously, never mind listened to it."

I nodded. "And there are lots of other young men in the world."

"I'm not sure I want another young man."

"Really?"

"Really. It's like breaking in a new puppy." She turned to me, pulling closer, her face animated in the firelight. "They're very cute and they wag their tails at you and bark and yip and lick your face and other places . . ." She giggled at her boldness. "But they leave messes all over the place. I think I'm one of those girls that likes older men."

"Lots of those around, too," I said, sighing. "Lots of other loose people around these days. I often wonder what they do for Thanksgiving."

She pulled closer, her hip touching mine. She took my hand. "Let's promise, right now, Norman, no matter what happens, that we'll always have Thanksgiving together."

"Done," I said, deeply touched.

"You know. I keep thinking about that video clip. You know, of the three people."

"Yes, it's strangely moving."

She gave a giggle. "You mean it makes you horny."

"Well . . . yes."

She tittered. "I love your reticence, Norman. It's so sexy."

"Oh, dear," I said, which made her laugh and give me an affectionate kiss on the side of the lips.

Perhaps to break the spell, to keep my heart and my lips from wandering, I brought up the Ossmann-Woodley case directly. "What I don't understand," I said as we both stared into the flames, "is why anyone would go to the trouble of trying to get their hands on a powerful aphrodisiac."

"What do you mean?"

"Well, for starters it's not possible for someone, even if they got the dosage right, to simply sell it to some company and make lots of money."

"Okay."

"The whole research file has to be available, and those files are usually several feet thick."

"Okay."

"It's all very cumbersome, involved, and expensive."

"But it wouldn't have to be legal to make money as a drug."

"What do you mean?" Lights were starting to go on in my dim brain.

"Good God, Norman, there's like a huge, multibazillion-dollar illegal drug business out there."

"Even for a drug, if there is one, that induced Ossmann and Woodley to kill each other with sex?"

"That's why people do Ecstasy."

"Ecstasy?"

"It's a drug that makes you feel good about everything. It opens you up, especially if you do it with something else. I still have a little stash . . ."

"Oh, right," I said, remembering the autopsies. I wondered for a bewildering moment of she were proposing we try it. "Is that what you and Sixy . . . ?"

"Yeah, sometimes." Then she put her put her hand to her mouth and gave an embarrassed laugh. "God, the things we used to do."

"Really?"

"Yeah. One afternoon me and Shelly, she was going with Danko, the drummer, we popped some meth and did a little blow and the guys swallowed some Viagra and I don't know what else . . . Anyway, we ended up doing the whole band."

"Had sex with them?"

"You don't think the less of me for that?"

I sighed. "The things I've missed."

The ensuing heavy silence I broke by saying, "So, Di, you think there would be a market?"

"Are you kidding? I mean once they get it right, if that's what they're trying to do. Think of all those Chinese who can't get it up unless they're eating parts of endangered animals. You whip up a concoction, call it Tiger Balls or something like that. I mean the Asian market alone is incredible. They all seem to suffer from limp dicks."

The light went on very brightly. I sat forward. "You're a dear," I said. I leaned over to give her a little kiss. "You're a very smart dear. And now I must go to bed before I have another one of these and make a fool of myself."

Diantha stood up with me and gave me a real kiss. "I'll never think of you as a fool, Norman."

But of course I am a fool, an utter, low fool. The very next morning I watched her as she left the upstairs bathroom with a small towel draped so haphazardly over herself that I could not but help seeing her naked form in its every robust detail. My breathing all but stopped. I suppose she doesn't realize what this does to me. I am not one of those casual males where displays of this kind are concerned. As someone once said, the beauty of women makes good men suffer. Not that I count myself good. Because I find myself utterly infatuated. Can one love two women at once? Can one love a mother and daughter simultaneously, love them like a man loves a woman?

We came back on Saturday to find that Amanda Feeney-Morin had done a long "think" piece in the *Bugle*, dredging up the

Bert-Betti and Ossmann-Woodley cases, linking them together, of course, rehashing the details with insinuating, subtle invective, and speculating about the management of the Museum of Man, "which has resisted efforts by the university to provide modern institutional leadership." She then quoted President Twill of Wainscott to the effect that he has "ongoing concerns with the policy directions underway at present in the Museum of MOM [*sic*]." The man doesn't even know what we're called.

I have written to Don Patcher asking him to assign a more unbiased reporter to cover the university and the museum. I pointed out to him that Ms. Feeney is married to Mr. Morin and is doing nothing more than serving as a mouthpiece for Wainscott in its continuing attempt to take us over. As it stands, I wrote, you might as well put Malachy Morin's byline next to hers. I don't know whether that will do any good or not, but it is right and proper to respond to these matters.

25

Well, Lieutenant Tracy and I have taken the bulls by the horns, so to speak, and confronted Dr. Penrood and Celeste Tangent about their relations with Professor Ossmann.

In turns out that Ms. Tangent's possible involvement takes on added significance in the light of certain aspects of her background. Indeed, the lieutenant's briefing on the matter provoked in me a heuristic arousal bordering on the unseemly. According to his sources in New York, both of the establishments mentioned prominently in her CV — the Caucasian Escort Service and the Crazy Russian — were controlled or owned through dummy corporations by one Moshe ben Rovich, a leading figure in the Russian-Jewish mob in Brooklyn with connections to Tel Aviv and Moscow. A leading figure, that is, until he crossed Victor "Dead Meat" Karnivorsky and disappeared a couple of years ago.

The lieutenant and I discussed strategy at some length. We decided to try to "break" Penrood first, using tactics somewhat less than gentlemanly. To that end, I put in a call to Dr. Penrood first thing yesterday morning, saying that I needed to see him in the Twitchell Room on a matter of some urgency. He said he could spare some time around eleven. I said that would be fine.

Penrood's evident if subtle English annoyance turned to a decided wariness upon his arrival at the Twitchell Room, where I introduced him to Lieutenant Tracy. I said the meeting was part of our investigation of the Ossmann-Woodley case. We needed him to look at some video footage. The play's the thing and all that.

So after I had closed and locked the door and turned down the shades, we watched for several minutes in silence Professor Ossmann and two other persons in sexual congress. There was enough light for me to notice that Dr. Penrood's complexion went from considerable color to a decided pallor and back again.

When the tape ended, I turned the lights back on. Lieutenant Tracy pulled his chair closer to Dr. Penrood's and leaned into him. "This footage is dated September eighth. The man facing the camera is quite obviously Professor Ossmann. And we have reason to believe, Dr. Penrood, that the woman involved in this arrangement is Celeste Tangent — and the man with his back to the camera is you."

I took my seat to one side and watched Dr. Penrood wrestle with what to say. Finally he shook his head. "I don't want to say anything without a lawyer present."

Lieutenant Tracy leaned back, nodding as though in sympathetic agreement. "It's that bad?"

"No, it's not that bad."

"Of course, Dr. Penrood, you have the right to remain silent and the right to consult an attorney . . ."

Marvelous, I thought, the way the detective was using the Miranda warning as a kind of insinuation.

He leaned even closer. "If you do decide to get an attorney before helping us, as my colleagues in your country would put it, it could get very messy. You won't have to tell us much, true. But you see, Dr. Penrood, Ms. Tangent has documented connections with organized crime in New York. That will help us considerably when we go before a judge, show him this footage, and ask for all different kinds of surveillance as part of our investigation into the Ossmann-Woodley murders."

"Murders . . . ?"

"That's what we've announced."

"Of course, of course," Dr. Penrood said, his nervousness obvious now.

When Dr. Penrood had lapsed into silence for a good while, the lieutenant quietly leaned forward again, his voice low and nearly cold. "I can also assure you, Dr. Penrood, that if you help us we will make sure that no one else gets to see this footage. Because, as Mr. de Ratour can tell you, the Seaboard Police Department can turn into a regular sieve when it comes to leaks. Despite our best efforts."

Dr. Penrood stiffened. "Are you threatening me, Lieutenant?"

"No. I'm only trying to reassure you. I want to know what happened the night you and Ms. Tangent and Professor Ossmann had sex together."

Dr. Penwood wavered awhile longer. It was obvious, I think, that he was trying to figure out what to tell us and what not to tell us. Finally he sighed. "First, I want it established that my relations with Ms. Tangent are strictly my own business and I am only telling you what I know to help clear things up."

"Of course."

"On the night in question, Dr. Ossmann and Ms. Tangent dropped by my office for an after-work drink."

"Had you been intimate with Ms. Tangent before this incident?"

Dr. Penrood hesitated. "Yes."

"When did your relations with her start?"

"About six months ago."

"After she came on board?"

He hesitated. "Before that."

"Did you hire her?"

"I . . . As a matter of fact . . . I mean I was only one of several to interview her."

"Had she been intimate with Professor Ossmann before the incident with the three of you?"

"I don't think so. But . . . she has a life of her own."

"As do you."

"Yes."

"Tell me, Dr. Penrood, what did everyone have to drink on the evening in question?"

"Sherry. That's all I keep in the office."

"Who poured it?"

I think I detected a look of cunning come into the researcher's eyes. "Actually, it was Professor Ossmann. He was well acquainted with the cabinet where I kept the sherry and glasses."

"You knew Professor Ossmann well then."

"Not in any real social sense. He was always in here, usually complaining. The drink placated him."

Lieutenant Tracy looked up from the notebook he had been writing in. "How much sherry did you have?"

"A couple of glasses each."

"And Professor Ossmann poured all of them?"

"Yes."

"Over at the cabinet?"

"Yes."

"And in each case he could have slipped something in the glasses had he wanted to?"

"Yes."

"Tell me exactly what happened after you each had several glasses."

Dr. Penrood colored a little and cleared his throat. "It's hard to remember exactly. Celeste . . . Ms. Tangent . . . was sitting

between me and Professor Ossmann on the couch. We all just
. . . started getting amorous."

"Are you bisexual, Dr. Penrood?"

"No. It wasn't that way. I and, I think, Professor Ossmann
were only interested in Ms. Tangent."

"What happened then?"

"I said something to the effect that if we were going to get
carried away, I knew a better place in the building."

"The staff smoking room?" I asked.

He nodded.

"So you went there?"

"Yes. It's just down the hall from my office."

The lieutenant took the edge off his voice. "Did you ever feel
at any point that you were under the influence of some . . . drug
. . . or potion?"

Dr. Penrood did a very good job right then of feigning what
might be called the ignorance of innocence. He shook his head,
appeared to think back, made a grimace. "I can't really tell. It
did happen quite . . . suddenly. At the time I just thought it was
. . . Celeste."

"Do you know if Professor Ossmann was working on any
kind of aphrodisiac? I mean, on the side."

Again he hesitated, but only for a moment. "He could have
been, but I doubt it."

"How's that?"

"Professor Ossmann was a serious scientist. He tracked assiduously every last tittle he contributed to any project. I doubt very
much he would have been involved in something he couldn't put
his name on."

"But it's not inconceivable?"

"No . . ."

The lieutenant looked up, glanced at me, and said, "I think

that's enough for now, Dr. Penrood. I'm going to have this typed up, and I would like you to sign it."

"But . . ."

"It won't be under oath. If, later, you want to add or subtract something, we'll understand completely. People often leave out things, details."

"Is it really necessary?"

"No, not really. But it will look a lot better for you if . . ."

By the time Dr. Penrood left he had lost that air of superiority that mantles so many British of a certain class.

I tackled, and that is the operative verb, Celeste Tangent next. Lieutenant Tracy suggested that I speak to her alone. He was of the opinion, and I agreed with him, that, given her background, Ms. Tangent might open up more with me, say things she might not say in the presence of the police.

So this afternoon, when Doreen ushered Ms. Tangent — "Oh, please, Celeste" — into my office, the dear girl showed all the awed deference she might have held for a movie star. I was a little awed myself, frankly, with the way Ms. Tangent's rich blond hair swept up from a regal neck, the sudden, brilliant smile lighting from behind the cornflower eyes, the formfitting slacks and how she sat herself just so into the chair I held for her in front of my desk.

She was instantly alive with throwaway chatter in an accent I couldn't quite place, Oklahoma, perhaps, with an overlay of Brooklyn. "Oh, but I do love this part of the museum. I mean parts of it are creepy, you know, but really fascinating."

I nodded, half hypnotized not so much by the way her turtle-neck of fine wool molded her ample bosom, but by her eyes and voice and how they played off each other, the effect like some exquisite sonata. A lab assistant, indeed.

I cleared my throat. "Ms. Tangent . . ."

"Oh, please, Celeste."

"I'm afraid I'm going to have to call you Ms. Tangent."

She smiled. "Actually, coming from you, it sounds really nice. But then call me Miss Tangent. Ms. always sounds like someone who wears heavy shoes."

I cleared my throat again. "Miss Tangent, as you probably know by now, we have a somewhat compromising tape of a person we know to be you with Dr. Penrood and the late Professor Ossmann involved in . . ."

She gave a tut of mock self-reproval that, as she leaned toward me, turned into a kind of confiding embarrassment. "Oh, our little threesome. It was all my fault. I know you think Pen — Dr. Penrood, isn't that a silly name — told me to tell you that. But it's true. Sometimes, Mr. . . ."

"De Ratour."

"Mr. de Ratour, now, that's a name. Anyway, there are times when I feel lonely with just one guy. But not with every man, Mr. de Ratour. There are men who are up to it. I can sense it in them. Even some older guys . . ."

"Miss Tangent . . ."

She smiled, gave a laugh. "So they have it on tape. Oh, my God, I hope my mother never gets to see it. She's born-again. She has Jesus for breakfast. Can I get a copy? I could have been a porn star . . ."

"But instead you became a lab assistant."

"Yes. Isn't life amazing?"

"Why?"

"Why is life amazing?"

"Why did you become a lab assistant?"

"It's where the action is, isn't it? I mean the men doing this work are the modern giants, aren't they? At least I thought so. There's a lot of teeny-weenies out there."

"What are your connections with organized crime, Miss Tangent?"

She did miss half a beat on that one. She shook her head.

"You can talk to me, Miss Tangent, or we can involve the Seaboard Police Department directly. I'm sure you know the drill, the interrogation, the fingerprinting, the surveillance . . ."

A different Celeste looked at me, as though with a loathing that had been there all the time. "What do you want to know?"

"What was Professor Ossmann working on that would interest Moshe ben Rovich?"

"Moe? Big Moe? Moe Rovich? You gotta be kidding. Nobody's seen Moe in years. They say he sleeps with the gefilte fish."

She was a good actress, but I didn't find her convincing. I had to conceal the sudden excitement of having hit a raw nerve. She overplayed it. She went on, elaborating when she didn't have to.

"Big Moe. Yeah, he used to hang around the Crazy Russian all the time. You'd think he owned the joint."

"He did own the joint, Miss Tangent."

"Really. Nobody ever told me."

"He also owned the Caucasian Escort Service."

"Yeah, that doesn't surprise me. The guy was always using the escorts, sometimes two at a time."

"You have something in common, then, don't you."

As Mr. Shakur would have put it, she blew her cool at that remark. "Listen, Mr. Little Mustache, I don't have to take this shit from you. I know guys who could buy and sell you all day long and stick you in a hole at the end of it."

I nodded. "Perhaps if you would tell me what guys, we could be of help to you, Miss Tangent."

She stood up. "It's the other way around, pal. Take my advice. Pretend you never saw that little tape you probably keep around for jacking off. Pretend we never had this conversation. I'm doing you a favor. You can regard this as a health warning."

And with that she flounced her admirable behind out of the office, leaving the door open for dramatic effect.

Lieutenant Tracy and I met for an hour in the late afternoon going over each interview in detail. We came up with what might be called "degrees of complicity." Miss Tangent had indirectly admitted, with her threats to me, that something very untoward was or had been happening in the Genetics Lab. We surmised that Dr. Penrood was in some manner implicated, but to what extent we could not quite determine.

At one level we found it maddening that we had no real evidence pertaining to a solution of the Ossmann-Woodley murders, if that's what they are. At the same time, we knew for sure that a conspiracy of sorts existed in the Genetics Lab, and we knew at least two of the principals involved in it. I mentioned Diantha's observation about the potential illegal market for a powerful aphrodisiac. "Exactly," the lieutenant said. "That's exactly what I think is happening."

On another matter, he informed me that the SPD had received a lot of pressure to tell everything it knows about the disappearance of Korky Kummerbund and the reappearance of his column in a way that amounts to a kind of sick parody. Both the SPD and Don Patcher of the *Bugle* have kept mute on the subject, leading to wider and wider speculation. I hate to say it, but I'm grateful to both of them that they have kept my name and the museum's out of it.

But Celeste Tangent. I must confess that I keep thinking about her. I don't believe I've ever met a woman more palpably sexual. It wasn't just her looks, but a sense that she is, in her hour-to-hour life, a hair trigger away from amorous initiation or response. I have now watched that video clip with her and the two researchers several times, telling myself, of course, that I was looking for some detail that might help with the case.

Just last night, when I knew Elsbeth was asleep and thought Diantha had gone to a movie, I was about halfway through it when the latter came into my old study where we have the enormous television. I hit the STOP button, and the unmistakable image stayed on the screen.

She took a long look and laughed, "Oh, wow, a real *ménage à twat*. So you're into amateurs, huh? I do think it's better than the professional stuff, you know, where the bimbos fake like they're really into it."

"Actually, it's evidence," I said, regaining my composure. "The man being fellated is Professor Ossmann."

"The one who got murdered?"

"Yes." I hit the PLAY button.

"Too cool. So you're not just getting your jollies."

Or was I? I sat there, my heart in a wringer, reminding myself that Diantha was my daughter, my stepdaughter, it's true, but still my daughter, as she sat next to me on the couch and as lust, in all its confusing eddies, swirled around in me.

26

I have had some good news that's shocking in its own way. Lieutenant Tracy phoned this morning to tell me that Korky Kummerbund, in a state of near starvation and in considerable disorientation, was found staggering along a back road in Worthington State Park, some twenty-five miles north of Seaboard. I called Elsbeth immediately and gave her the good news, although lately she has been in such a weakened state, I'm not sure she understood the import of what I told her.

And what a different human being I found when I walked into Seaboard General, where they took Korky for tests and recovery. He recognized me, lifted his hand to shake mine, and said, "How's Elsbeth?" His concern touched me nearly to tears, and I sat by his bed, reassuring the nurse that I would not stay long.

"You're safe now, Korky," I told him. "The worst is over."

He nodded. "The worst thing was . . . the music."

"Music? I thought you said it was noise on a loop?"

He nodded, and a look of horror crossed his wasted face. "They played it twenty-four hours a day, over and over."

"What was it?"

He wavered a moment, as though reaching inwardly for courage. "Stockhausen," he managed. Then, "Cage." Then, "And the dodecaphonic works of Schoenberg. Over and over."

"You poor man," I said. "From the unspeakable to the unfortunate."

I was still trying to comfort him when Lieutenant Tracy

showed up with Sergeant Lemure in tow. The sergeant scowled at me, but the lieutenant asked me to stay.

He conducted his interrogation with an incisiveness and gentleness I found to be the epitome of investigative professionalism. In a halting voice, Korky told us that he indeed had gone to the White Trash Grill to meet a friend. When asked what friend, he replied, "Any friend."

"You mean a pickup?" the sergeant put in rather bluntly.

Korky nodded.

"Did you meet anyone?" the lieutenant asked.

Korky nodded again.

"Can you describe him?"

"Yes. But I think he was in disguise."

"What do you mean?"

"He wore dark glasses and a fake mustache."

"Yeah but how big was he? What was he wearing?" The sergeant bulked over the bed.

Lieutenant Tracy waved him back. He asked, "Was it anyone you remember seeing before?"

"I don't think so."

"Then what happened?"

Korky shook his head. His voice was growing weak, as though powered by a fading battery. "I got into his car . . ."

"Do you remember the make?"

"No. Some kind of SUV . . . blue or gray . . ."

"So you got into the car."

"Yes. Then someone in the backseat put a handkerchief over my mouth and held it there. I think it had chloroform on it."

He told the detectives that the room he was kept in was as he had described it in his article. The only distinctive detail he could recall was that during the very infrequent times he was fed, the person who brought him his food was accompanied by one or two large dogs, because he thought he could hear, over the piped-in noise, the clack of their paws on the concrete floor of what he assumed to be a cellar.

When Sergeant Lemure started to follow up, I intervened, saying I thought Korky needed his rest. The sergeant looked like he wanted to punch me, but Lieutenant Tracy agreed. They would be able to be more thorough later on.

Out in the corridor, we held a brief conference. I repeated to the lieutenant that it might be useful to have someone in the SPD go over Korky's more recent reviews to find out whom he might have offended. At least to the point they would want to wreak this kind of revenge. I didn't want to make obvious the fact that the Seaboard Police should have already followed up.

The sergeant said he didn't have that kind of time and, besides, "It's probably just some kind of fag thing. I mean, they're weird people."

Lieutenant Tracy nodded to his man. "Yeah, and you've got to fly to New York and run down what you can about Celeste Tangent's mob connections."

Still, the sergeant wasn't very happy when I volunteered to call Don Patcher at the *Bugle* to have him pull copies of Korky's reviews and send them over to me. I soothed his ruffled feathers somewhat by saying that Korky was a very close friend of my wife, and that I would be doing it as a favor to her. We did agree that we were dealing with someone possessed of a distinctly malicious sense of humor, that we had entered that realm where evil and the darkly comedic batten on each other.

Speaking of which, I had another call this afternoon from Mr. Castor of Urgent Productions. He sounded a very conciliatory note, saying that he understood completely my position in regard to the museum as a backdrop to the film they were making. But not only would they treat any setting with the utmost respect, they would also clear any perspective with me personally. He assured me as well that the film would be sensitive in every possible way.

I demurred again. But in a like conciliatory spirit, I held out some hope to him, telling him I would shortly be taking the matter up with Professor Brauer.

27

Bobette Spronger called me yesterday around noon to confess something I had suspected all along. In that contemporary, and to my ears graceless, accent, she went on at some length. "I know I like should have told you sooner, Mr. Ratour, but I did use the soy sauce I found in one of those little plastic tubs someone left in the fridge."

"Why," I asked, "didn't you tell me this before?"

"Because like it was against like my diet and I didn't want anyone to know I was cheating. And Mosy like likes it with soy sauce."

"Is there any of it left in the refrigerator?"

"I don't think so."

I rang off and called Lieutenant Tracy. He came over immediately, and together we drove to the library. We met in the nondescript little room where we had talked before, and Ms. Spronger and Mr. Jones gave him a full statement. We were in the process of checking the refrigerator with the help of Mr. Jones, who wheeled around the place with admirable mobility, when the Director of the library, a Mr. Dewey Jackson, arrived on the scene.

Our encounter with him represents an example, I can see in looking back, of the difference between real and fictionalized detective work. In that ethereal realm of Inspector Dalgliesh, for instance, the police show up at a library and are treated with respect, even deference. In reality, Mr. Jackson, thinnish, balding, bristly beard, and stringy ponytail, a child of the sixties, demanded to know exactly what we thought we were doing in his library.

Lieutenant Tracy showed his badge and suggested we retire to Mr. Jackson's office, a request that had to be given considerable thought. Mr. Jackson made it clear he considered the police at best a necessary evil. We finally returned to the stark little room and sat around the table.

Mr. Jackson demanded to know if we had a search warrant.

The lieutenant patiently explained that we were merely trying to ascertain the origin of any soy sauce brought into the building over the past several months.

"Then you are searching for something."

"Mr. Jackson . . ."

"Dr. Jackson."

"Dr. Jackson, we are only making preliminary inquiries . . ."

"I don't want you interrogating my staff without counsel present."

"We are only asking some basic questions."

"I think I should talk to the dean about this."

There he was, I thought, *Homo academicus* at his worst — petty, picky, and, despite all the bluster, timid. And what galled me to the quick was the realization that, not so long ago, I would have acted exactly the same way.

Lieutenant Tracy sighed. Then, with an edge in his voice like cold steel, he said, "Dr. Jackson, we can go at this two ways. We, in your presence, can question the staff in a very casual way. Or you can call the dean and the lawyers. I then go and obtain search warrants. I bring in a squad of investigators. We turn the place upside down. We maybe take you in for questioning. The public has a right to know, so we have to issue statements. The media circus starts. People talk. Rumors spread."

Dr. Jackson got the point.

For all that we came up with precious little. A staff party in June had been catered by the Jade Stalk Restaurant. There had been leftovers, including little tubs of soy sauce, which, as everyone knows, have a shelf life comparable to that of salt.

In the end we agreed it was no breakthrough, but another important confirmation of what we already suspected. And there seemed little that we could do in a practical way. Issue a public health warning or a recall of all local soy sauce? That, surely, would only create a panic. Our "lead" had dwindled to a long shot, which the lieutenant said he would follow up.

On the way back to my office, he told me that Celeste Tangent had been seen several times entering the gift shop associated with the Green Sherpa during the past week or so. It probably meant nothing, he said. But he suggested that I drop by there some time inconspicuously and get a sense of the place. He had heard the FBI had been interested in its owner, one Freddie Bain, for some time. But then, the feds never tell the locals anything.

I agreed to, but with more a sense of foreboding than alacrity, a sense I couldn't really explain to myself.

28

It swear that the Christmas glitter gets gaudier by the year. It really ought to be called "the Shopping Season." I was acutely aware of the prevailing incandescent banality when, with Diantha accompanying me as a kind of cover, I visited the Nepalese Realm late this afternoon to do a little sleuthing as requested by Lieutenant Tracy. I didn't tell her very much as to what I was about, but said I was curious about the gift shop that forms part of the Green Sherpa restaurant. We had, in fact, some shopping to do. But what can you give, alas, to someone you love who is dying?

According to its squib in the Yellow Pages, the shop trades in "imported spices" and "the art and artifacts of Nepal." Both the restaurant and the shop, sharing a single awning, are located in Clipper Wharf, a renovated part of the old harbor, which, truth be told, had a good deal more charm when it was the haunt of fishermen with their boats, tackle, and smells. Now redbrick and boutiques with signs painted in old lettering on weathered board are starting to predominate.

"It's all so terminally cute," Diantha observed after we had parked and were strolling along. Her tone and words gave me a turn. It was exactly the kind of thing Elsbeth would have said.

I agreed, but pointed out that large trawlers, small freighters, and oceangoing barges still docked nearby.

We wandered into the shop like shoppers, glancing over the collection of what seemed to me an ordinary mishmash of orientalia — lacquered bowls, painted screens, batik prints, and a large selection of decidedly aromatic spices. The wrong note, if there was one, lay in the fact that, despite the season, we were the only customers in the store save for an older woman who looked like a street person.

We hadn't been there long when the proprietor came out of the back room and approached us. I noticed again how his closely barbered hair gave him an old-fashioned Germanic look. I also noticed, above the not unpleasant reek of spices, the distinctive musk of his cologne. *He* had been in the room with the green baize door. I was sure now he belonged to the *Société*.

This time I remarked the way his tawny eyes shifted about with the animation of a predator, even as he said, "Mr. de Ratour, how gratifying that you should visit us." Perhaps I am prejudiced, because he took an immediate interest in Diantha, turning on her a practiced charm.

"Are you gift shopping?" he asked, his voice deep, his accent again striking me as familiar and foreign.

Diantha flashed him a high-wattage smile, meeting his frank sexual appraisal with one of her own. "Yes, it's such a chore when it should be . . ."

He left her hanging.

"Joyous," I supplied.

"Yes, joyous."

"Mr. Bain, this is my daughter, Diantha Lowe."

She extended her hand and he took it the way an old-school European would, keeping it in both of his, as though she had given him a token to hold. He brought his heels together. "*Enchanté*. I'm Freddie, Freddie Bain."

Diantha bowed her head and withdrew her hand. *Enchanté, aussi,* she said and laughed, as though at a private joke.

"Joyous, yes," he echoed. "Then let us make it joyous for you." He produced a pair of small jade figurines, dancers, I would have guessed, but in poses more erotic than thespian. "You have a beau, perhaps. These would remind him of you in those days after Christmas."

Diantha looked at the price tag. "Pricey," she said.

"But these are for you. A mere token. Our mark-ups are . . ."

He had a very mobile face, so that one moment he was all smiles and the next nearly feral, the eyes askance then very direct.

"Thank you, but I simply can't."

"I must insist."

She laughed again and looked at me. I shrugged even as I gritted my teeth. Mr. Bain was not the sort in whose obligation I would want to be.

"I'll put them to one side for you, Miss Lowe . . ."

"Oh, please, call me Diantha. You have quite a spice collection."

"Yes. Thank you. And always fresh. We get in shipments all the time. We use them in the restaurant. You must join me for a cup of tea."

There was no escaping it. He ushered us most proprietarially into the Everest Tea Room, an alcove lined with a large photo mural of the famous peak. He rang a bell; a moment later a slight young woman appeared with a samovar and glasses in old silver holders. Tea Russian-style.

"These are so beautiful," Diantha exclaimed, holding one of the glass cups in her hand. Then, "Whatever made you think of opening a place with a Sherpa theme?"

Mr. Bain's agile face shifted from quizzical frown to a smile that came and went like a tic, then back again, staying in place. "I had occasion to spend time in Nepal. I became interested in the Sherpas. They are a fascinating people. They do what they have to do and never lose a particle of their pride or dignity."

"What took you to Nepal?" I asked, nodding toward the mountain in the photograph, indicating my question as rhetorical, to give him the opportunity to announce his alpinist proclivities and achievements, should he have any. He glanced at me sharply for a moment, perhaps sensing my ploy.

"I was going through my Buddhist phase," he said, directing his answer to Diantha, as though only she were present.

She laughed. "I'm still waiting for mine."

He bowed toward her. "I don't believe you will need it, Ms. Lowe." He poured our tea and offered around the sugar.

"So you came back enlightened and started this restaurant and shop?" She returned his glances in a way that made me feel extraneous.

"You could say that. As an exercise in enlightenment."

"Why the Irish . . ."

"Oh, a sheer whim. My grandmother Katie O'Flaherty was Irish."

It sounded to me like a blatant bit of fabrication, but Diantha nodded, charmed.

"Now you tell us about yourself, Ms. Lowe. Are you new to Seaboard?"

"Yes, but I feel I have been here forever."

"Or perhaps in another life?"

"Maybe. Deep in the gene pool."

"We all have past lives, Ms. Lowe."

They went on in that vein for a while, Diantha telling him really nothing, intriguing him the more as he made no secret of his interest in her.

Then he veered off suddenly, addressing me. "Has there been any more news of Professor Chard's fate?" he asked.

I was able to answer with technical honesty, saying, "None whatsoever. I'm sure that Mrs. Chard, his widow, would have called me had she heard anything from the State Department."

"Then perhaps there is hope."

"There is always hope," I said, mostly to make conversational noise.

"But don't you find the . . . silence intriguing? Mr. de Ratour?"

Diantha was about to say something when I shot her a quick glance. "Not at all," I said blithely. "To disappear among cannibals is to truly disappear."

The man laughed wickedly at my inadvertent *bon mot,* rubbed his hands together, and said he had things to attend to.

As we dawdled back to the car, I noticed the garish Christmas lighting blinking and winking all around us. I recalled that Malcolm Muggeridge had once remarked how he would like to show Christ around the Vatican. I think I'd rather show Our Lord the shopping areas of Seaboard and the way they get all tarted up like some old New England spinster trying to pass for a Las Vegas showgirl. Not that I disdain it. I was instead ineffably sad because Elsbeth loved it, even — especially — the front-yard displays. And I knew that next year she would not be here to share it with me.

"So, is Freddie Bain your villain?" Diantha asked, teasing me and bringing me out of my gloom as I drove us home in the creaking Peugeot.

"Possibly. I doubt very much that *Freddie Bain* was his original name."

"What's in a name?"

"Sometimes everything."

"I don't care. I found him fascinating."

"As he found you," I said, unaware of how dispirited I sounded.

She laughed, her wonderful, silly little laugh as we pulled up to the house. "Oh, Norman, I think you're jealous. How sweet of you." She gave me a peck on the cheek before getting out. We spoke of dinner and plans for the evening. But I sensed that before long she would have a love in her life.

As I drove back here to the office, I was filled with a distinct unease. The lingering smell of those pungent spices hung in the car like motes of suspicion.

29

My darling Elsbeth died this morning just as the fog lifted and dawn broke over Mercy Island, which we can just see from the bedroom window when the trees are stripped of leaves. When she woke about five thirty, I asked her if she wanted an injection for pain. She could scarcely talk. She smiled at me and shook her head. "Lie down with me," she said with an effort. I got under the covers and put my arm around her as she turned to me. Somehow I knew what was happening. I didn't need the cuff to sense that her blood pressure was dropping, that her kidneys and her valiant heart were failing. We lay like that for some time as I stroked her head and gave her as much love as I could. But again, it was as though Elsbeth were comforting me, was telling me she was okay, that she had entered some blissful peace before the final darkness descends.

Elsbeth whispered her final words, "Take care of Diantha. I love you, Norman." Her breathing grew uncertain. It stopped. Then started again. Finally it stopped and didn't start again as, holding my own breath, I waited and waited. I hugged her to me, but she was gone. I called her name, "Elsbeth. Elsbeth. Elsbeth." But she was gone. And in my sorrow I experienced the faith of disbelief: I could not believe that this woman, this being, my love, had ceased to exist. *You are not nonexistent*, I said to myself, holding her lifeless form, *you are only gone, gone somewhere else*. But where? "Come back," I murmured. I wept quietly. I sighed. I got up and went down the hall to tell Diantha.

I pushed open her door and sat on the side of her bed. "Diantha," I whispered, "Di . . ."

She sat up and turned on the bedside light. "Mom?"

I nodded.

She came into my arms, her tears running together with mine as I held her. And I had the strangest sensation, a sensation like a revelation: Diantha was Elsbeth. This is where Elsbeth had gone. It lasted only a moment, of course. No one is anyone else. But it lingered as we walked back to where Elsbeth lay, as Diantha knelt by the bed and ever-so-gently stroked her mother's wan, still face and moved the wisps of hair to one side.

Then Diantha said a strange and provocative thing. She looked directly at me. "I want a baby. I want a baby girl. I'm going to call her Elsbeth."

I nodded as though I understood, but didn't really, except in some abstract sense of knowing that we all have an impulse to answer death with life.

We got dressed and attended to the doleful necessities. I called the Medical School to whom Elsbeth had left her body. A couple of hours later a vehicle arrived from Flynn's Funeral Home and bore Elsbeth away after Diantha and I, alone and then together, spent a few more moments with the still and still-beautiful form lying on the bed.

Diantha called Win Jr. and remained some time on the phone with him. "Like talking to an imitation human being," she told me. She hugged me again, to assure and be assured. "It's amazing. He wanted no details, no times, or what she said, or anything else. Let me know, he said, when you've made arrangements for a memorial service. But Win's never quite connected with his own species, never mind his own family."

For some reason we found ourselves both quite ravenous. So together, already like a long-established couple, we made ourselves an old-fashioned breakfast — bacon, eggs, toast, orange juice, and coffee. But I'm afraid it only gave us the energy for grief, at first together, talking about Elsbeth, her vitality of old, her foibles, and her knack for turning life into an occasion.

Then alone. When I went upstairs afterward, the mystery of death persisted. Where had Elsbeth, where had life gone?

I spent the rest of the morning making phone calls to our little network of friends. I phoned Lotte and Izzy, who were very kind. "Come to dinner tonight, you and Diantha," Lotte insisted. I accepted for both of us.

I called Alfie Lopes, who said he would say a prayer for Elsbeth, "though, frankly, Norman, I doubt that she really needs one. I have feeling she's already the life of some heavenly party."

I called Korky and left a message. I fear for the dear boy's reaction. He already has so much to contend with.

I called Father O'Gould, and he said he, too, would say a prayer.

Upstairs, in the drawer of the little desk she used for her correspondence, I found a sealed envelope addressed to me. Inside was a letter written several weeks after we had learned the terrible news of her condition.

> Norman dearest,
>
> I know you are sad right now (or, at least, I hope you are!), but time, I know, will heal your heart. Along with my dear children, the best part of my life has been you. I thanked God every day for the chance to spend these last few, blissful years as your wife. Perhaps it is only the courage of fatalism, but I find myself less fearful hour by hour of what lies ahead. My only worry is for you and Diantha. It would be mawkish to nudge you into each other's arms, but I only pray that you will,

in some loving way, take care of each other. I am gone, Norman dearest, but I have every faith that somehow, somewhere, I will be waiting for you.

With love forever,
Your adoring Elsbeth

I wept again, and then again later at dinner, with tears and with that inner weeping of the heart, with a kind of sorrowful joy, exacerbated, no doubt, by the generous hand of Izzy, who kept filling my glass at dinnertime with a wonderful new Malbec from Argentina. Indeed, as I write this now, my head and my heart both thump painfully, and I feel the first faint yearnings for that void where I might go in search of Elsbeth.

30

Oh, Elsbeth, where are you? Why did you leave me again? My house is empty. My heart is empty. My soul is empty.

Grief is never comic. But it can be grotesque. I writhe on a rack of loss and lust. The ghost of Elsbeth beckons but so does the living presence of Diantha. I have had to all but manacle myself to keep from leaving my empty bed and falling at the foot of hers, on my knees, imploring, take me, hold me, give me life again.

But Diantha has grown distant in her own grief. She spends more time at her work now, a fixture in front of a fixture. She has promised to go to the Curatorial Ball with me, but that seems a pathetic sop to what I now crave in the core of my being. I feel like one of evolution's bad jokes, surviving only to suffer. A poor forked animal. Forked, all right. Diantha has been gone nearly every night and does not return until the wee hours. On what debaucheries, I can scarcely, in my fevered state, imagine. I suspect she's going out with that mocking fraud of a restaurant owner. Perhaps it's a reaction to her mother's death. I am powerless to do anything, to help her in the way she needs help.

I'll probably excise this outburst later on, but I needed to get that off my chest. A reluctant Calvinist, I am of the old school, neither a Papist who can bare his soul to some sympathetic priest nor a dupe of the therapeutic racket that exacerbates, while purporting to cure, the pathologies of self-absorption. And I have, despite my many good friends, none I want to bother with my troubles. And self-pity is a poor form of self-reliance.

I've found work a solace. The very furniture seems welcoming. The contents of my in-basket have proved a balm where I can lose myself in detail, the pickier the better. And Doreen is being extra sweet to me. Not to mention that I am knee-deep in a murder investigation.

Indeed, I arrived to find an e-mail from Nicole Stone-Lee. She reports that it's clear from notes and memoranda deftly hidden on Professor Ossmann's hard drive that he was working on some kind of aphrodisiac. It seems likely that in reviewing research done by Professor Tromstromer and Dr. Woodley, he stumbled across a combination of compounds that had "a profound effect" on the sexual activity of various small mammals. She noted that there seemed a lot more to plow through and would report back as soon as she had anything else of interest.

I forwarded the e-mail along to Lieutenant Tracy, made a hard copy for myself, and then erased it. I left word with Ms. Stone-Lee thanking her and asking her to refrain from e-mail in the future as I was not all that sure how secure it was. I'm wondering whether it would be helpful if the lieutenant and I paid a visit to Professor Tromstromer. I can think of several insinuations to lay before the big gnome. How much did he know about Ossmann's use of his research? Were Tromstromer and Woodley working on something that Ossmann stole? Does Tromstromer stand to gain with the removal of Ossmann and Woodley from the scene?

And speaking of Mr. Bain, I had a fruitful conversation with Professor Brauer early this afternoon. I had left word at his office to drop in when he got a chance. He came by just after lunch. Our relations have always been cool, and we didn't pretend any great cordiality beyond a business-like handshake.

We indulged a minute or two of small talk before we got to the point.

"I understand," I said, "that a production company making a film of your book would like to use the premises of the MOM for background shots."

"That's true," he said. "I believe Malachy Morin is taking care of details."

"Mr. Morin isn't taking care of anything," I said, "despite what he might be telling you to the contrary."

Professor Brauer wrinkled his smooth pate in frowning. "He tells me it's a done deal."

"It is not a done deal, Professor Brauer. The university in general and Mr. Morin in particular have no say whatsoever regarding the premises of this museum. But it doesn't surprise me that he has been less than straightforward with you. He has always had a tendency to tell people what he wants them to hear regardless of the truth."

"Did you ask me in here just to tell me that?" His expression was decidedly baleful.

"If I had, you could take it as an act of courtesy."

His frown turned to puzzlement. "Then what did you ask me here for?"

I cleared my throat. "I'm willing to consider some very restricted use of the museum for the film in return for some information."

"What information?"

"I want to know who, in the Long Pig Society, funded Corny's trip to the headwaters of the Rio Sangre."

He did something of a double take. He had the expression of one suddenly thinking quite deeply about something. "Well, that's privileged information."

"I understand. And these are privileged premises. And as

you know, I have very good relations with the Seaboard Police Department. I'm quite sure I could arrange to keep your crews from getting anywhere near the place."

He sighed. "If I do tell you, it's strictly, strictly confidential."

"Of course."

"I want to be able to use the Skull Collection."

"Okay."

"And the Oceanic exhibit."

"With restrictions."

"Understood. And outside shots, doors and one or two window shots."

"Within a period of no more than . . ."

"Say three weeks."

"Two and a half."

"Done. You'll get a call from Mr. Castor."

"Yes. I've spoken to him before. And now . . ."

"Yes. You know this is in absolute confidence."

"Understood."

"For your protection as much as anyone else's."

"I understand."

"Most of the funding came from Freddie Bain."

"Freddie Bain," I said. "The restaurateur?"

"Yes. Among other things, the proprietor of the Green Sherpa."

"Yes. Of course. He makes quite an impression. When did he join the club?"

"Not long after the trial. Of the Snyders brothers. He's quite a man about town, if you didn't know."

"I didn't. Are his interests in matters anthropophagic purely scholarly?"

"I'm not sure. He's the kind of person who talks but doesn't say much."

We left it at that. I felt I had learned something valuable, but I wasn't sure what. I also remained under the distinct impression that Raul Brauer was holding something back. What else did he know about Freddie Bain and what the man was up to? How did he get the kind of throwaway wealth to fund an expedition like Corny's? Not from a restaurant, surely. What, if anything, were his connections with Ms. Celeste Tangent? Why was the FBI interested in him?

Not that it matters. Not that anything matters. I continue this weird, bifurcated existence. I fill my life with this stuff only to find it empty at the end of the day. I suppose the only thing to do in these situations is to invent another life for yourself. But I don't want another life. I want what I had and what now exists only in the sunshine of memory.

But what memories! Into little more than two years we packed a lifetime. We had the most marvelous little wedding at the Miranda Hotel overflowing with friends and champagne. We honeymooned for three glorious weeks in France. (Izzy has remarked that people in relationships go to therapists; people in love go to Paris.) Elsbeth, I have come to realize, was like a magnifying lens, shaping, brightening, and intensifying my life.

No more. No more! It is like the sad old days again. I think I'll make my way over to the Club. There are people there. Someone might ask me to join their table. If nothing else, the waiters talk to you, they smile, they bring you things.

31

Diantha, dressed alluringly in slacks, a clinging jersey, and a tailored jacket, came in to see me at the museum this afternoon. My delight at her appearance vanished when I learned she wanted to borrow the car to drive out to Eigermount, Mr. Bain's country place. I was perfectly willing to let her take the old thing, but then she had another idea. "Why don't you drive me out instead? That way you can see Freddie in his natural habitat. It's surreal, to use one of your words."

When I declined, she persisted. "Oh, come on, Dad, you need an outing."

I couldn't really refuse, even though I was busy with year-end budget matters. Dealing with surpluses, I've found, is quite as tiresome as dealing with deficits. So we took a cab home, where Diantha packed an overnight bag.

We then drove northwest out of Seaboard to the Balerville Road and the picturesque little town of Tinkerton. Where the road forks just beyond a bridge that crosses Alkins Creek, we went right. The route climbed for several miles through gloomy stands of pine and hemlock and brought us eventually to a turn-off that would have been easy to miss. We drove into it and made our way along a narrow paved drive.

Well, Diantha was right about one thing. Seemingly out of nowhere, like a castle conjured in a tale about sinister fairies, rose a great round structure of cut granite. Nestled in a rug of evergreens, it towered at least four stories against the side of a steep declivity. The windows, narrow vertical slits with Gothic arches, blinked at the visitor uncomprehendingly, bringing to mind that line in Yeats about the pitiless sphinx.

A baleful kind of folly, I thought immediately, but let that impression seem, in my outward expression, a kind of awe. "A Martello tower writ large in the woods," I said, as though giving it some kind of architectural context might blunt the sense of foreboding I felt wafting from it.

We pulled up across from the main entrance — two massive oak doors with studded hinges set in a portal with pointed arch and curved surrounds of weathered stone. I wanted to drop Diantha and scuttle back to the office. I wanted really to keep Diantha in the car with me and drive away. But as in a dream bordering on nightmare, the oak doors opened, and Freddie Bain, in loose trousers and one of those Russian tunics cinched around the waist, came forth.

The man positively clung to me. He wouldn't hear of my returning without coming in for a cup of tea or a glass of wine.

I parked the car, and we crossed over a virtual drawbridge spanning a dry moat before entering through the great doorway. Such places are not really my cup of tea, but I admit the basic design had a vulgar grandeur to it. Indeed, it reminded me of the museum, only circular, the central core an atrium around which rooms led off from balustraded balconies. Sconces in the form of torches alternated with large oils on the walls, which, made of marble or synthetic marble, gave off a dark shine. An octagonal skylight opened dimly at the top.

Diantha, apparently knowing the place well, went into a kitchen off the main floor to see about tea. Mr. Bain showed me around. He was particularly proud of the immense fieldstone fireplace that, situated on the side of the building against the mountain, rose up through three stories, narrowing as it went before disappearing into the wall. Somewhat prosaically, the heads of mounted game — mostly deer — looked down with glass-eyed serenity from over the fireplace.

"I had a moose up there, but he was too . . . how do you say . . ."

"Lugubrious," I suggested.

Then, as though on the same subject, he said, "Permit me to express my condolences on the death of your wife, Diantha's mother."

I nodded and murmured my thanks, feeling oddly compromised. "This is quite a space," I said, sweeping my arm around the area. There were sofas and several armchairs upholstered in black leather on a raised stone area before the fireplace and a dining table with chairs not far from the kitchen door off to one side. Otherwise, the remainder of the ground floor, a vast expanse of polished hardwood that gleamed, remained bare. "What do you use all this for?" I asked.

"Human sacrifice," he said, and laughed, making a sound devoid of humor. With a sharp glance, he went on. "I hear you have a very interesting tape from the late Professor Chard." We had stepped up onto the raised area, and he was indicating an armchair to one side of the fireplace.

I tried to dissemble any double take. "Diantha told you?"

"She says you call it quite . . . sensational."

"That's one way of putting it."

"Strange that you didn't mention it to me when I first asked you."

"The widow wants it kept private."

"Ah, yes, the widow." Mr. Bain pursed his wide mouth. His frown was nearly confiding. "I don't know quite how to put this delicately, Mr. de Ratour, but I believe that tape is my property."

He turned and scarcely had to stoop to enter the fireplace, where he tended to the lighting of paper, kindling, and logs.

"On what grounds do you base that claim?" I asked as evenly as I could.

"As you know from Professor Brauer, the Green Sherpa funded most of that expedition."

"He told you he told me?"

"He did."

"In that case Professor Chard should have sent the tape to you. Yet he very clearly sent it to the museum."

"We had an understanding."

"In writing?"

"We are men of the world, Mr. de Ratour. We are gentlemen. We don't need lawyers to keep ourselves honest."

"Perhaps, but I'm afraid you'll have to discuss this with the museum counsel. I have given the family my word as a man of the world that the tape will be kept sealed in a vault for the next fifty years."

The fire now roaring dramatically behind him, as though he had stepped, a blond Lucifer, from the flames, Freddie Bain smiled grimly. "We will discuss this matter at a more appropriate time . . . Norman. You don't mind if I call you Norman?"

"Not at all." But I did in a way. The inner cringing that people like Mr. Bain provoke in me had reached my throat. I glanced around. To change the subject, I said, "You built this yourself?"

"I did. With an architect indulgent of my whims."

"Which are also many, I presume."

"They are."

"Your restaurant and gift shop must do well to be able to afford this kind of whimsy. Not to mention . . ." I left it hanging.

"Whimsy?" he repeated, perhaps offended. "Oh, I have many

other . . . resources." He moved out over the coffee table across from me. "Would you like to try a cigar? From Havana."

"No, thanks. I never learned to enjoy tobacco."

"One of life's little pleasures." He toyed with a cigar but didn't light it.

"You seem to have a penchant for things Russian."

"I have a penchant for many things." He looked in the direction of Diantha, who was emerging from the kitchen in the company of a little old lady in head scarf and frumpy clothes, a veritable babushka. "Among them beautiful women."

"I would think Diantha worthy of more than a penchant."

He glanced at me anew, his mobile face — his mouth and the finely wrinkled flesh around his eyes — registering a realization and some faint amusement. "That is very well said."

Diantha came over with the tea and the babushka. "Nana's teaching me Russian," she said with a little laugh. "*Spassiba,* Nana."

The old woman smiled a gummy smile and retreated.

Diantha, whom I found to be disconcertingly at home, sat in the armchair across from me and poured tea. "Isn't this an amazing place," she more exclaimed than asked.

"I've never seen anything like it," I said honestly.

We made small talk. Mr. Bain, standing in front of the large, busy fire, was very much the man of the manor. He was definitely Diantha's point of reference, the recipient of her smiles and small attentions. It dismayed me that she could be so taken with him. His charm struck me as an elaborate pose, a kind of parody he put on for his own amusement. He smiled as he related, with a kind of mock homage, how he had visited the museum several times over the past year.

"I like primitive art because it is primitive," he said. "Its savagery has an honesty we have lost."

I nodded, but noncommittally.

Diantha said, "Dad thinks that all art forms have their own integrity."

With a knowing laugh, Mr. Bain said, "Except for that noise your friend Mr. Shakur makes."

What didn't he know already about Diantha and me? I wondered.

At intervals Mr. Bain's pocket phone would ring, and I found it curious that he usually hung up after a word or two in a foreign language that may have been Russian or German, then excused himself to use a regular phone. At one point a man with a head of shorn, pelt-like hair and wearing a hip-length leather jacket appeared near the entrance and beckoned to Mr. Bain to join him elsewhere in the building.

I suppose I am too scrupulous in these matters to have taken the opportunity to disparage Mr. Bain and his effects in his absence. I doubt Diantha would have listened anyway. She seemed utterly oblivious to any of the more indirect cues I offered her as to my real feelings about the man. And each time he returned, her eyes would brighten and she would hang on his every word.

As I was making motions to get up and go, Mr. Bain produced a bottle of expensive vodka and insisted I join them in a shot for good luck. That led to a second small glass, knocked back with ceremony. And while still capable of driving home, I was inveigled into staying for dinner. It didn't take much convincing, I'm afraid to say. The thought of returning to an empty house left me vulnerable. And I nursed a faint hope that Diantha might change her mind and return with me to Seaboard.

You may imagine my surprise when the babushka, answering the sound of a gong, went into the small foyer at the main door and returned with Celeste Tangent in tow.

I expected from the lab assistant a start of surprise, a frown, a look of alarm, even. But after she had finished a loud and elaborate exchange of greetings with her host, she turned to me with an irresistible charm of smiles, voice, and gesture. "Norman, how delightful to see you again."

"Miss Tangent," I said, inclining my head, standing my ground.

She gave a quick, toothsome laugh. "'Miss Tangent!' Oh, I love it. So full of restraint. Not that this place is a stranger to restraints. And, Di, princess!" She turned to Diantha. "How are you? You're so right about Norman. He is precious." Then to me again, her hand sweeping the vast room, her silver bracelets jingling. "Isn't this wild! Don't you love its . . ."

"Extravagance," I offered, finding my voice. I was, despite myself, under the woman's spell.

"Yes. Yes." She took off her long thick fur to reveal attire that, though quite casual, slowly mesmerized me. I mean the pre-faded expensive jeans over nylons and thick-heeled pumps, a low-cut black jersey that molded her breasts just so and displayed her gorgeous throat and neck. And then her lustrous blond hair piled wantonly on her head.

"You will stay for dinner?" Freddie Bain intoned.

"Of course. Norman needs a date."

So I had a partner for dinner while not really wanting either. I should have made some good excuse for excusing myself. I could have pleaded guilt or insanity or grief or all three. I felt complicit in some tawdry enterprise, but nor could I withstand the fantasy to hand, so to speak. Because Miss Tangent had me quite bedazzled, sitting next to me on the sofa, her shapely limbs articulate as she shifted around. In what remained of my detective's instincts, I understood then how she could have made slaves of Penrood and perhaps Ossmann. With my proclivity for self-delusion, I told myself I might be able to get her, in a weak moment, to tell me about what was happening in the Genetics Lab. But I can see, looking back, that all the weak moments were to be mine.

For the nonce, it was Mr. Bain who saved me from any overt foolishness. For reasons I cannot fathom, the man seemed determined to impress me. Glasses in hand, we began a tour of the art that hung both in the main room and along the balconied walls. Diantha kept glancing to me now, as though trying to divine whether I approved. I didn't. To me the stuff — Dalíesque vistas foregrounded with muscle-bound blond men and great-breasted naked Valkyries with heroic buttocks doing violence to subhumanoid forms — appeared to be utter kitsch. Or kitsch so kitschy it achieved a kind of parodic authenticity. Art as a serious joke, so to speak. Not that Mr. Bain betrayed any self-amusement as he led us around.

"And what do you think, Norman?" Miss Tangent had hooked her arm in mine, had taken virtual possession, and now delighted in putting me on the spot.

Influenced by Dalí and perhaps by Wyeth, N.C., not Andrew, I responded, fending her off with a smattering of erudition.

The works on the third tier included a Werner Peiner landscape, an Ivo Saliger nude, and a large mural of muscular Aryans, men and women, at various kinds of outdoor work. "Looks like Communist art," I said to Miss Tangent out of earshot of our host. "I suppose you could call it National Socialist Realism." But my *bon mot* did not appear to register.

Instead, Miss Tangent unhooked her arm and took me by the hand. "You want to see my favorite room?" I didn't have a chance to answer as she led me along the balcony to a door behind where the fireplace chimney joined the wall. It opened into a large bedroom with a row of pointed Gothic windows on either side. A rug comprising two polar bear pelts lay in front of a smaller fireplace while a bed capacious enough for giants to copulate on stood to one side under two angled gilt-framed mirrors. These hung from a ceiling where the beams stood out bold and formed with the joists a coffered effect. A painting over the fireplace depicted a knight in shining armor and a large-limbed maiden vaguely of the Pre-Raphaelite school.

I didn't try to conceal my wonderment at it all. Because it wasn't until I glanced out of one of the windows that I realized we were in a kind of wide bridge between the main pile and the side of the mountain in the back.

"Is this the master's bedroom?" I asked, deliberately employing the Saxon genitive.

"Oh, no, that's upstairs. That's restricted territory. It looks like this only . . . it has a winding staircase that goes up to the top where there's a greenhouse and a pool." She gave her wide-mouthed laugh. "Maybe we'll all end up there . . . for a swim."

Which left my head swimming a little at the prospect. I walked over to the fireplace and, pretending some interest in Sir Galahad kneeling before the diaphanously clad beauty, asked, "Do you work for Freddie?"

"Don't we all?" Her laugh had a bitterness to it this time. "Oh, Norman, stop playing detective. It's a real turnoff."

"Miss Tangent . . ."

She had taken both of my hands in hers, and it seemed unmannerly to shake them off. "Seriously, Norman, you're off duty. Officially. Until morning. Then we'll straighten everything out for you."

But Miss Tangent remained very much on duty. She let go my hands and reached up to give me a kiss, opening my mouth with hers and for the barest moment entwining her tongue around mine. At the same time, she reached a hand down and brought it up softly against the crotch of my worsted trousers with a gesture so light and fleeting it might never have been. "I can tell, Norman, you're not the kind of older guy who needs much help."

I maintained enough presence of mind to ask, "Perhaps that's something you could tell me about?"

She pulled away. "If you're going to be a bore, I'm not going to get naughty with you. Or perhaps I'll just have to spank you."

It would be less than honest to say I wasn't tempted. Most immediately by this attractive woman, by the thought of a night with her on that vast bed, along with God knows what combinations of Diantha and Freddie Bain, the two polar bears, and the little old babushka, for all I knew. Because Miss Tangent's jean-clad haunches swung before me with maddening palpability as we descended the stairs to the main floor. And as real as they seemed, I felt a deeper, more irresponsible temptation. To simply let go. To smile, finally, to laugh, to loosen my bow tie and give in to the allurements shimmering around me.

Strangely enough, it was Freddie Bain who saved me. Not that I didn't have misgivings, about Diantha's situation, for instance. What kind of sordid, silken rat's nest had she gotten herself into? Perhaps, I kept thinking, I should have been more forthcoming about my suspicions before we went snooping around his gift shop.

All the while, vodka, and then wine from Georgia — the republic — kept flowing. We arranged ourselves at the dining table, which was nearly square. I sat across from the host, the host from hell, as it turned out. I was sober enough, though, to realize that the meal the babushka set out on the dining table was far better than anything Mr. Bain served in his restaurant.

As we finished supping a chunky borscht and began some delectable piroshki, the discussion turned to the music issuing from well-hidden speakers. I recognized it as Wagner, but couldn't place it as his music seems to me one long continuum.

Mr. Bain and I reenacted the Wagner–Brahms debate in a minor key. I stood my ground, saying that Wagner was for hearing and Brahms was for listening to. Mr. Bain, imbibing heavily and growing ruddy of face, waxed dogmatic and craven at the same time, boring in on me, as though desperate for my affirmation of his tastes and ideas. Was it Diantha? I wondered. Did he want me to approve of him for her sake? Or was he just one of those men who cannot imagine others holding opinions different from his own?

I tried to involve the girls, as I thought of them, in other topics, including the food. The lamb shanks, baked to a turn in rosemary and served with a subtle gravy and garlic mashed potatoes, had me asking Diantha how to say thank you in Russian.

But Mr. Bain proved relentless. He wanted to talk about art, which turned out to be a subterfuge for talking about politics. I didn't mind when he excoriated twentieth-century art, especially the abstract stuff, calling it the greatest hoax of all time. I have heard those sentiments before. I comfortably demurred, confessing that I found a lot of the early Picasso delightful. I declared a partiality for the works of Max Beckmann, saying I paid homage to his *Self-Portrait in Tuxedo* whenever I went to Cambridge.

"Beckmann!" He spit it out like an expletive along with bits of food he was chewing.

"And Gustav Klimt," I went on, baiting him a little. "I find his prostitutes touching and beautiful."

"Degenerates," he said dismissively. "Weimar scum."

The pot, I thought, calling the kettle black. But I simply shook my head and tried to dissemble a distinct repugnance as I remarked to myself the congruence between my host's opinions and the shirt of scarlet silk beneath his tunic and the welling Wagner and the flames from the roaring blaze in the fireplace reflecting off the polished walls and the deplorable oils, the whole effect creating a hellish Valhalla.

It got worse.

Mr. Bain leaned across the table and shook his head with exaggerated effect. "Do you know, Norman, who is the greatest artist of the twentieth century?"

"I have some opinions, but I'm not very passionate about them," I replied.

"Adolf Hitler." He paused for effect. "*Der Führer.*"

"You're not serious," I said, rising to the bait with that queasy disquiet such topics elicit. Just a bad joke, I hoped. Because, guest or no, Miss Tangent or not, drunk or sober, I was not to be suborned into anything like admiration for or understanding of, however ironic, that archvillain.

Mr. Bain's smile had that Mephistophelean curve I had come to know. "Think of it, Norman. Think of it in terms of what we are told art must do. *Épater le bourgeoisie.* Well, *Mein Führer* épatered them to the roots of their little beings. He épatered them like no one else has before or since. He made us stop and think what it means to be human.

"Or inhuman . . ."

It was not really a conversation. My host had turned declamatory, his words coming like something he had gone over in his mind or rehearsed with others again and again.

"War is not art," I said.

"On the contrary. World War Two was his masterpiece. The world itself was his canvas. He drew his brush across it. He carved and painted with men and machines . . ."

"And madness."

"Yes, but inspired madness. *Der Führer* was modern way beyond his time. While Picasso and the others were dabbling at their little experiments with reality, Adolf Hitler conceived and executed a fantastic, glorious war. He created new levels of reality. Do you have any idea of what life was like during the battle for Stalingrad? Do you know that human beings experienced there another order of existence?"

"Is that art?"

"By today's standards, certainly. Think of it in conceptual terms. Think of it as a kind of installation . . ."

"Not a permanent one, thank God." I turned to Miss Tangent, thinking she would at least smile at my rejoinder. But she was under the man's spell.

Mr. Bain leaned across the table and jabbed the air with his fork. "What do those poncy little critics keep telling us every time someone slices a cow in half or buggers himself with a crucifix? They tell us it is art. And if we protest, we're told it's *supposed* to disturb us. Well, by that standard . . . I mean *Der Führer* disturbed all of us, didn't he? He still disturbs us, doesn't he?"

I looked to Diantha and, even allowing for the amount we had all drunk, was appalled to see her apparently impressed with the rantings of this charlatan. Perhaps she had heard this all before. Which made it worse.

"You are pushing the limits of irony," I said, hoping for some relieving laughter.

Freddie Bain shook his large head, and his expression showed a twist of demonic anger. "Irony? What makes you think I would stoop to irony? Art is supposed to show us as we really are. *Der Führer* held up a mirror to mankind and we remain horrified at what we've seen in it."

"But the Holocaust," I said, my answering anger making me stumble over the words.

"The Holocaust." The man laughed, a laugh I can still hear. Then serious, boring in again. "The Holocaust was Hitler's masterstroke. With the Holocaust he made himself immortal.

Look around you, Norman. His monuments are everywhere. Every time the Jews put up another memorial or try to get the Gentiles to acknowledge their suffering, they honor Hitler's achievement."

I took my napkin off my lap and put it on the table preparatory to rising. "Who are you?" I asked.

He ignored my question. "Think about it, Norman. Think of those he killed. The Jews. Stalin killed more people, many more. Stalin had them shot. He had them worked and starved and frozen to death. But who did he kill? Kulaks. For Christ's sake. Peasants with a couple of cows. A few intellectuals. Poets. Bureaucrats. Do you think if Hitler had killed twenty million Chinese anyone would care? Mao killed many more than that. No, Hitler killed Jews. The best and the brightest, no?"

I was reduced to shaking my head.

His eyes, cold and mocking in his inflamed face, bore into mine. "They wanted, my friend, to be chosen. Hitler chose them."

"I am not your friend."

"As you please. I regret to upset you."

But he clearly didn't. He was leaning even farther across the table, his voice a loud whisper. "Do you know what every Jew fears deep in his heart?"

"People like you."

"No, no, I am not jesting. They fear, my friend, deep in their hearts, that Hitler was right."

"That kind of fear is only human," I replied with some fervor. "Most people know in their hearts that Hitler was wrong."

"Don't be so sure, Mr. de Ratour. You would like to think, wouldn't you, that you would never have joined the *Schutzstaffel*, that you and those you know would be incapable of such a thing. But under different circumstances, in different times . . . People who thought of themselves as decent and law abiding and progressive joined the Nazi Party. The same kind of people joined the Communist Party . . ."

Incredibly, he laughed. "They both got more than they bargained for, didn't they? They got right up to their noses in the blood of others. And when the party was over and the fingers started pointing, they scuttled for cover like cockroaches." Then he turned serious. "But my father never did. He never hid what he was."

"Diantha, I think you should come along with me now."

"You see, Norman, what we really don't want to admit to ourselves is that evil can be fun. Think of all those films that have Nazis and ex-Nazis in them. That shiver of excitement when the swastika fills the screen."

"Hitler is dead."

"Then why do we have to keep killing him?"

I coughed to clear my throat. "I'm finding this conversation more than distasteful." I stood up to leave.

He rose to his feet as well. "You're running away, Norman. You're running away from yourself."

"You are not I."

"Do not be so sure, Norman." He made my name sounded like a mockery. He stood up as well and leaned across the table. "Tell me, are you a Christian?"

"I'm an Episcopalian," I responded, not sure I had answered his question.

"Yes. Then tell me, sir, where was your Episcopalian God when the trains pulled into Treblinka? Where was He when Stalin and Kaganovich, a Jew, by the way, deliberately starved to death six or seven million people in Ukraine? Where was He when the machine guns of the special units overheated at Babi Yar? Where was your Episcopalian God when Stalin worked and starved and froze to death those millions in the mines of

Magadan? Where was He when Pol Pot murdered a quarter of his countrymen? When the Hutus sharpened their pangas and hacked to death half a million Tutsis? Tell me, sir, where was your almighty Episcopalian God then?"

Had I only heard the man's voice it might have sounded like a *cri de coeur*. But Freddie Bain was smiling broadly, was on the verge of mirth.

"God is not cruel."

"Then why did He create us as we are?"

"Man is free to be evil," I said.

"Then God, too, is free to be evil. Think about it, Mr. de Ratour. If we are made in the image and likeness of the Almighty, Mr. de Ratour, then like us He needs a good laugh now and again. And what could be funnier than looking down on mass murder? Hilarious. Knee-slapping. God-roaring. A scream. Face it, God is a joker. If He made us for anything, He made us for His amusement." At which point he laughed himself, his noise bouncing like the reflected flames off the surfaces curving around us.

"That, sir," I said though a clenched jaw, "is the most damnable blasphemy I have ever heard."

"Not so, Norman. If not laughing, what else could He have been doing? And if God doesn't exist, then what difference does it make? We are but infinitesimal specks on a speck, our greatest and worst moments of history of no more significance than what happens on a petri dish."

"History judges," I said, grasping at straws.

"History comes and goes."

"You're mad" was the best I could do.

"Bah" was all he said to my pathetic response. Then, "And I want my tape." With that he turned unsteadily, but with a certain melodramatic flourish, and walked across to the fire. There, backlit by the flames, he stood and toyed with a cigar.

A moment later Miss Tangent went over to join him. I looked at Diantha. "I think you should come home with me now."

But she seemed under a spell. She looked across at Freddie Bain and said, "Oh, Dad, Freddie's just pulling your leg. He has his little rants. Everybody does. You should have heard Sixy get going about gays. He wanted to kill them all."

I implored her again, knowing it was futile. I was torn myself, in turn afflicted with the lowest form of lust, with enough anger to want to burn the place down, and with an awful foreboding. Though I had no real proof, I was now certain Freddie Bain had a lot to do with what was happening at the Museum of Man. But I couldn't stay.

It was freezing and dark outside, with the upper reaches of his preposterous domicile looking like battlements against the night sky. I got in and started my cold old car. I had been shocked into sobriety but still drove with the exaggerated care of the technically drunk. I was full of rebuttal. In the after-arguments running in my head, I stood back, remained dignified, and said things like, *If Hitler was an artist then art has no meaning.* Or, *The profundity of nihilism is an illusion.* Or, better, *Nihilism is the profundity of the unimaginative.* Why? he would ask. And I would respond: *Because it is easy to imagine nothing, and evil is a form of nothingness.*

I stopped at a roadside diner to drink coffee and calm myself. I kept trying to convince myself that God is good. That the world is good. That people are good. The worst kinds of self-doubts gnawed at me, the kind from which you cannot escape into nice big abstractions like nihilism. Could I, I asked myself, have been a Nazi under other circumstances? No, I said, no. At the same time, I knew my denial was an indulgence in the moral luxury afforded by hindsight.

I also wondered, as a more immediate concern, if I had done

the right thing in walking away. Am I a coward? A moral coward and, where Miss Tangent is concerned, a sexual coward?

I am confused. With Elsbeth gone only days, I scarcely know my own heart. I know I loved Elsbeth. I thought I loved Diantha. And perhaps I do. But now that love has been polluted with lust for another. I sit here writing this with my head on a poker of pain wanting, in the depths of my corrupted being, feeling her lips and her touch, to be in that big bed with that mocking, maddening Lorelei.

32

It is Monday, December 18, and Diantha has not returned home since Friday, and, frankly, I have become concerned for her welfare. She did call yesterday, mostly to tell me she wouldn't be going with me to the Curatorial Ball, which we held last night. She hinted and then proposed outright that she come and bring Freddie Bain and Celeste Tangent. I hesitated a moment, but then said no, that I didn't think it would be a good idea.

My evening at that grotesque fortress-*cum*-mansion still resounds within me. I want, of course, to dismiss everything that madman said, but it lingers, like an intellectual infection. I keep running it around in my head. If we are made in the image and likeness of God, what percentage of our DNA, ontologically speaking, overlaps? Is God a joker? I'm sure the question is hardly a novel one, but I have wrestled with it repeatedly since that weird evening. Did God simply set in motion the awesome machinery of natural selection, then sit back and watch? Does He laugh at us?

It would have been worse, I'm sure, had I stayed the night. But I sometimes wonder. Miss Tangent, her eyes, her hair, her touch, also lingers, so that I suffer a kind of low-grade erotomania in which she and Diantha and Elsbeth tease and tempt and leave me. They invest my sleeping dreams, night visions bizarre and poignant, from which I awake in torments of lust and despair. I would have thought grief something pure, a kind of suffering that renders one innocent.

And then it's all mangled and mingled with my workaday life, the heavy routine of being a museum director. Not to mention my role as a part-time murder investigator. Who is Freddie Bain? Had I stayed Friday night, might I have found out? Is he Moshe ben Rovich? It hardly seems likely, given his proclivities. How does Celeste Tangent fit into all this? It's obvious she works for him as a seductress. And Ossmann? Penrood? And myself, had I not suffered the rectitude of indignation that night? What would he want with a powerful aphrodisiac? To sell it as an illegal drug, obviously. What might Diantha be able to tell me when she comes back? If she comes back.

Korky and I went to the ball together, not as dates, of course — I certainly didn't dance with him. Still, we raised a few eyebrows when we came in. I could hear their thoughts. Is Norman coming out or just swinging on the closet door? But as time goes by, I find myself caring less and less what people think. It has occurred to me, finally, that the standards of yesteryear, for better or worse, no longer apply.

Korky appears to be doing well, considering what he's been through. We had a drink at my house before setting out. Elsbeth's absence shouted at us from every cornice and corner. We clung together for a small tearful moment. But said nothing. One word and neither of us would have shut up for the evening. Which might have been cathartic in its own way.

As we drove over together, he confessed he suffers bouts of acute depression. He said he is still very interested in what he calls "the marvelous world of fine food," but that he can no longer tolerate the thought of anyone going hungry in the world. "I'm torn, Norman, about what to do with my life. I feel like volunteering for an international relief agency, you know, where you fly to one of those wretched villages in Africa to hand out food to the starving. But it wouldn't be me."

"A man doesn't live by bread alone," I murmured inanely.

Which made him laugh. "No, he needs, baguettes, bagels, boules, franchese, focaccia. It's the difference between feeding and eating. But I still can't write about it. I don't know what I'm going to do."

The Curatorial Ball wouldn't have been the same anyway. Rather than dismantle the Diorama of Paleolithic Life in Neanderthal Hall, as we've done for the past couple of years, we decided to hold the party in one of the function halls of the Miranda Hotel. We decorated it ourselves with streamers and those collapsible ornaments. We had a papier-mâché menorah, some Kwanzaa symbols, and a pagan display provided by a local coven. We moved Herman the Neanderthal into the foyer and decked him out in his traditional Santa suit. And the Warblers, getting just a bit creaky, sang all the old favorites. But it wasn t the same.

Korky, I was glad to see, met a friend and left the party early. I lingered and drank too much, turning wine into water at a miraculous rate. Rather than drive, I left the car in the parking lot, declined several offers of a lift, and walked home under a cold clear night, looking up at the heavens, a speck on a speck, and remembering Elsbeth.

33

I have been made privy to some disturbing information regarding Freddie Bain, information that makes me more anxious than ever for the safety and well-being of Diantha. As I was sitting in my office this morning in a practically deserted museum — everyone who can has already officially or unofficially taken holiday leave — Lieutenant Tracy called and said he wanted to drop by with Sergeant Lemure and Agent Jack Johnson of the Federal Bureau of Investigation.

I said certainly, and not long afterward they arrived. Dressed in a plain but sharply pressed dark blue suit, Agent Johnson evinced the practiced no-nonsense demeanor of a veteran law enforcement officer. He took in, I noticed, some of the more *outré* items decorating the office but said nothing. He gave my hand a short, brisk shake and sat down in one of the three chairs I had pulled up before my desk for the meeting.

Flanked by Sergeant Lemure in rumpled suit and Lieutenant Tracy in tweed jacket and holiday tie, Agent Johnson started right in. "Mr. de Ratour," he said, getting my name right, "I hope you understand that the Bureau seldom shares information with a private citizen regarding an ongoing criminal investigation . . ."

"Or even with local police departments," Sergeant Lemure put in.

"That's right. But it seems the Bureau, the Seaboard Police Department, and you have a keen common interest in the activities of one Freddie Bain."

"That's right."

"Could you tell me why?"

"For several reasons. But one of them involves confidentiality and the others remain conjectural."

"If it involves criminal activity, Mr. de Ratour, I'm afraid I won't be able to comply with any request for confidentiality."

I nodded. "I don't believe it is criminal. But I will leave it to your judgment." I waited for him to nod and then continued. "A couple of months back one of our professors — or, I should say, one of Wainscott's professors who was affiliated with the museum — undertook a highly dangerous expedition to South America. Given the nature of the trip, we here at the museum refused to fund any substantial part of it. We did underwrite his medical supplies and his insurance for medical evacuation."

"How was it dangerous?" Agent Johnson, a man in his forties, regarded me steadily with cool hazel eyes.

"It was very remote to begin with. A lot of outsiders have disappeared while exploring the territory. The situation, apparently, has been exacerbated recently by road-building and logging activities near the tribal lands. The Yomamas are reputed to be cannibals as well as very fierce. Indeed, Professor Chard went there with the express purpose of witnessing an anthropophagic ritual."

"That's cannibalism," Sergeant Lemure put in.

Agent Johnson ignored the sergeant. "And he got eaten instead?" There might have been the slightest touch of ironic humor in his tone.

"Yes."

"How do you know?"

"We have it on tape."

"I see. And how does Freddie Bain fit in to all this?"

"Mr. Bain funded most of the expedition."

The agent nodded. "Well, there's nothing illegal in that, is there? At least on the surface." He paused for a moment as though considering. He shifted in his seat. "And your other conjectures?"

I must say I felt a bit self-conscious detailing for this experienced FBI agent what amounted to little more than hunches. I had a sense as I reviewed my suspicions regarding the "love potion" deaths and Korky's kidnapping that Lieutenant Tracy and Sergeant Lemure wanted me, for professional reasons, to do the speculating for them.

Whatever the case, Agent Johnson listened with unnerving attention. When I finished, he said, "First off, Mr. de Ratour, I would advise you to be very careful in any dealings you have with Freddie Bain."

"Yeah, he ain't called 'the Bear' for nothing," Sergeant Lemure put in.

Agent Johnson betrayed only an instant's irritation with the interruption. "It may help you if I fill you in on some of his background."

I nodded, waiting.

He glanced down at a notebook. "Freddie Bain was born Manfred Bannerhoff in the city of Omsk in the former Soviet Union. According to Interpol, Israeli police intelligence, and other sources, his father, Gerhardt Bannerhoff, was an officer in the Wehrmacht in World War Two. He was taken prisoner when von Paulus surrendered at Stalingrad. He survived the gulag, stayed in Russia, and married a Russian woman by whom, though well into his forties, he fathered Manfred. When he came of age, Manfred Bannerhoff changed his last name to Bannerovich. Then came *glasnost*. When Gorbachev opened the Soviet borders during the eighties to Jewish emigration, Bannerovich had himself circumcised, changed his name to Moshe ben Rovich, passed for a Jew, and made his way to Tel Aviv. Apparently a good number of Gentile Russians found themselves to be the sons and daughters of Israel during that time."

"Yeah, a lot of Aryan-looking guys were walking around with sore dicks right around then," Sergeant Lemure said, as though this time to deliberately irk the agent.

"History," I murmured, "is full of ironies."

Agent Johnson went on. "What Russia also exported to Israel was a criminal culture so cynical and cold-blooded in its operations it makes the Cosa Nostra look like a gentlemen's club. Anyway, Moshe wanted bigger fish to fry than what was available in Tel Aviv. And besides, the Israelis are not that easy to exploit."

"Yeah, they've all got guns and know to use them," Sergeant Lemure said.

"So he emigrated to America?" I asked.

"Exactly."

"How could he do that? I mean if he was a criminal."

"He's also a businessman. He had accumulated substantial capital, enough to make himself respectable. His papers were in order. He didn't have a record. He landed in New York, eventually morphing into Freddie Bain, all-American boy. Along the way, incidentally, he picked up fluent German, Hebrew, French, English, and some Nepali, along with his native Russian, of course."

"He still has no record, officially," Lieutenant Tracy put in.

Agent Johnson leaned back as though to give the floor to Sergeant Lemure.

"Right," the sergeant said, "no priors, but he's got a rap sheet as long as your arm. Extortion, armed robbery, prostitution, drug dealing, murder. But no convictions and no outstanding warrants."

"Amazing," I said.

The sergeant shrugged. "He has good Ivy League lawyers working for him. Anyway, he got in thick with the Russian mob in Brooklyn. Got right in up to his neck. The word on the street is that he crossed Victor 'Dead Meat' Karnivorsky on a million-dollar drug deal. Karnivorsky put out a contract on him. He's called Dead Meat because once he says you're dead meat, you're dead meat."

"But he's still alive," I put in, stating the obvious.

"Right. Freddie made a deal from what we've heard. He was allowed to live once he paid Karnivorsky twice what he owed him and agreed to disappear."

"So he came up here."

"Eventually. First he took off for Nepal for a couple of years. I mean he disappeared."

Agent Johnson had the floor again. "Right. Then he landed here and quickly took over the Seaboard mob."

"Seaboard has a mob?" I asked with some amazement.

"Every place has some kind of mob," the agent said with weary cynicism. "Anyway, we can't pin anything on him, but we think he's mixed up in narcotics, prostitution, extortion, and probably quite a few legitimate businesses. He's a very shrewd operator. He knows who to pay off and who to scare off. We suspect he may run a major pipeline for drugs moved around here and all up and down the East Coast. We think he uses the spices as a cover, but we haven't been able to prove anything."

"But why would he bother with Corny's expedition?"

"He's that kind of guy, Mr. de Ratour. He likes getting involved with things, weird things."

"He certainly has Nazi leanings," I said.

Agent Johnson nodded. "That's been noted. But he's also been a rabid Buddhist, an advocate for alien abductions, and a devotee of astral travel."

"And now cannibalism," Sergeant Lemure said.

"One other thing, Mr. de Ratour. Would you mind telling me how you know for sure that your professor is dead?"

"I was sent a tape. It's quite graphic."

The agent nodded. "I figured as much. And given that Freddie Bain paid for the expedition, don't be surprised if he doesn't come looking for that tape if he gets wind of it."

"He already has," I said. I hesitated and then said, "I know him personally. I've even been out to his place. It's in the Hays Mountains, west of here."

"The Eigermount." Agent Johnson nodded, very interested in what I had to say. "Could you describe the interior for me?"

I did so in some detail. I also told him about the shady characters and how there seemed a lot of coming and going for an ordinary household. I admitted that my stepdaughter, Diantha Lowe, was out there with him as we spoke.

Agent Johnson nodded as though he already knew. Of a sudden I realized why he was here, why he was telling me all this, and what he wanted. "Is there any way you could get in touch with her?" he asked.

"She has one of those pocket phones," I said. "Why do you ask?"

The agent appeared to muse to himself. "Perhaps she could look around for us."

"That could be very dangerous," Lieutenant Tracy put in.

"Too dangerous," I said. "I don't want her exposing herself like that. I want her home."

The FBI man nodded, not at all rebuffed. "When she comes home, I would like to talk to her if that's possible. She might have learned something. She might be able to provide us with a pretext for a search warrant." He took out a card and put it on the desk.

They left a short while later, the federal agent mixing banalities of caution with those of reassurance. I wasn't reassured in the least. To me it seemed a sump hole of evil had opened right up under my feet. I wouldn't have been surprised if Freddie Bain had had something to do with Elsbeth's death.

So I sit here now, in my own little eyrie, on the longest night of the year, resisting an overwhelming urge to take my father's gun, drive out to that ridiculous stone bastion, make that gangster listen to my rebuttals, and rescue my stepdaughter. But I fear that, upon arrival, Diantha would answer the door, laugh at my intentions, and invite me in for a drink.

34

It is Christmas morning, the wee hours, and I have received the best present imaginable under the circumstances. Diantha has returned home. Late yesterday afternoon, as I was fidgeting around this big empty house feeling mocked by the glitter of the little tree I managed to set up, as I mourned as never before Elsbeth's absence, as I thought of ginning myself into oblivion, Diantha came through the front door. She threw herself into my arms, she pulled me to her, and she wept hot tears on my neck. "Oh, Norman, Norman, I am so glad to see you. I will never leave you again. You are like . . . civilization."

I was nearly at a loss for words. I couldn't exactly chastise her for being away so long. Yet I felt constrained in returning her effusions, as for me there is a very thin line between certain kinds of affection and darker, richer, more palpable feelings. I did manage to gaze smilingly into her eyes and express both great joy and great relief that she had returned safely.

"Let's have a cup of tea," she said, "and I'll tell you all about it. I want one of your English cups of tea, real tea out of a pot with milk and sugar. You know, the way you learned to drink it when you were in . . ."

"Jesus," I said, "Jesus College, Oxford."

So we retired to the kitchen while Diantha, perched on a stool, looking the worse for wear, to judge from the dark circles under her eyes, told me what she had been doing.

"Well, you were there . . ."

"Yes. It was like a fortress of sorts," I said, keeping my remarks neutral as I got the electric kettle going. "Eccentric, to say the least."

"You don't know the half of it, Dad. I mean he's got these killer guard dogs and some really creepy-looking guys around. And these secret rooms."

"I see." Though it was Diantha, my stepdaughter, I had already started taking mental notes. "But what happened? I mean to send you home like this?"

"Well, at first Freddie was all sweetness and light. Walks in the woods and philosophizing. He said you need to lead the Nietzschean life or none at all. You heard him go on about Hitler. I mean the guy is obsessed. He talks about how you have to live life on the edge, all that sort of stuff. He's into filmmaking. He kept bugging me about that Corny Chard tape. He said he'd use muscle if he had to in order to get it. He says he paid big time for it."

I poured hot water into the pot to scald it. Then I ladled in two heaping teaspoons of loose tea before filling it with more water, which I had brought to a boil. I sighed, shook my head. "You really shouldn't have told him."

"I know. Yeah, but at first, he comes on like a regular guy. He wanted to know all about you. Then, you know, like, you have a joint and start talking. I was just kind of bragging. About you."

I smiled, flattered in an odd way. "Does he use drugs?"

"Is the pope Catholic? I mean, he's into it . . . big time."

"Do you think he sells drugs as well as uses them?"

"I couldn't swear, but I think he does. One night, when I couldn't sleep, I wandered into this place that leads off from a bookcase that's really a door on the second floor behind where the fireplace goes up. It was like something out of a movie. I was looking for something to read. I pulled out *Northanger Abbey,* you know, I've always liked Jane Austen, and the bookcase kind of went in. Then it just opened, right into a dark passage. It was really creepy with no lights. I went down to the kitchen and got a flashlight. I went in, I don't know how far, maybe fifteen feet, and just as I got to this big vault-like door cut into solid rock, lights started flashing. Freddie and two of his creeps showed up with guns and dogs. I couldn't believe it. Freddie was really pissed. He accused me of snooping. I told him that was bullshit. I told him I went up to the bookcase to look for a book because I couldn't sleep. I said when I pulled out a book the bookcase started to swing open."

"Did he believe you?"

"He didn't have any choice. Besides I was telling the truth. But I think he deals and I think that's where he keeps his stash."

"On a large scale?"

"Yeah. Now that I think of it. He was always getting beeped on his cell phone, then he'd go and use a special phone that probably had some kind of scrambler on it. Then some creepy-looking type would show up and they'd go upstairs."

"And he uses it himself?"

She shook her head to indicate incredulity. "You wouldn't believe it."

"Too much for you?"

She sipped her tea. "I don't mind doing a joint, you know, like, to get things going or slow things down, but he is really into heavy stuff."

"Like?"

"Cocaine. H. Ecstasy. Meth. You name it. It was everywhere."

"So when did things start to go . . . bad?"

"Some friends showed up. Business associates, he called them.

Real scaggy types. They had like these girls with them. I think they were hookers. That's when the handcuffs and the whips came out. You know, dog collars and chains."

"Was Celeste Tangent there?" I tried to sound casual.

"Yeah . . ." Her voice got wistful. "They have a thing."

"They?"

"Freddie and Celly. We all had a thing."

"The three of you?"

"Yeah. But it was too druggy to be real. Sixy would have loved it. You know, like his cut, 'Orifice Rex.' But it's not my scene. I mean they were putting dildos on dogs and trying to get a chain going. And then they had this mock wedding between a midget ballerina and one of the German shepherds. I'm so sick of that stuff. It's all fizz and no wine. And . . ."

"Yes?" I prompted after a pause.

"I think Freddie's starting to lose it." She pointed to her head.

"So you decided to leave?"

She sighed, as though it had cost her something. "Yeah. He wasn't going to let me go, though. He said no way, not now."

"How did you do it?"

"I took a walk and called a cab."

"With your walkaround phone."

"Yeah. The cabbie had a tough time finding it. Freddie was really pissed when he found I had called one and given it directions. He's like a dictator. He didn't want to let me go. But he knew you knew I was up there. It's like he owns people. And everyone's a slab of meat."

"He's a criminal, you know," I said.

"I can believe it."

"I don't say that just because he thinks Adolf Hitler was a

great artist. I mean he's a real criminal. He's part of organized crime."

Diantha stuck out her lower lip and nodded, but skeptically.

I related to her then what Agent Johnson and Sergeant Lemure had told me about his background. I went into some detail. One has to be careful these days in talking to young people. Criminality has taken on such glamour. But Diantha listened as though taken with my seriousness.

She got up to rinse her cup, and I noticed the way she wore her slacks, just like her mother had so many years ago. She turned to look at me. "Hate to rain on your parade, Dad, but I know firsthand that Freddie's not circumcised."

What is it about that kind of detail that cuts to the heart? Because I suffered then a keen and entirely inappropriate stab of retrospective jealousy. I can't explain it. Was I that smitten by my own stepdaughter? Was I to live in torture now until she found some suitable young man and went off to start a life of her own?

"Perhaps he faked that when he went through his 'conversion,'" I said, trying to keep my voice neutral.

"It wouldn't surprise me. Reality to him is what he says it is. The guy really is . . ."

"Solipsistic . . . self-absorbed."

"Yes. You always know things, do you know that?"

She smiled at me then, melting my heart, touching me in ways I'm sure she couldn't imagine. I was looking again at a young vibrant Elsbeth, and again experiencing a kind of temporal dislocation.

We decided we would go Christmas shopping together for some last-minute things. We would dine out first, shop, and then go to the midnight carol service at St. Cecilia's, the rather High

Episcopal church I attended with some regularity before Elsbeth arrived on the scene and changed my life.

I managed to get us a table at the Oriole in the Miranda, an old-fashioned place that serves excellent, old-fashioned food. Diantha had wild goose and I had tame steak, and we finished off a bottle and demi-bottle of decent wine. She couldn't quite stop talking about Freddie Bain, at the same time reaching over to touch my hand, as though clinging to me, as though torn between a rollicking life on a sybaritic if sinking pirate ship and austere survival on an odd bit of eroded rock jutting from the water.

We shopped halfheartedly for an hour or so, mostly walking off the wine, before making our way to the incensed interior of St. Cecilia's. There, for more than an hour, we lifted our voices and our hearts, bracing hope and beauty against the solstistial darkness. Elsbeth and I had come here each of the last three years, and my eyes watered when we sang the verses of one of her favorites:

In the bleak midwinter,
frosty winds may moan,
earth stood hard as iron,
water like a stone;
snow had fallen,
snow on snow, snow on snow,
in the bleak midwinter, long ago.

God is good, I thought. Had He not sent His only son as a reassurance? Of course, we had nailed Him to a tree and left Him to die. And we've celebrated His death ever since. I put such thoughts aside and thanked fate that Diantha was with me and safe.

Afterward, outside, I noticed that Diantha had tears shining in her eyes. I tried to comfort her.

"Oh, Norman," she cried, clinging to me again. "I don't know what to do."

"About what, darling?" I said.

"About Freddie. I know he's a creep. I know he's crazy. I know he's a monster. It doesn't matter. I can't help it. I love him."

35

Something horrific has happened, something so personal, so shattering, and yet so poignant, I scarcely know where to begin. Indeed, I would not begin at all were it not pertinent to account for the strange happenings that have rocked our little community to its very foundations.

I have just returned from the Seaboard Police Department headquarters. (I'm sorry if this seems disjointed, but I am agitated beyond words.) We've finally had a real break in the case, but at an awful price. I sit here in my high study, my father's .38-caliber Smith & Wesson at the ready, my hands afflicted by a telltale tremor.

Let me start at the beginning.

Earlier this evening Diantha and I returned from a meeting with the Reverend Lopes and Father O'Gould to make arrangements for Elsbeth's memorial service at Swift Chapel. Such matters are draining. They take an emotional toll the worse for not being expected. What order of service? What hymns? (For instance, one of Elsbeth's favorites was Mendelssohn's "Why Do the Heathens Rage?" But it didn't seem appropriate to the occasion.) Who speaks? What about the reception?

At any rate, upon returning home, we felt simply too tired to cook anything for ourselves. Indeed, we were too drained even to contemplate going out for a quick bite. Ordinarily I do not enjoy sent-out food, the kind that arrives in white cardboard containers with plastic accoutrements and little pouches of condiments.

But to indulge Diantha, whose spirits had ebbed woefully low, I agreed to call the Jade Stalk and order from a veritable laundry list of Chinese food. We ticked off black bean shrimp, some kind of shredded beef, sweet-and-sour something or other, and rice, of course.

I presently poured a glass of chilled white wine for Diantha and made myself a martini of lethal potency with at least three shots of good gin and a fair dollop of vermouth, which I chilled briefly over ice before pouring it into a frosted glass with an unpitted olive. I had just had the barest sip when the bell rang. I opened the door to find a young man of Asian aspect holding a white bag stapled shut with the cash register printout attached. I paid him the requisite amount, gave him a generous tip, thanked him, and closed the door. I took the bag of food and my drink into the television room, where Diantha was arranging plates and silver on the ample coffee table between the couch and massive screen of the television.

"Smells good," she said, smiling at me. "I'm famished."

"Yes," I agreed. "It's quite appealing when you present it on a dish." We were each ladling generous amounts onto our plates. Some sort of police drama from the big city was on the television, one of those improbable tales of murder and mayhem with people yelling at one another and exchanging significant glances in between scuffling with criminal types. I never really pay much attention. To me most of what's on television constitutes a kind of moving wallpaper with noise.

"The black bean shrimp is divine," I remember Diantha saying. In one of those endearing, almost intimate gestures that occur between two people who are close, she held over a heaping forkful for me to take. We ate in greedy silence for perhaps ten or fifteen minutes. Diantha had switched the channel to what's called a situation comedy, a low form of humor in which people make wisecracks about their bodily functions, contort themselves like idiots, and mug for the camera, all to the sound of canned laughter. Yet I was glad to see Diantha respond even to this meager fare, because of late she had become withdrawn and moody. I had taken just the merest sip of my martini, saving it for a postprandial. I remember thinking I should have made tea instead when Diantha turned from the television, let out a low moan, put down her plate with a clatter, and turned to me. "Norman, Norman," she said breathlessly, her eyes going wide, her mouth opening. In one quite amazing gesture, she reached under her skirt and peeled off her panties and nylon tights. She leaned back, opened her legs to me and implored, "Norman, please, Norman, please."

I might not have resisted even if, a minute or so later in time that had gone out of focus, the most powerful erotic sensation I have ever experienced had not rocked my entire body. I cried out a futile "no" but was already unbuckling myself, had turned into a veritable satyr, engorged as I have never been in my life. I was in the grip of a passion too urgent to allow for anything as basic as pleasure let alone the more tender delights of love-making. We conjoined with a thrusting, uncontrolled violence, a frenzy beyond passion or love, a kind of injuring madness as we pounded at each other, snarling and biting like panicked animals.

Don't ask me what made me do what I did to save us. In the midst of the madness, as I pummeled Diantha and she pummeled back, our voices shrieking and groaning like two demented demons, some minuscule particle of ordinary sense remained intact in what was left of my mind. Because, on some inexplicable impulse, springing no doubt from that tiny remnant of normalcy, I reached over, grabbed my martini, and, before much of it spilled in the heave and shove of our frenzy, managed to swallow it down, nearly choking on the olive, which lodged for a moment in my throat before I managed to swallow it.

Mirabile dictu, it worked. Not right away, but a minute or so later, I experienced a prodigious, prolonged emission. I immediately lost the insane compulsion I was under, but detumesced only slowly. I was then able to subdue Diantha enough to get her to swig from the gin bottle that I hastened to bring her. She convulsed orgasmically as well, then fell weeping into my arms, her tears dampening the top of my shirt. When she lifted her swollen eyes to mine, she said, "They're trying to kill us, aren't they?"

"Trying to kill me, at any rate," I said, treading between the risk of sounding self-important and the need to reassure her.

"It's horrible, horrible," she cried, ready to weep again. Then she said something that startled me. "That's not the way I would have wanted it to happen . . ."

"I know," I said placatingly.

We were silent for a moment as acknowledgment registered. Neither of us, I think, was sorry that it had happened — only how.

She gave a tearful little laugh. "You're quite the stud, Norman, you know that?"

I stammered something about overplaying the part. By then I had made myself presentable. Before I left her so she could do the same, I told her to stay in the television room while I checked the doors and windows.

"You mean they could still be around?" She pulled on her panties without any false modesty. It seemed as though, in some strange way, we were already a couple.

I went then and fetched the revolver. I loaded it carefully and put it in the holster, which I had strapped on under my arm. The holster still smelled reassuringly of new leather. I went downstairs and, on some instinct, opened the front door to check outside.

Surprise, strangely enough, is often sharper when you expect something rather than the reverse. I all but jumped at the sight of the deliveryman coming up the front walk carrying what looked like a video camera. But I wasn't nearly as startled as he was. He turned immediately and ran out the gate and up the street. I pursued, drawing my revolver, and calling for him to stop. I saw him climb into one of those truck-like station wagons and drive away. I suppose I could have, as in the films, fired at him, making him skid out of control and crash dramatically into an abutment. But I lack the killer instinct, or whatever it takes to do that. I did manage to get the first four numbers on the license plate.

I rushed back into the house and quickly explained what had happened to Diantha. She stood by calm and collected as I telephoned Lieutenant Tracy on his private line. I gave him as dispassionate an account of what had transpired as I could muster, telling him about the suspect, where he worked, the kind of car he was driving, and what I had of the license plate number.

The lieutenant was most sympathetic. He asked if there was anything we needed. He said he would call headquarters right away and then call back in a few minutes.

Diantha and I sat on the couch holding hands for a while. Though we were both scared and excited, I think we were both thinking about what had happened, about the intimate aspects of it, and how that might change our lives. It might mean, for instance, that she would no longer be able to live in the house with me. As though intuiting my thoughts, she touched my face. "Norman, I don't want this . . . to come between us. I mean it doesn't have to start anything or stop anything. I don't want to move out."

I nodded. I said, "I don't want you to. I know Elsbeth is hardly gone from us, but . . ."

Diantha laughed. "She would mind much less than you think. She told me to take care of you."

"But not like that."

"Who knows?"

Just then the phone rang. It was Lieutenant Tracy. He said he would come by to drive us down to Keller Infirmary to have blood samples taken. He said not to touch any of the leftover food. He would bring a crime scene crew to go over everything. He said they also had a safe house where Diantha could spend the night if she felt threatened.

When I related the lieutenant's offer she shook her head. "No way. I'm staying with you."

Well, to make a long story short, we went to Keller, gave blood, and then went with Lieutenant Tracy to the home of the delivery-man, which the police had ascertained through his employers. I counted no less than five cruisers on the scene, some of them with their lights flashing. It turned out to be a lavishly appointed condominium in one of the better downtown neighborhoods, certainly not the kind of place one would expect to be inhabited by a delivery boy from a restaurant.

The lieutenant told us, on the way over, that the restaurant owners had been very cooperative. They said Bob Fang, the deliveryman, had worked for them nearly a year, had been reli-able, but had wanted to remain a delivery boy even though they offered to make him a waiter, which pays much more.

Sergeant Lemure was already there with another crime scene crew. There were signs of a hasty departure, with drawers pulled open, items strewn about, the back door ajar.

"He looks like he was searching for something to take with him," the lieutenant remarked. "Perhaps we'll find it instead."

After a few moments there, he drove us home. He arranged to have a cruiser drive by every hour. I carefully locked all the outside doors. I have left the door to my attic eyrie open to keep an ear, so to speak, on Diantha. She finally drifted off into a deep sleep in her room, which is down the corridor from mine. What a night this has been.

I can only be thankful there was no one else here to join us for supper, say Alfie Lopes or one of the neighbors. It boggles the mind what might have happened.

36

It is New Year's Day and I am in a hellish quandary. Diantha
has gone back to that ridiculous gangster and that absurd pile in
the woods, and I don't know whether she has been kidnapped
or not. She may simply be suffering from the common illusion
that love conquers all. There must be some evolutionary advantage to self-deception. How else to explain its prevalence among
the human species? Especially when it comes to love. Especially
among women.

Well, not just women. Since the incident with the doctored
food, I have harbored the hope, however unrealistic, that
Diantha would take Elsbeth's place in my life. Several times I
have been on the point of declaration, suggestion, even action.
But I have not been able to turn myself into a gallant suitor,
bringing her roses and lighting candles. I have been, as I should
remain, hamstrung by scruple. I am in mourning for my beloved
wife. The figurative black band is around my heart as well as
my arm.

At the same time, I fear that in temporizing with Diantha I
have lost her as I lost her mother so many years ago. For courting
too slow, as the song has it. Not that Diantha has been open to
any real advances had I made them. She has been in turn flirta-
tious, gay in a semi-hysteria, drawing me on then laughing me
off when I have reciprocated in the slightest way; and then silent,
her eyes avoiding mine. I have heard her talking at length on that
little phone of hers behind the closed door of her bedroom.

All the while I have been subject to a kind of sensual haunting. Diantha did love me, after all, if only under the sway of that pernicious potion. And I almost willingly delude myself that, despite the grotesque circumstances, we had made love rather than merely raped each other.

Our coexistence without Elsbeth here would not have been easy in any event. It is difficult and soul trying to stay vigilant. It was a strain to be cooped up, especially given the way things were developing between us. I did go to work, impersonating myself as museum Director. When absent from home I made sure that a cruiser drove by the house at regular intervals. I called to check on Diantha to the point, I'm afraid, that I annoyed her. But what else could I do? An attempt had been made on our lives.

Indeed, Lieutenant Tracy called yesterday at the museum with some preliminary results on the food brought to us from the Chinese restaurant. It was saturated with the compounds that had been given to Ossmann and Woodley, Bert and Betti, and probably Spronger and Jones. It had been, in short, nothing other than attempted murder.

Something had to give, and it did. About midmorning the day after New Year's, Diantha called me at the office to let me know that she was driving over to the supermarket at Northgate Mall to shop for groceries. And, in fact, we had run quite low on things. I cautioned her to be careful. I told her to park as close as she could to the door of the store, even at the risk of getting a ticket. She said she would be very careful, and I believed she would be.

I came home in the early afternoon to find she hadn't returned. I called her pocket phone number several times. It rang and rang, the last time in sync with a faint echo coming from upstairs. I went up and found it on her bureau. I didn't know what to do. I perhaps should have called Lieutenant Tracy then, but Diantha is, as they say, a free agent.

I finally took a cab down to a car rental outlet and obtained the use of a small inconspicuous sedan. I drove over to the mall and searched every conceivable parking place for my little car, but to no avail. Then, with my heart lurching, I drove out to that monster's lair in the woods, all the while rehearsing my rebuttals to his provocative remarks about God, art, Hitler, and history. I composed stinging ripostes that sent Freddie/Manfred Bain/Bannerhoff reeling.

Until, arriving there, I found I really had no words. Because what could I say, I wondered, as, through a gap in the trees some distance from that ludicrous bastion, I could clearly see my little Peugeot docilely parked next to an expensive English car. I suppose she could have been carjacked, as they say these days. Mostly, I hate to admit, I was fearful of appearing like some old besotted fool, knocking on the door, hat in hand, a beggar for love. Because however trenchant my speech to him, what claims, really, could I make on her?

Perhaps I should call Lieutenant Tracy, but I have no real proof of anything. I would be loath to tell him what may be the truth: that Diantha prefers that ogre to this ogre.

Because now my imagination works in feverish double time conjuring all sorts of debauchery out at that ridiculous place where Sir Walter Scott meets the Third Reich. Manfred Bannerhoff aka Freddie Bain is not circumcised. Why does her knowing that torture me? Why can I visualize so acutely her fondling, her submission, her hunger for that prick's prick? There, I have, finally, been reduced to vulgarity. I want to take my gun and . . . I am nearly mad.

37

The nature of Diantha's absence became terribly apparent when I answered a knock on the door yesterday morning to find one of the boys who live in the neighborhood standing there with a note in his hand. "I'm supposed to give this to you, mister. Number sixty-eight, right?"

"Right," I said, taking the plain white envelope. "Who gave it to you?"

"A guy on a motorcycle."

"What did he look like?"

"I couldn't tell. He had his visor down. He gave me ten bucks and told me to wait ten minutes before I rang your bell."

"Can you remember anything about him?"

"No, but he was driving a really cool Hog."

"I see. Well, thank you."

I don't know how I remained so outwardly calm as premonitory alarm made my hands shake. When the door closed, I tore open the envelope. In block print script it said:

IF YOU WANT TO SEE YOUR PRECIOUS DI AGAIN, OLD MAN, BE HERE PRECISELY AT NOON TOMORROW, ALONE. WE'LL TRADE. HER LIFE FOR THE TAPE. ANY WHISPER OF THIS TO THE AUTHORITIES AND SHE'LL BE DEAD MEAT.

At first I did not know what to do other than call Lieutenant Tracy and leave the matter in his competent hands. But I knew

Manfred Bannerhoff and what he was capable of. I knew I was dealing with a psychopath. I also knew that if I simply went there, he would probably kill us both. The hopelessness of the situation made me fall into a lethargy of despair. The only real recourse was to call the police and take the chance that they would find her and rescue her before this maniac could wreak his revenge on her. But I could not bring myself to do it.

I struggled for some time with these demons. Poor Diantha, I thought. What terrors she must be going through! And I helpless to help her. Half of the time I was on the verge of calling Lieutenant Tracy; half, on the verge of making a big pitcher of martinis and rendering myself insensate.

Then the determination to rescue her myself fired me with resolve. Absurd, yes. But in nightmares begin responsibilities. I had my father's trusty gun. I am physically in shape thanks to my daily walking back and forth to work. It's true that I'm not particularly fearless. But love and desperation gave me courage, however phantasmal. Like one of those revelations that make you into another person, I realized I was willing to die for Diantha.

But also, I'd like to think I'm smart, smarter than Freddie Bain, anyway. So how to go about it? How to storm that fortress-like den of depraved absurdity? After a few moments of pacing and thinking, I drove out to an older mall located on the south side of the city. There, as I remembered, was an establishment called Things for the Wild. It's been taken over by a chain, clearly, but it still had most the items I needed.

"Camping," I said to the young lady who approached and asked if she could help. "I'll need rugged hiking boots, thermal underwear, some climbing rope."

For rescue purposes, I suppose, much of the outerwear came in bright colors. I managed to find some that were nearly white. We spent a good hour and a half at it. I bought crampons, an ice ax, a wrist compass. By the time we finished, I could have ascended Mount Everest, especially if Diantha were up there for me to fetch. I doubted my chances at the Eigermount would be any better.

My final item was the US Geological Survey map of the area. "Near Tinkerton," I told her. It took us a while, but we finally found one. It was the last copy. Fate, I thought, was on my side. I paid at the register and took my considerable bundles out to the car. Standing there in the innocent parking lot, quotidian life bustling all about me, I wondered if I was simply indulging a silly fantasy. Then I thought of Diantha, of the suffering she must be going through, and my determination returned stronger than ever.

At home I laid out the map on the kitchen table. It was relatively easy, starting in Tinkerton and following the road to where it crosses Alkins Creek, to locate the wretched place even though there was no little black square to indicate its existence. From the contour lines, I determined that the building was set against the west side of a high long hill, as much a ridge as a small mountain. The approaches from the other side of the rise were steep, forming two mounts with a dip in between, a saddleback. Below that, down a short, steep slope, I would find the back of the structure. I saw how I could drive in on another road from the east to within two and a half miles. I could arrive at dawn, climb through the woods to the back, and take them by surprise.

By surprise? Wouldn't he have some kind of security system? Those awful lights that go on when they detect movement? Video cameras that see in the dark? All of the above as well as dogs? The thought of dogs daunted me the most. Dogs like me, but I have never been comfortable around them. Dogs, I thought, pacing the kitchen lengthwise. Then I remembered how, in some film I had watched with Elsbeth, the good guys had neutralized the vigilant canines with doped meat.

Why not do the same? I drove out immediately to a local grocery store and purchased two pounds of very lean hamburger. I also bought myself some of those high-energy snacks. On the way home I stopped to fill my little rental car with gas and check the oil and tires. Back in the kitchen, I retrieved some of the pain medicine, a potent form of synthetic morphine, that Elsbeth had taken in her final illness. I took all but one of the pills and rendered them to a white powder in the small stone mortar and pestle my father had brought back decades ago from Central America. This I mixed with about three-quarters of the hamburger. I then wrapped the doped meat in a plastic bag and put it in the rugged little knapsack I had purchased.

I also fetched the tape of Corny's death from an old safe I have here in the house. I wrapped it twice in plastic bags and secured it in a side pocket of the parka.

For a meal I took the remainder of the meat and made myself a big hamburger, which I slathered with mustard and ketchup, put between two pieces of bread, and ate with a beer.

I moved as if in a dream. I laid out my kit — boots and crampons, thermal underwear and socks made of something called polypropylene, the long-handled climbing ax, the wrist compass, my revolver with an extra box of steel-jacketed rounds, the high-energy snacks, a headlamp of the kind miners wear, Gore-Tex overalls and hooded jacket, insulated gloves, and an old hunting knife I received one Christmas as a teenager.

It was late afternoon when I unplugged the phones and set a couple of alarm clocks to ring at two the next morning. I went upstairs, took the morphine pill with a glass of water, and got into bed. To my surprise, in retrospect, I fell asleep not long afterward.

The two clocks brought me up from an energizing nightmare about dogs and darkness. Fully conscious within seconds, I turned off the alarms and went downstairs. I dressed effectively and quickly while the coffee brewed. It was snowing when I opened the door to load the car. It had been snowing for some time, and I wondered if the roads into the mountains would be passable. It didn't matter. I would get there one way or another.

How warm and comfortable I felt in my mountaineering clothes! How snug the revolver felt just under the jacket, under my arm in its leather holster. I also tucked in the small portable phone Diantha had left on a bureau upstairs. I thought it might come in handy.

I had not counted on a real nor'easter, blowing and snowing like the end of the world. The rented car, wearing snow tires, did very well in the snow. We poked our way out into the ghostly swirl, the streetlights glowing through the moving veils of the storm, the *chunk, chunk* of plows sounding along the bypass.

Nibbling at a snack, sipping coffee from the thermos cup, I got in behind one of those rumbling monsters and let it lay down a swath of sanded salt for me to follow. It all seemed both dream-like and very real. I was nearly hyperconscious. I knew I could take the interstate to an exit not far from Tinkerton. I would walk from there if I had to!

Surprisingly enough, I was able to drive relatively close to my projected destination. I didn't do anything theatrical like try to hide the car. I simply found the inlet to a logging road, stopped, backed up, and gave the vehicle enough momentum to plow its way well in off the road.

In the dark and the silent snowfall, I sat in the car, the lamp on my forehead playing a spot of light over the survey map. I esti-mated I was just short of two miles on the Remsdale Road from where it crossed Biggins Brook, a tributary to Alkins Creek. The map showed the logging road as a track. If I followed it about a mile and then turned north, it would bring me to the foot of the hill I needed to ascend to get to the back of the house.

Wondering again if I wasn't demented, I started into the dark along the logging road. The wind blew, and the snow bit into my face. The illumination from my headlamp played feebly but adequately over the terrain ahead. I realized I should have bought a pair of those small snowshoes because in places my boots broke through the crust, and I found myself struggling, floundering, and almost foundering several times. I should also have carried a GPS device. I nearly lost heart several times, my progress seemed so slow even while on the remnant road. How could I surprise anyone if I arrived in full daylight?

I became so warm I had to open my coat. The wind picked up high in the trees, and the snow deepened the farther I penetrated into the wilderness. I stopped to rest several times. I finished the coffee and put the thermos into my backpack. The whirling snow grew so thick at times, I had difficulty keeping on the road. But I kept going. I kept thinking of Diantha. Even if I were to fail, it might be of some comfort to her to know I had tried.

After what I took to be a mile, I turned off the rough road and started through the woods in a northward direction, checking the compass as I went. The going got very difficult indeed. Beneath the newly fallen snow was an older layer, treacherous, holding firm one moment and then letting me fall through to my waist the next. Looking back, I don't know what possessed me to keep plowing on. The wireless phone in my pocket suddenly seemed like the most important thing I had brought along. It was my out, as they say. I could always call the operator and get through to the SPD and Lieutenant Tracy. Tell him what the situation was and what I was doing.

I kept going. The hill grew increasingly steep. I stopped to strap on the crampons. In places I had to hook the spiked end of the climbing ax on trees ahead of me to pull my way up. Under a rock ledge I hunkered to eat an energy snack and drink from the canteen hanging from my belt. It was already nearly six o'clock, and I knew that, even with the snow and overcast, it would be light by the time I reached the madman's lair; the advantage of darkness would be gone.

I kept climbing. I felt at times as though I had entered a kind of twilight zone, a realm of unreality in which I was dead and would, with the pain of hope in my heart, spend eternity climbing through snow, wind, and darkness toward an ever-receding destination.

Inwardly, as in a hallucination, I ranted at Freddie Bain and heard his smirking replies. Hitler did not triumph! I shouted at him. Then why, Norman, are we still talking about him? Hitler is dead! Then why, Mr. de Ratour, do we need to keep killing him? Because, you swine, it's fun. Hitler was a failed artist! Not by twentieth-century standards, *mon vieux*. God is good! God is smiling, my friend, as you fumble toward your doom.

But the wind eased, the snow abated, and the lilac light of dawn filtered through the trees like an ethereal mist. Its subtle splendor would have enchanted me under other circumstances, would have made me ponder the mystery of so much gratuitous beauty, had it not disheartened me as an impediment to my plans. I struggled on, the dawn brightening into day, until I noticed, up ahead, through the trees, a patch of blue sky.

I came out finally onto a clearing, and my heart faltered once more. I could clearly see the twin peaks and the saddleback they formed between them. But they seemed so far away. And the sun shone in full reflected glory. Jays called. Chickadees came down to visit me. I checked to make sure I still had my revolver and continued my grim journey.

It was seven o'clock before I reached the low point between the two modest summits. I tried to keep under cover, but I'm sure anyone on the lookout could have seen me. Exhausted, but with adrenaline pumping through me painfully, I gained the actual ridge and peered down through the trees to the bastion below. It looked well nigh impregnable. Indeed, it appeared like a fortress anchored to the mountainside by the wide bridge, forming the shape of keyhole.

I took out my birding binoculars and swept over the scene several times. The long drive into the place and the walks had been shoveled. It struck me that I could just as well have driven over, parked down the drive, and walked in. Still, it looked peaceful, the narrow mullioned windows glinting and winking, the greenhouse shedding its cover of white so that the blue dazzle of pool water showed through a clear pane. I saw no movement as I panned the scene for several minutes. Then I noticed, looking up at me, as though expecting me, a huge German shepherd. It had come out of a kennel near a door toward the back, where a deck off the lower bridge part led to a path that went along the slope.

I ducked back under cover and took off my knapsack. I would drug the beast using the doctored meat. But first I took out the wireless phone. After a few attempts I got through to the switchboard at the SPD. I gave them the three-letter emergency code for Lieutenant Tracy. They put me through to his home. The connection wasn't good. I explained to him where I was and what I was doing.

"Norman, stay where you are," he kept saying. "We'll handle this from here. Don't go any farther."

"You don't know how insane he is," I said. "The first sign of a police cruiser and he'll go berserk."

"Norman, don't do it."

"I'm going in, Lieutenant," I practically shouted into the receiver as the wind, picking up again in that open space, made a racket around me. "It's her only chance."

"Norman . . ."

But I had clicked it off.

I made the bag of doped hamburger handy, hoisted my knapsack back on, took a deep breath, and started, as furtively as I could, down the steep slope toward the back of the house. I stopped every once in a while to check through my binoculars. The dog clearly knew I was there, but it didn't bark. *Nice puppy,* I said to it softly, *nice puppy.*

The going was rough, precarious. The wind had scoured the area of fresh snow. Iced-over ledges showed through the sparse vegetation. I must have been no more than a hundred feet from where the dog waited when I lost my footing and took an awful spill. I managed, almost by instinct, to complete a self-arrest using the ice ax. I bruised my arm and scraped my face. I watched helplessly as the bag of meat in its fragile covering slid down the smoothly crusted snow toward the dog.

For a moment I was utterly disheartened. Surely the animal would bark now and give the alarm. Instead, miraculously, it left the small deck and with clumsy determination, made its way up to where the meat had snagged on a bush poking through the snow. I watched with bated breath as it nosed the pack, pawed at it, and finally freed the hamburger from the plastic bag. It wolfed the meat down in a matter of seconds.

It didn't take long to have an effect. The dog looked up to where I crouched, turned, and started back toward the house, its footing unsteady. Not far from the deck it stopped, sat down, and then lay down. I reached it not long afterward. I think it was dead. But I had no time for regrets about a dog, whatever its innocence. My blood pounded so fiercely I could scarcely think.

As stealthily as I could, I made my way to the deck where the dog had its kennel.

A formidable oaken door, studded and barred like those of a medieval keep, led into the house from the deck. For a handle it had a great wrought-iron ring. As quietly as I could, I twisted the ring, felt it give and click. With an ominous creak, the door swung open. I found myself in a dark passage, the darker for my pupils being contracted against the sunstruck snow. I paused a moment. A kind of pantry, curved with the exterior of the building, led off to the right into what I presumed was the kitchen. A bathroom opened to the left. I could see light coming from under the door ahead of me.

I did not have the presence of mind to take out my revolver. I did not have the presence of mind to skirt around the main part of the house through the kitchen. I simply went ahead and started to push open the door in front of me.

It was opened for me with a sudden jerk. I was taken roughly by the arm from the side and propelled into the center of the vast circular space I remembered, as in a nightmare, from my previous visit. Over against the fireplace, on the raised stone area, seated like some kind of petty potentate, was Manfred Bannerhoff, aka Freddie Bain. Near him on the couch sat Diantha, her face drawn and worried.

"Welcome, welcome, Mr. de Ratour. You're just in time for breakfast. We've been expecting you, haven't we, Diantha. That's okay, Fang, you can let him go. He's not going to do anything."

"Norman!" Diantha cried, rising as though from a deathbed trance.

"Diantha." I started toward her.

"Stay where you are, both of you, unless . . ."

I stopped. It wasn't only the mesmeric powers in his striking eyes. Fang, whom I recognized as the delivery boy from the Jade Stalk, and two well-muscled young men hovered in the background.

Bain pointed to a large television screen next to the fireplace. "We have been enjoying the show, Norman. A jolly good show." He flicked at a remote control. A moment later I appeared on the screen, emerging from the woods above the building. "Such a hero. Such a fool." I was looking down with my binoculars. "We've all had a great laugh, Norman. There you are. Now we can't see you. You must be behind the rock, getting ready for your assault." I watched, glanced over to Diantha. *Are you all right?* I mouthed silently. She nodded. I turned back to the monitor. At least they hadn't seen me making the phone call.

"Now here's the best part," my awful host announced. On the screen I was trying to get down the steep, windblown slope of iced-over snow. Suddenly, I fall and tumble over several times before I stop myself. The view cuts to a wide angle, and the dog can be seen making its way up to the doctored meat. "Poor Mitzi," Freddie Bain said. "What did you put in the meat, Norman?"

"Morphine," I said.

Bain laughed his mean laugh. "She overdosed, like so many of my good friends." Then his laugh died to a snarl. He came toward me. "Mitzi was my friend. She took good care of me. You killed her. And I'm going to kill you, old man, with my bare hands. But first, did you bring the tape?"

"I have it."

"Give it to me."

"I will leave it in the foyer as Diantha and I leave."

Madness showed in his face. "You old fool! You give it now or . . . I will kill both of you with my bare hands." He laughed. "Or should we inject them with enough of our new potion and let them go at it in the cage, eh, Fang?"

Fang, who had moved away from me, gave a sycophantic laugh along with the other two.

As much to stall for time, I said, "Is that what you did with Ossmann and Woodley?"

"I'm afraid so. Professor Ossmann proved uncooperative in the end."

"So you're the one behind the whole deadly business?"

"Business is right." He smiled wickedly. "When I see a business opportunity, I take it."

"From whom did you take it?"

"Oh, from poor Ossmann, of course. But he, I'm sure, took it from someone else. Now, give me the tape . . ."

"What do you plan to do with the . . . potion?"

"Free trade, *mon vieux*, free trade. I will ship it by the carload to the Far East, and, of course, bring back various controlled substances by the carload . . ."

"A regular businessman, I see."

His smile became a scowl. He started toward me and stopped. "No, *Herr Directkor,* not a regular businessman. I will be a force to be reckoned with. I will wreak my vengeance."

"On whom?"

A thin smile shaped his lips. "On history, my friend, on history."

"I thought you said history comes and goes." Though fearful I had botched everything, that Diantha and I were both doomed, I still had this compulsion to argue with him.

"Yes. And I will make it stop."

"Make history stop? Of course, that is the essence of despotism, isn't it?"

"I am not in the mood for dialectical diversions, old man. Now the tape. I paid good money for it. Give it here."

"First — "

"No first!" he shouted. "You are not here to dictate terms. Perhaps if we started on Miss Lowe that would convince you."

As he turned toward her, I reached into my coat and took out the Smith & Wesson.

Manfred Bannerhoff stopped and threw back his head in a laugh. He turned to the others. "Oh, my goodness, fellas, look, Mr. de Ratour has a weapon."

"Listen . . . damn you," I said, determined to get my points across.

Turning toward me, his face malignant, he snarled, "No, you listen, Gramps. Face it, you don't have the balls to use that thing, so give it to me before you hurt yourself with it."

He was right. I felt like some small beast transfixed by the eyes of a cobra. I could not move. A fatal paralysis froze my limbs, my hands, my fingers. But not my mind, not the urge to beat him with words. "You're wrong," I snapped, fierce with refutation. Referring to something entirely different, I began, "Hitler —"

When he laughed, interrupting me, dismissively shaking his head, I felt the gun jump in my hand. The sound came like an aural shock from afar. More than anything, I think now, I was trying to get his attention. I hadn't even been aiming the thing, just pointing, but the bullet caught his left upper thigh. He went down on his knees, cursing and holding his leg. The other two started toward me and stopped when I swung the gun directly them. Fang uttered a cry and ran off behind the door I had come through, followed by the others.

"You son of bitch," Mr. Bannerhoff cried. "You old . . ." He reached under his tunic and pulled out a Luger.

I fired again, catching him in the right shoulder, making him drop the gun, which clattered to the floor in front of him. He looked at me, his rage turning to amazement. "You, you . . . ," he muttered.

"I mean it," I said, still wanting him to pay heed. "Adolf Hitler was no artist."

He lunged for the Luger, screaming in German. I fired again, aiming at his heart. He went down with a thump and lay still. Blood began to pool around him on the polished wood of the floor, just like in the movies.

"And God is not a joker."

I spoke loudly, with bravado, knowing I had won the argument. But I was far more certain of my first utterance than of my second. I also felt a strange vacuity. You cannot argue with the dead.

It turned into a blur after that. The three men had disappeared. I could hear a helicopter approaching. I took Diantha in my arms and held her. Then, the gun still in my hand, I led her out the way I had come in. We went out past the still Mitzi and up a way along the hillside. I gave her my parka, and we hid in a stand of thick hemlocks.

Presently a helicopter from the SPD hovered a hundred feet off the deck, its loudspeaker booming orders for everyone to throw down their weapons and come out with their hands up. Not long after that, several skimobiles rocketed out into the woods from a basement garage. We could hear gunfire, sirens, men shouting. Then, after what seemed an age, we were both in the back of a four-wheel-drive police vehicle. I was wrapped in a blanket. My teeth chattered, but not from the cold.

There's more. But I can't keep going right now. I'm dead, dead tired. I'm going to bed, to sleep.

38

The repercussions of the Love Potion Murders, as this curious tale has come to be called, are going to reverberate for some time for myself, for the museum, and for the larger Seaboard community. There has been considerable media hoopla. There were calls from some quarters for a full investigation of Freddie Bain's death even after it became apparent that I had "taken out" a major drug lord.

Then, as more details came to light, I had to endure the fickle adulation of the media. At the same time, there remains some concern for the safety of both Diantha and myself in terms of possible mob revenge. Actually, I am more worried that some distant relative of Mr. Bannerhoff/Bain will show up with a lawyer in tow claiming wrongful death.

I would like to have it generally known that I do not feel smug in the least about killing Freddie Bain, however richly he deserved to die. Though under duress at the time, though fearful for my life and Diantha's, I question my motives. Mostly, I fear that I shot him in the heat of an argument. And that is the way despots win arguments — by imposing the ultimate silence. I take some small comfort in the more likely possibility that I killed him because of Diantha; that it was, ultimately, a crime of passion. Who will ever know? In life, unlike in art, loose ends seldom get tidily tied up.

What happened to Celeste Tangent, for instance? Well, she simply disappeared. Perhaps she had divined earlier than most that her erstwhile colleague, Manfred aka Freddie, was going off the tracks. When the Seaboard police, armed with a warrant, searched her apartment, they found evidence that she was long gone. I trust that, given her wiles and other endowments, she will survive quite well.

Lieutenant Tracy tells me that the SPD, now pretty much under the thumb of the FBI in this investigation, has a good idea of how Mr. Bain conducted his business. For some time various federal agencies had been suspicious about the shipping coming and going at Clipper Wharf. The theory, promulgated by the FBI, was that he was using the import and export of highly aromatic spices to mask a far more lucrative drug trade. Apparently not. Instead the wharf, the restaurant, and the spice trade were merely a distraction. Most of his contraband came in on one of the larger trawlers using another dock. This ocean-going vessel "fished" specially wrapped and buoyed bundles of narcotics dropped off by tramp freighters far out to sea. Those little GPS devices come in handy for ill as well as for good.

Indeed, it turns out that Mr. Bain's castle in the woods contained only his private supply of controlled substances. This was found, cleverly hidden, in a chamber quarried out of the mountain's granite core, where he maintained a shrine to the memory of Adolph Hitler and the Third Reich. Along with bits and pieces of Wehrmacht memorabilia, the usual flags and rags, there was a fountain pen supposedly used by the *Führer* and an ornamental dagger with a handle of early plastic, remarkably like ivory, adorned at the top with a swastika inside a circle.

It's quite clear from the evidence gathered so far that Mr. Bannerhoff/Bain planned, as he told me on that fateful day, to export the powerful aphrodisiac being developed covertly at the lab in exchange for illegal drugs. What he intended to do with the enormous sums generated by such commerce remains a secret he took with him to his grave.

Dr. Penrood, I regret to say, has been deeply implicated in this matter. Among his papers in the Genetics Lab, investigators found a detailed account of how things transpired. It appears that Professor Ossmann, in his work on the hangover drug ReLease, came across a compound — first noted in the research of Dr. Woodley and Professor Tromstromer — which he dubbed JJA-48. It reportedly triggers the vascular dilation needed for an erection far faster and more aggressively than anything in Viagra, for instance. He combined this with other compounds and with a cocktail of psychoactive drugs that act directly on those parts of the brain involved with sexual urges.

Dr. Penrood found out about the experiments through a routine inquiry into the disappearance of the small mammals Professor Ossmann was working on. When Penrood confronted Ossmann with his suspicions and threatened a thorough review by a committee of his peers, the latter decided to include the Director in his scheme. Basically, they were to repeat some of the experiments openly and proceed through the usual channels in developing and testing the aphrodisiac.

Freddie Bain found out about the experiments through Celeste Tangent. She, in her role as a provider of escort services, had "escorted" Dr. Penrood on one of his trips to a research conference in Atlanta. Penrood, smitten with her, not only told her what was afoot, but took her on as a laboratory assistant. She, Bain's sex and drug slave, in turn made Penrood her sex and drug slave. I certainly cannot excuse Dr. Penrood's behavior, but I think I understand it.

There remain other details yet to be cleared up. Mr. Fang, who is very well lawyered, has said little to date as he maneuvers for some plea bargaining. It is not clear, for instance, how he knew Ossmann and Woodley would be in the lab together that fateful night. It's not clear how he inveigled both of them to eat the food from the Garden of Delights that he or someone unknown had doctored with the fatal potion.

Speaking of which, and perhaps not all that surprisingly, the Ponce Institute has already come up with the trade names Priaptin — the version being developed for men — and Lubricitin for women. Another team has taken over the project, and the Acting Director at the lab tells me it shows enormous commercial potential.

A thorough search of that monstrosity in the woods turned up the cellar room where Korky had been kept on a starvation diet. Korky appears, by the way, to have landed on his feet. With the cooperation of many of the *haute cuisine* restaurants in and around Seaboard, he has opened up a soup kitchen for the homeless dubbed "the Best Leftovers." It uses surplus food from the sponsoring eateries and aims at "personal redemption through fine dining." It's been so successful that he has reserved a part of the establishment for paying customers.

Other matters are resolving themselves in one way or another. Production of *A Taste of the Real,* Raul Brauer's self-aggrandizing film project, has come to a shuddering halt. It turns out that Freddie Bain was the principal backer. The government has seized all of his ill-gained assets, and I doubt it will feel compelled to honor Mr. Bain's obligations in that regard . . . although it's not beyond the realm of possibility that lawyers are working on it right now.

On quite another topic, my book about the MOM, *The Past Redeemed: The History of the Museum of Man,* has received some very positive advance notices. Indeed, on the strength of this reception, I have been asked by a well-known university publishing house to edit the considerable correspondence between Mason Twitchell and Lady Miriam Rothschild, the eccentric English aristocrat who kept a large collection of trained fleas. To date I haven't said yes, but I haven't said no, either.

In the interest of promoting the museum and my new book, I have made several guest appearances on national television talk shows. Elsbeth could watch them for hours and knew extraordinary amounts about the people interviewed and talked about. To me the shows all seemed the same — a ritual in which the host and the guest try to be funny or profound. And I have always found it annoying when the host or hostess lowers his or her voice, mimicking sincerity and signaling to everyone they were asking a searching question. But I must say they all treated me with respect and consideration. One fellow, in suspenders, reminded me of a sideshow barker, and the alpha female on one of the morning shows had very nice legs.

Which brings me to my own situation. Two days after the denouement in the castle, late in the evening, Diantha came into my room where, restless, I was trying to read myself to sleep. She sat on the edge of the bed and, in essence, confessed that she had returned to the Bain place "on an impulse." She said she was going to try to convince him to leave me alone. "I knew it was a mistake the minute I got there. At first he was amused. Then he turned freaky. I mean really freaky. He wouldn't let me go. He kept asking me where Celeste was. He wouldn't believe me when I told her I didn't know."

"Were you still in love with him?" I asked.

"Maybe. Until I got there and saw him again. Then . . ." She sighed and looked at me with her marvelous eyes. "I kept thinking about you."

Thus in quick succession she came into my arms, into my bed, and into my life.

Diantha, it turns out, is pregnant. A week ago she informed me she was late with her period and that an off-the-shelf test from the pharmacy proved positive. I didn't know quite how to respond, to tell the truth.

"It's yours, you know," she said as we moved around the kitchen, making dinner together.

"How can you be sure?" I asked as the realization sank in through layer on layer of denials, no, no, no, culminating in a large, smiling yes.

"Freddie was shooting blanks. He had a vasectomy years ago."

"Just like a nihilist would," I said, stopping to take her in my arms. "You're sure you're pregnant?"

"I am. I'm seeing the doctor, but I know I am. If it's a girl I want to call her Elsbeth."

"Absolutely," I said.

At the same time, I knew I would peruse the autopsy report of Mr. Bain, where the fact of his vasectomy might be listed. What strange beings we be.

It hasn't been all roses between Diantha and me, but the thorns have been few and predictable. It would seem that I am playing Professor Higgins to her Eliza Doolittle. But cultural transmission, so to speak, goes two ways. It's not simply a matter of, say, music. Like her mother, Diantha cannot abide Brahms. She can also be casual about meals. She doesn't like to cook, and I am still leery about ordering prepared food that comes in those white containers.

It also turns out that my nubile Galatea has certain preferences of an intimate nature that test both my capacity for stimulation and the limits of my taste. And while a few eyebrows have been raised regarding our arrangements, I couldn't care less. Not that I haven't tried to get Diantha to refrain from referring to me, in public, as "Stud."

In the wake of all this, I have initiated an ongoing discussion with Izzy Landes, the Reverend Lopes, and Father O'Gould. It could be that I have been seeking a kind of expiation for killing another man, however justified my action was in some lights. We often end up speaking about the nature of evil and the nature of comedy. What intrigues us, I think, is the way comedy relies in large part on pain, mishap, even cruelty.

The good priest has admitted that evolutionary psychology has yet to come up with a credible theory as to why humor developed among *Homo sapiens sapiens*. It's not entirely clear, he says, in what ways a good laugh enhances reproductive fitness. For his part, Alfie Lopes concedes that neither of his good books provides much insight. There really isn't, he notes ruefully, one good joke in either the New or Old Testaments. And as Izzy points out, we can no longer look to Freud in these matters. The Viennese doctor's work, more often viewed now as "a grand, inadvertent parody of the scientific method," is more a source of hilarity, however unintended, than an explanation thereof. Increasingly of late we have explored the possibility that comedy is a form of recognition — but of exactly what, I believe, remains a mystery.

And finally, and I mean finally, patient reader, you can imagine (you must imagine) my surprise this afternoon when, as I ruminated over this final entry in my office at the museum, the door opened. In hobbled none other than Corny Chard, missing a couple of limbs, of course. His ruddy face, shagged with a rough beard, beamed with a wild smile. "Norman," he said, clanking over and sitting down in the chair before my desk, his crutch dropping to the floor with a clatter. All the while I stood, speechless with incredulity, and watched as his eyes lit up with a demonic, triumphant glee. "Norman . . . Norman. Man, do I have a story to tell."